OTHER BOOKS BY LINDA O. JOHNSTON

– A BARKERY & BISCUITS MYSTERY –

BISCUIT

LINDA O. JOHNSTON

MIDNIGHT INK
WOODBURY, MINNESOTA

First Edition
First Printing, 2015

Book format by Bob Gaul
Cover design by Ellen Lawson
Cover illustration by Christina Hess

Midnight Ink, an imprint of Llewellyn Worldwide Ltd.

Library of Congress Cataloging-in-Publication Data
Johnston, Linda O.
  Bite the biscuit/Linda O. Johnston.—First edition.
    pages; cm.—(A Barkery & Biscuits mystery; 1)
  ISBN 978-0-7387-4503-9 (softcover)
1. Dog owners—Fiction. 2. Murder—Investigation—Fiction. I. Title.
  PS3610.O387B58 2015
  813'.6—dc23
                              2014047913

Midnight Ink
Llewellyn Worldwide Ltd.
2143 Wooddale Drive
Woodbury, MN 55125-2989
www.midnightinkbooks.com

Printed in the United States of America

To people everywhere who love their dogs and want to feed them the best and healthiest treats.

To people who have a sweet tooth of their own.

To readers who enjoy cozy mysteries, especially those involving pets and food.

And, as always, to my dear husband Fred. I think he fits into two of the three categories!

ONE

TWO NEW STORES! RATHER, one new and one redone. They were opening today, and both were mine.

I couldn't help smiling as I glanced out through the narrow expanse of windows in the shop where I stood.

A lot of people were outside on the sidewalk. Many stared inside expectantly, waiting for the doors to open. Others were involved in conversation, and the unintelligible crowd noises, though muffled by the windows and walls, seemed to be increasing in volume. Because more people were arriving?

Despite how proud I was of this new venture and how determined I was to make it work, I felt a rush of stage fright. I quickly shoved it aside and turned back to Brenda Anesco. This had previously been just one store—Icing on the Cake—and it had been all hers. I owed her a lot, including the courtesy of listening to her final instructions for the new Icing, the shop we currently occupied.

"I'm really going to miss this place," Brenda told me with a sigh. Her back was toward the window, perhaps intentionally. Did she realize how much the throng was growing?

I wished, for her sake, that there had been more crowds when she had been in charge. But the bakery's recent decline in sales wasn't why she was leaving. No, the decline that caused her departure had to do with her mother's health.

"I know you'll take good care of it," she continued. "Won't you, Carrie?"

"Of course."

Ignoring the crowd and how nervous it had started to make me, I stepped toward her along the gleaming new vinyl tile floor I'd just had installed in Icing. It was patterned in a patchwork of pale gold and dark brown, which I hoped would lure people to buy similarly hued pastries for themselves. The blissful aroma of baking cakes and cinnamon and chocolate that wafted through the air would attract them a whole lot better than the decor, though. Even my mouth was watering, and I'd been inhaling the enticing scent long enough to become inured—somewhat, at least.

"And you'll remember all I told you?" Brenda continued. "I mean, what draws people in. How to keep them coming back. All of that."

Short and a bit plump, with uneven ash brown hair—not to mention endlessly gesturing fingers with blunt pink nails—Brenda was much more of an expert than I, at least about Icing. She knew how to bake great stuff even if her business skills had wavered a bit recently. Plus, even though she was in her early forties, around ten years older than me, she was my dearest friend. So of course I was listening to her.

But as eager as I was for all to go well for Icing, I was a lot more concerned about the other store, my half of the newly divided bakery: Barkery and Biscuits, which featured my own very special baked and otherwise cooked products.

For dogs.

Were any members of the crowd waiting for the Barkery to open? I thought so. I *hoped* so.

"Mmm-hmm," I responded, giving Brenda a quick hug of reassurance. But despite how much I wanted to make her feel better, my gaze had wandered over her shoulder toward the closed door that led to my favorite area, the new part. I ached to go there to make sure it, like Icing, was thoroughly ready to receive whichever members of the group outside wanted to attend its launch.

Maybe that would be all of them.

"Listen to me, Carrie Kennersly," Brenda demanded, stepping back. Her arms, in the light pink sweater she'd knitted herself, were folded as she glared at me. Uh-oh. Busted. She must have realized how sidetracked I was. Not that she should be surprised.

"I am." I shifted uncomfortably in my seldom-worn blue stilettos. Above them, I wore a flowing dress in the same azure shade, one of my few party outfits.

"What was the last thing I told you about our products, then?"

Brenda, despite being my friend, could be really pushy. But I got it. She'd let me remodel the store she loved, but Icing remained her baby.

"Make them sweet and make them good," I said, and she grinned.

She went over a few things again, like the popularity of her red velvet cupcakes, which were in a prime location in the large refrigerated display case crammed attractively full of the bakery's other products too.

She finally finished. "Okay, it's time. Go on into the Barkery and get the party started."

I gave her another brief hug and hurried to open the wide wooden door into Barkery and Biscuits.

My little golden toy poodle–terrier mix, appropriately named Biscuit, flew at me, and I knelt to take her into my arms after closing the door behind me. At the moment she was loose, but I'd have to restrict her now so she couldn't run out when the front door was open.

"Hi, sweetheart," I said as she stood on her hind legs and licked my face.

I glanced down at the floor beneath my knees. I'd had it redone also. The materials were similar to those used in Icing—sturdy but attractive vinyl tiles. But the main area was all blue, and the center decoration was huge and appropriate and beige, in the shape of—what else?—a dog biscuit.

There was an alluring aroma in here too, though not sweet like the one in the bakery. This one suggested a hint of meat. Otherwise, this part of the shop was a mirror image of the other. I'd planned it that way.

Both retail parts of the stores were fairly compact, just large enough to house the wide display cases and have room for people to line up if necessary. Plus, each held an area where customers could sit at small tables to rest and eat.

But the joint kitchen? It was huge and necessary and modern and wonderful!

"Are we ready?" asked Judy Zelener, correctly interrupting my reunion with my dog. We had things to do here. All of us.

"I think so." I rose, holding Biscuit.

Judy was one of the shop assistants I had inherited from Brenda. The other one, Dinah Greeley, was back in the kitchen making sure the trays containing samples of my dog treats were ready.

Judy was in her late twenties, with a long face, high forehead, and shoulder-length wavy hair in a shade of medium brown that resembled cherry wood. She always seemed serious, especially when involved in a discussion with Brenda or argument with Dinah. The latter, unfortunately, happened too often.

Now, though, she smiled, and it lit up her whole face. "Are you going to open the door?"

"Definitely." Taking a deep, calming breath, I put Biscuit down, looping the end of the black leash I'd pulled from my pocket over my wrist to keep her close. Then I unlocked the Barkery's glass front door, pulled it wide open, and hollered "Welcome!" to the sound of the ringing bell I'd had installed on top to notify us of customers.

In moments, the crowd began pushing inside.

It was happening! One of my most cherished wishes was at last coming true. I'd trained to be a veterinary technician, a job that I could love—did love—even though it meant working for someone else to earn a living. But owning my own business, being my own boss—that had always been my dream. Especially when it also involved the other love of my life, dogs.

I, Carrie Kennersly, was now a store owner. Not only that, but most of the products I was about to sell were my own creations.

"Now I'll go open Icing," I said to Judy, but Brenda appeared in the doorway leading to the other side.

"I've just opened it," she said, holding out a round metal tray of dog biscuit samples. "Dinah gave me this from the kitchen. She's greeting everyone in Icing for me. The party has begun!"

She was absolutely right. People were flowing into the Barkery. I needn't have worried that everyone there wanted to visit Icing. I hadn't been able to see the crowd's feet earlier, so I hadn't known that many had their leashed dogs with them—very welcome in the Barkery, but not in the human-focused bakery.

A lot of our visitors were familiar—friends, even. I'd met quite a few of them when their dogs were patients at the Knobcone Veterinary Clinic; I still worked there, part-time now, as a vet tech. And some of these people were also neighbors who lived near my home.

I greeted as many as I could by name, welcoming them and ensuring that they received samples of baked goods for their pets to try. Biscuit, at my feet, helped too in her limited way, wagging her tail at both people and dogs.

At least some of the people I didn't know had to be tourists visiting our lovely town of Knobcone Heights, California. I'd had help making sure that word had gotten out.

"Hi, Carrie." Les Ethman, a moderate-height guy with eyes that turned down at the corners and a forehead that kept expanding, was a member of the City Council and was owned by an English bulldog named Sam. I wondered whether he had dressed up to make an impression at the party or if he had some official business to conduct, since he wore a blue shirt with a striped necktie and nicely creased slacks.

"Hi, Les," I said. "Where's Sam?"

"Left him home for today. But I want to bring him some of your treats. Give me a recommendation."

"They're all good, of course." Would I really say otherwise? Never. But it happened to be true. I raised my voice, since some people around us had started to listen in. "I use all natural ingredients. The treats come in different flavors, from liver to peanut butter to chicken, beef, or cheese, and even some dog-healthy fruits and veggies. They're all labeled."

Saying "excuse me," I wended my way sideways with Biscuit enough to be able to gesture with my free hand toward the large refrigerated display case, which was identical to the one in Icing. Both shops also had shelves along their back walls that held treats less likely to go stale fast, like small cookies in glass jars. Like the refrigerated case in Icing, the one in the Barkery was filled with baked delights—but all for dogs. "See?" I asked my audience, pointing to the sizeable ingredients labels stuck on toothpicks on each plate. I also hoped they noticed that some of the items had "B&B" etched into them, representing "Barkery and Biscuits."

"They sound good enough for people to eat." Another member of City Council had just joined her colleague. Wilhelmina Matlock, who preferred to be called "Billi," was also an acquaintance of mine thanks to her frequent visits to the veterinary hospital. She owned a couple of dogs, but I knew her more for her private shelter where she took in rescues. She was one busy lady, since she also owned a day spa that catered to the wealthy human residents and tourists who came to Knobcone Heights.

"You can always sample them yourselves," I said. "The ingredients are just as good for people as for their pets—although there are a few you should avoid if you have a peanut allergy. I'd be glad to point them out."

Some of those around us made faces that suggested they'd rather do anything than taste any kind of dog treats.

"Please come over here," I called to Judy, to whom Brenda had handed the sample tray. "This first tray contains our cheese biscuits," I told the crowd. "As gourmet as your dog could ever want, with three kinds of cheese as well as wheat germ, pureed veggies, and other highly tasty ingredients baked until nice and crunchy." I loved them. So did Biscuit and every other dog I'd given a taste to.

By the time Judy got close to me, only half a dozen bone-shaped biscuits remained on the tray.

"Looks like they're popular, so grab what's left," I told our patrons, "and we'll bring another flavor out soon."

I saw that some people were forming an irregular line at the cash register on the counter, most pointing at treats in the adjoining display case.

"Please serve those folks," I told Judy in a low voice. She nodded. I figured that Brenda and Dinah were handling sales on the bakery side.

The men and women around us, including the two I'd been speaking with, managed to take samples before they were all gone. I laughed. "I think it's time for me to get the next tray."

But I couldn't bring Biscuit into the kitchen. That was one restriction in the city permit that had allowed me to divide the original Icing on the Cake bakery into two parts. Pets were permitted in Barkery and Biscuits, but only the store area, since the kitchen was used for cooking products for both people and pets.

I'd divided the equipment and counters up in the kitchen, and put in a special ventilation system so the aroma of meaty animal treats wouldn't contaminate people-goodies containing things like sugar and chocolate, and vice versa. And I'd made it absolutely clear to my assistants that those ingredients had to be kept separate, for taste reasons but also for dog health, since chocolate was dangerous to them.

Right now, I wasn't about to let Biscuit loose while I entered the kitchen, especially as this throng of people also held open the front door. The area I had planned to keep Biscuit in wasn't completely set up because of the party. What could I do with her while I got the next round of dog treats?

Fortunately, one of the people just coming in was Neal, my brother. He wasn't looking toward me but back outside as he gestured for someone else to enter.

"Hey, Neal!" I called. Somehow he heard me over all the conversations going on among the shoulder-to-shoulder people.

I couldn't have been happier to see him. Not only could he take care of Biscuit while I went into the kitchen, but he could also help with crowd control, starting to get this group flowing in and out.

Neal is twenty-eight—four years younger than me—and quite a few inches taller. Like me, he's got the Kennersly longish nose and blunt chin, plus some fairly sharp cheekbones as well as our family's typical medium-blond hair. An athlete and leader of fun tourist expeditions, as well as one of the front desk receptionists at the Knobcone Heights Resort, Neal keeps his hair short and a shadow of a light beard on his cheeks and chin.

He lives with me. We're about as close as siblings can be, which is a good thing. We're all we've got.

And he's used to taking orders from me.

It took him a minute to scooch through the crowd, not only because he had to keep excusing himself but because, friendly guy that he is, he greeted everyone, mostly by name. His job at the premier local hotel meant that he'd even met many of the tourists. In fact, at my urging, he'd told a lot of tourists about my grand opening.

"Hey, Carrie," he said as he reached me. "Hi, Bug," he added, bending over to rough up Biscuit's wavy fur. He stood straight again and looked down at me. "Good crowd, huh?"

My bro was wearing a snug, navy Knobcone Heights Resort T-shirt that showed off his muscular build, and jeans. Dressing up wasn't in his vocabulary—unless he had a hot date who demanded it. And since lots of women seemed eager for his attention, he apparently could have one of those hot dates whenever he chose.

"It sure is," I said. "I need to get something in the kitchen, then pop in on the Icing side. Will you take care of Biscuit for me?"

"What do you think, Bug?" He looked down at my dog again. "You gonna take good care of your uncle Neal?" Without waiting for Biscuit to answer, Neal held out his arms and I gently turned my pup over to him.

But before I could inch my way to the kitchen, I heard the undercurrent of excited party voices ramp up to a crescendo, then stop. What was going on?

I turned to look toward the door.

Two people I recognized were shoving their way in. They were relatives of Les Ethman, but Les remained standing at the side of the store talking earnestly with Billi. And unlike their uncle, they clearly had an attitude—one they'd merely hinted at over the last months of my remodeling. Was it about to erupt?

"Happy opening day," shouted the woman, Myra Ethman, in a sing-song sarcastic tone that sent a tendril of dismay creeping up my spine.

"We hope you close tomorrow," called her husband Harris.

And I wondered if the party was already over.

TWO

Myra slithered her way through the crowd and reached me first. She was slender to the point of near emaciation, although I bet she considered herself gorgeously svelte. Her brown hair, filled with gleaming highlights, formed a wispy cap surrounding a face so perfect that I had no doubt she'd availed herself of cosmetic surgery at least once. She was, after all, at least fifteen years older than me.

I made myself smile at her, although I knew the curve of my mouth wasn't reflected in my dubious eyes. "Thanks for your good wishes, Myra," I said. She had, after all, said something positive about my party, even though I knew it had been sarcasm.

At least Harris had been genuine in his statement. But I had no intention of closing tomorrow or anytime in the next zillion years.

Harris had followed Myra over to me and now edged his way in front of her, confronting me.

Like Councilman Les, Harris was an Ethman, a member of one of the town's most wealthy and privileged families. His eyes looked similar to Les's, turned down at the edges; on Les, those eyes appeared a bit wistful and invited people to say something nice to make him feel better, but on Harris, they looked angry and challenging. Or maybe I was just reading the obvious mood in his eyes today.

"Would you like a sample of my treats to take home to Davinia, Harris?" I asked sweetly.

As with most people I knew in this town, I'd met Harris and Myra when they brought their pets into the veterinary clinic. They owned a black standard poodle named Davinia and a Manx cat named Beauregard. I wondered how the animals got along together in the same household, but maybe they'd formed an alliance to deal with their nasty owners.

"No, thank you." Myra was the one who responded. She almost sounded polite—until she continued. "All of the dog treats and other products at Knob Hill Pet Emporium are of much superior quality to any of your poisonous little pieces of garbage here." She made a face like she had just ingested dog feces.

I wanted to slap that face. More realistically, I wanted to shout at her to get out of here. She didn't have to come to my opening party. And I thought I'd made it clear enough, when she and her nasty husband had appeared to oppose my application for a permit to remodel this building, that they weren't any more welcome here than I was now at the pet store they'd established a couple of years ago.

But Myra was Neal's boss. She was the executive manager of the Knobcone Heights Resort. I hadn't turned around to see how he was reacting to this conversation, but I was sure my usually devil-may-care brother was listening closely with his teeth gritted.

Before I allowed myself to show any reaction, I glanced at the unrelated guests surrounding us. Several faces looked horrified. Others seemed caught up in fascination, as if the people enjoyed fights and were waiting for the next ugly round. A few who held their dogs in their arms appeared to have turned, so that if the situation came to blows their beloved small family members would not get creamed. I knew most of these people and understood their loving concern.

Those friends and neighbors, more than anyone else except Neal, caused me to take a few deep breaths and order myself to calm down. I wanted pet owners to come here for the benefit of their fur-kids. I wanted them to try, and then buy, treats that I'd been baking the past few years for the patients at the veterinary clinic, which included products for dogs with special dietary needs. The vet patients had been my guinea-dogs, and it was because they and their owners seemed so happy with my products that I was now sharing them with the world.

Or at least the world of Knobcone Heights.

I decided to show everyone what a good sport I was. "You know, Harris, I won't be in direct competition with the Pet Emporium," I said. "I have a limited supply of products, and they're not the same kinds of things you carry anyway."

I'd visited the Emporium several times in the past, while I was still welcome, to get stuff for Biscuit—and to check it out. Like Barkery and Biscuits, it fronted on the Knobcone Heights town square, but it was at the opposite side from my two shops on Summit Avenue, and therefore a couple of blocks away. Both were in the town's premier retail area. The Emporium was one among many upscale establishments that catered to wealthy tourists and the town's elite.

The rest of the people around here, including me, drove out of town a ways to some of the nice but cheaper strip malls. One of the chain pet supply companies maintained a store there, and they too carried brands of healthy foods.

"We sell treats," Harris huffed back. "Better than this junk."

"There's nothing in the area—no, in the world, the universe—that's better for dogs than my home-baked dog treats," I retorted, through gritted teeth that I bared as I pretended to smile. "Anyway, you're entitled to your opinion, but I can assure you there's room in this town for both of our stores. But I think you've worn out your welcome here. Hadn't you better go back to your emporium to see if there are any customers there you can browbeat—I mean, wait on?"

I turned my back on him, but not before I noticed his nasty frown.

Myra had maneuvered away, and she was standing in the corner of the Barkery talking to Les and Billi.

Even though Harris was the born Ethman of that couple, when they'd married Myra had apparently donned the cloak of eliteness and done her best to outdo the blood-related kin. Harris might have the money, but Myra appeared to have the brains. I'd heard that she had been the one to purchase the Emporium, to give Harris something to do besides spend their kids' inheritance. Their human kids, that is. They had two, a girl and a boy. The girl was off at college and the boy was still in high school—the best private preppy school in the San Bernardino Mountains.

I noticed that Judy, behind the counter, appeared a little frazzled, so I went over to help her, which also got me far away from Harris.

"I'm fine," she whispered to me. "But we need some more sample treats out here."

"You're right," I said, recognizing that my nasty exchange with the Ethmans had delayed my retrieving more treats. I moved around Judy to duck into the kitchen and brought out a second tray full of my dog treat samples—some small, crunchy training rewards that contained beef, yams, and more. I began moving slowly through the crowd, allowing people to take more than one

14

of the treats, particularly acquaintances who had their dogs with them. I chatted casually with most of them, sharing smiles and thanking them for their good wishes.

When I got near the corner where Myra stood, apparently holding court since she was the only one talking, I felt myself freeze.

She was continuing to act as nasty as her husband, while apparently trying—unsuccessfully—to maintain a civil demeanor. "But this place looks so tacky now, don't you think?" She was looking at Billi with an expression that suggested the kind of disgust she might feel at finding a tick on her dog. "I mean, I still don't know why our city granted a building permit for this remodel."

She did know, though. Despite her fighting it, my permit had gone through. I assumed she was now criticizing Les and Billi, as representatives of the town, just as she had criticized me.

"I thought from the first that dividing one store into two was a bad idea," she continued, "and even the appearance of this poor quality remodeling job proves it. Maybe it would have been better if she had at least hired locally, a really good contractor like our own Walt Hainner. He and his crew just do wonders around here, both constructing new buildings and remodeling. But, no, Ms. Kennersly had to take her building permit and wave it at a lesser contractor, one of those outfits from Big Bear." She said the latter as if she was speaking about some inner city slum instead of a very nice neighboring town in the same mountain range.

Fortunately, Billi just smiled and said nothing while Les rolled his eyes. "You know, Myra," Les said, "we Ethmans have occasionally hired contractors from Big Bear. In fact, didn't you find one you liked when you and Harris remodeled your house two years ago? What was his name? J—"

"Never mind that," Myra snapped. She must have recognized that her audience had expanded beyond the two City Council members, and also beyond me. "I just don't like the look of this place. But the worse thing is the crap—er, products—she's selling here. I mean, homemade dog biscuits. I just hope our poor pets aren't poisoned. I'm certainly not taking any of this home to my Davinia."

Why was her attitude so over the top? Because I was an upstart, a relative newcomer to Knobcone Heights, and not a member of one of its top-echelon families? Because she really was concerned about the potential competition to her pet shop? Some other reason I couldn't even guess? I had no idea, but I had to deal with it.

It was time for me to step into this conversation. "You absolutely don't have to take any samples, Myra. But that doesn't mean Davinia hasn't tried them. I've been baking treats for our patients at the veterinary clinic for a while now, and sending some home with them when appropriate. Didn't you bring Davinia in a few months ago when she'd apparently eaten something in your yard that didn't agree with her? She'd been throwing up, and after making sure there was no indication she'd eaten anything poisonous, Dr. Kline prescribed some meds and also sold you some of the bland and soothing treats I developed to help our patients with tummy problems."

"Well, that's different from giving them garbage made from untried recipes like the stuff here, and—"

"They. Are. Not. Garbage." Okay, I was losing my cool now. I took a deep breath. "And I have tried them out, on Biscuit, my friends' dogs, and our veterinary patients. As I've said, they're all made with only the finest ingredients and no preservatives like most of the crap sold in your store. And—"

I made myself stop. I had previously taken the position that there was room for both establishments here, and I intended to continue on the high road, not criticizing the Ethmans despite what they were trying to do to me. "Sorry," I said. "I know you only sell foods and treats made by reputable manufacturers. It's just that my homemade products are even better. But there are fewer of them. They might even complement what you're selling. So, like I said, our two businesses can coexist."

"Like hell they can!" Myra took a step toward me, her hands clenched at her waist into fists.

I felt my eyes widen. I might despise this woman and the malicious position she was taking, but I didn't really want to fight with her. Not physically, at least.

Before I was attacked, though, my dear boss wended his way through the crowd.

Dr. Arvus Kline—known by all as Arvie—was in his sixties. He looked even older, with all that remained of his hair, silvery wisps, hanging over a face filled with deep wrinkles. "Carrie, my dear, how wonderful this is. Congratulations on opening your store." He reached out toward where I still held the new treat tray—now nearly empty—and took a couple, then rubbed my upper arm in a short, friendly pat.

"Thanks, Arvie." I gave him a warm and genuine smile. I owed so much to him. He had allowed me to experiment with giving my treats to his patients, for one thing. Of course, we'd always talked about each dog's needs and the ingredients I was using and why, so he'd basically helped me work out some of my recipes.

In addition, he had funded my remodeling of the building into two stores. I'd only borrowed the money from him, of course, and would start paying it back with interest next month. But getting a bank loan would have been iffy and a lot more expensive.

Arvie had also allowed me to keep my job at the vet clinic part-time. I'd wanted to make sure I maintained an income as I started my new venture. Plus I loved being a vet tech.

But not as much as I loved opening my own business.

"Are all these the same kinds of treats you've distributed around our clinic?" he asked.

"Pretty much, but with some additional ones too." I glanced around with a smile, knowing that people around us were still eavesdropping. They might find this upbeat conversation less exciting than the ones I'd had with the Ethmans, but this was the kind of stuff I really wanted them to hear. "They're all made with the ingredients that you and I talked about in advance, and since you're one heck of a veterinarian, I knew I was doing things right." Since not all the people here would know who Arvie was—townsfolk, yes, tourists, no—I'd made sure to mention his job. His credentials lending credence to my work couldn't be beat.

"Hi, Arvus. Hi, Carrie." Another vet had just joined us.

Dr. Reed Storme had only started practicing at Arvie's clinic a couple of months ago. Although I was still employed there part time, I'd been here at my new shops a lot, supervising the work, and hadn't been around the veterinary hospital as much as before. I'd had coffee with Reed several times and wouldn't have minded getting to know the new vet better. I'd heard rumors of his background in the military. He looked like one hunky guy. But even more important, I had observed his caring attention to his patients, including a dog who'd been hit by a car, and I believed he was a really good doctor.

For the moment, I just returned his greeting. I also answered a few questions about why I'd done this—loud enough for those around us to hear. "As you know, I opened Barkery and Biscuits partly because I love dogs and want to treat them specially, not only medically the way I do as a vet tech at your clinic."

Reed nodded. There was a strange expression on his handsome yet somewhat rugged face. Maybe I'd said too much and he thought I believed him stupid, which I didn't.

I glanced around. "I just want to make sure our guests here know that too," I explained. "Anyhow, my friend Brenda Anesco ran her Icing on the Cake bakery out of this place before I divided it into two shops. I think I mentioned to you that she has to move away to care for her ailing mother and was looking for someone to take over her bakery, and I got the idea of keeping it going yet starting Barkery too."

Arvie nodded while Reed's dark brows rose in apparent interest. He had rich, wavy black hair and just a hint of a five o'clock shadow, which made sense since it was late in the day.

I talked a little more about my idea for the Barkery and my love of dogs, and about putting together my recipes, some of which I'd already described before. But Arvie and Reed hadn't heard it. Neither had everyone around us. In fact, I'd seen Neal, still in charge of Biscuit, working on increasing the flow of visitors so that as many were coming in as leaving. Which meant I now had a new group of people near me, some with dogs. I would have to get a third tray of samples from the kitchen soon.

I also needed to duck into Icing and make sure all was going well. While the Barkery might be my baby, Icing was now a beloved stepchild. Plus, despite some decrease in its business lately, it was the tried-and-true part, and I had to make sure I took good care of it. It was a critical part of my exciting new venture.

I finished my current spiel, glad about the interest on the faces around me.

"Thanks for coming," I told their owners. "I'll be back here with more samples soon, but I need to visit the bakery next door."

"I need to get back to the clinic," Arvie told me.

Impulsively, I gave him a hug. "I'll be there for my shift tomorrow afternoon as promised." I glanced at Reed, wondering if he'd be there then. No matter.

But Reed said, "I'll see you then."

Which made me smile.

At least until I glanced at the corner where the Ethmans still stood talking with their uncle and Billi Matlock. Why hadn't they left already? They didn't like my place, and I didn't like their being here.

As if she felt my glance, Myra looked in my direction and scowled.

Maybe I needed to give her a hint. I maneuvered my way through the crowd toward them. "I'm so delighted that you're still here," I lied, raising my voice so people could hear. "It shows how much you support my new venture."

"You know we hate it," Myra responded icily.

"Then you are very welcome," I said sweetly, smiling all the more, "to leave."

THREE

I GESTURED GRANDLY, LIKE a TV hostess, in the direction of the door, then turned away quickly without confirming whether my now-even-more-unwelcome guests were heading toward it. It was time for me to go into the kitchen.

Leaving the mostly happy rumblings of my customers behind me for a second, I stepped into the Barkery side of the kitchen and approached the center dividing shelves to fill another tray with sample dog treats. I headed back just long enough to lay the tray down on the counter near where Judy was working the cash register. Then I hurried into Icing.

This shop was just as crowded with guests as the Barkery, and I knew some of them here too. I was thrilled! People were shoulder-to-shoulder even as my other assistant Dinah maneuvered her way among them with a tray of human treats: chocolate chip and sugar cookies and mini-scones and more.

Brenda was still there too, schmoozing with our guests, handing out samples of our sweets, saying farewell to those she knew. I decided just to observe before stepping in and showing that I was now the boss—at least, Dinah's boss. When and if Brenda would ever return was still up in the air. I'd promised Brenda she could always come back and help me—knowing that would only happen if her mother didn't survive.

In any case, I'd officially purchased her business, thanks to Arvie's loan.

I crossed my arms and rested my back against the jamb of the door into the kitchen, grinning as I observed. Dinah seemed in her glory, giving out the samples, smiling and encouraging people to taste and then buy some of the people-focused baked goods.

When I'd first met Dinah, I'd thought her awfully young for the job of full-time bakery assistant. She looked as though she must still be in high school, with her huge blue eyes, slightly acned skin, and a body that appeared to bear some baby fat. Turned out I was wrong. She had even finished college, gotten her degree in English, and considered herself a writer in her spare time. For now, she said, she was not only studying baking while working with Brenda, but was using Knobcone Heights as a research venue while she studied people.

I liked her. I also liked Judy.

What I didn't like was their incessant sniping at one another. When Brenda had started talking about having to leave to care for her mom, both assistants thought their boss would turn the bakery over to one of them. And each felt certain that she'd be the chosen one.

Instead, Brenda had chosen me, as well as my modifications to the store—partly because she couldn't keep the business, and also so she wouldn't have to choose between Judy and Dinah.

So far, neither had quit. Both were acting as if their former allegiance to Brenda had transferred to me—even though Judy had started dropping hints about wanting to open her own bakery one of these days.

Would their truce last? I wasn't sure, but one thing I did know was that I appreciated the knowledge and dedication of both of them. Despite how much I loved to bake for dogs, my training and experience were all as a veterinary assistant. Though I'd fantasized for a long time about becoming an entrepreneur and being in charge, what I knew about running a store was only as a patron, not as an owner/manager. Till now.

So far, both Dinah and Judy had been great about showing me how things were done. They knew the pastry recipes Brenda used and had each demonstrated how to bake cupcakes and muffins and more. Even though Brenda had tutored me on how to use the identical cash registers on the counters beside the display cases in each store, as well as how to do the bookkeeping on the computer kept in the office at the rear of the kitchen, the two assistants vowed to make sure I didn't flub processing credit cards or cash when I rang up sales.

The office was new, and very small. I'd added it during remodeling just so I'd have a door to lock my computer, credit cards, and accounting information behind. It held only a small desk, with a laptop computer that was usually closed, plus a chair and a two-drawer file cabinet.

And my assistants? I suspected that having only two of them to help run two shops wouldn't work well, especially when we'd be open every day and I worked part-time elsewhere. But both Judy and Dinah had seemed eager to give it a try, so I hadn't spent the time or money to hire anyone else—yet. I'd just have to see how things worked out now that both stores were open.

I'd been observing long enough. Smiling, I strode into the shop and approached Brenda. She was clasping hands with an older lady I didn't know. When the lady looked at me, Brenda followed her gaze. Tears shone in her eyes.

"Carrie, I want to introduce you to Cecilia Young. Cece is a teacher here in Knobcone—sixth grade—and she's been a fan of Icing on the Cake from the moment I opened the doors."

"Great to meet you, Cece," I said, holding out my hand. She grasped it in her own light and cool grip. She was a slight woman, clad in a shapeless gray party dress with a frilly hemline.

"Likewise." She looked up at me from brown eyes peering out among myriad wrinkles. "Are you going to do as good a job of baking as my friend Brenda?"

I couldn't help an uncomfortable laugh. "No one's as good as Brenda, but I'm going to do my best. And fortunately she's left her wonderful assistants to whip me into shape."

The woman nodded, and only then did she smile at me, baring teeth so white I wondered if they were implants. "Well, my favorites are the blueberry scones. If they're not as good, I'll let you know."

"Thanks," I told her, actually feeling sincere. I'd rather someone tell me to shape up than to lose customers without knowing why. "Do you happen to have a dog?" If so, I'd make sure she got some of my canine treats from next door.

"No, but I just adopted a kitten from Mountaintop Rescue."

That was the shelter run by Councilwoman Billi Matlock. Billi had already gotten a small selection of my treats as samples to take to her canine wards when she'd brought some of them into the veterinary clinic. Now that my Barkery was open, she would get even more.

"Then maybe I'll see you at the veterinary clinic," I told Cece. "I still work there part-time as a vet tech."

"Just make sure you don't bite off more than you can chew, Carrie," she said. Her gaze now was hard and assessing, and even a little unnerving from such a small and wizened woman. I suspected that she had no trouble at all keeping her students in line. Even I nearly swallowed hard and promised to be good.

But all I said was "Never!" punctuated with a friendly grin. "I'd better mingle a bit, so please excuse me, Cece."

She nodded and I moved away, glancing encouragingly at Brenda. Her smile this time appeared genuine, but I knew how hard this must be for her.

I followed Dinah for a couple of minutes, seeing which members of the crowd chose which items to taste. I didn't recognize quite as many people here as I had in the Barkery—not surprising, though. I'd lived in Knobcone Heights for about five years and met most people through their pets. Those who chose to visit Icing didn't necessarily have animals at home.

I stayed for maybe twenty minutes, saying hi and introducing myself and welcoming everyone—and inviting them to come back and buy more. The bell at the top of the front door to this shop rang often, making it clear that a lot of people were coming and going. I'd had the bells installed so that if we were in the kitchen or just one of the shops, we'd be aware of customers' entries into the shop that we weren't watching.

Since I was much more used to chatting with dogs and cats these days than with people, I was growing exhausted. I ducked back into the kitchen to check on our supplies of samples and saw, unsurprisingly, that they were disappearing fast. But fortunately I'd told everyone, when I'd invited them, what the hours scheduled for our party would be: we would close at five, which was only half an hour away.

I planned to reopen at seven o'clock in the morning for the breakfast pastry crowd, not to mention provide treats for their pets. Which meant I'd have to rise hours earlier to start baking—fortunately, with one of my assistants joining me soon. On weekends, when both Judy and Dinah would work full-time, they would alternate which one came in first. At other times they would alternate which one had the day off.

I felt fairly certain that I'd be able to work things out so I'd be able to keep my part-time vet tech job. Worst case scenario, I would hire more helpers, also part-time. I'd have to make sure I could afford them, though.

Sleep? I'd fit it in somewhere. Most important was that I'd be able to have Biscuit with me when I was working here, even though I'd have to make sure she stayed in the Barkery.

Speaking of which, I decided I'd been in Icing long enough. Before we kicked everyone out—er, ended the party—I wanted to make sure things were still going well in the other half of my new venture.

I hadn't seen Neal in Icing, but even so, the crowd was flowing the way he'd initiated in the Barkery: in the door, circling the shop, then leaving. I squeezed my way into the line and began flowing toward the exit with everyone else. As I got outside, I saw with relief that there were only a few people now in line waiting to get into each of the stores. We should be able to end the party without hurting anyone's feelings.

The sidewalk on both sides of the stores looked busy, which was a good thing, as did the town square across the street, where people enjoyed the park with its grass and knobcone pine trees or just passed through to get from one area of shops to another. This upscale shopping district in this upscale town attracted a lot of customers. They and their dogs needed refreshment. Treats. And drinks. We had coffee and soft drinks available in Icing, and water bowls on the floor along one wall inside the Barkery as well as outside of it.

My smile was pasted onto my face with overuse today, but that was okay. I still had to greet the remaining party attendees. I got into the line that was entering the Barkery, knowing I'd have to cut in without waiting but still wanting to greet people.

A man edged up as though he, too, wanted to ignore protocol and courtesy and follow me in. I raised my brows in what I hoped looked like a chiding-but-friendly glance.

"Carrie?" he asked. "Are you Carrie Kennersly?"

I nodded. "Yes. Can I help you?"

"I really hope so. My name is Jack Loroco. I've already been inside looking the place over, bought some samples, and got someone to point you out. I'd like to talk with you—just for a minute now, although I hope we can speak again later."

My curiosity was piqued, if only a little. "All right," I said.

"How about if we sit down over there?" He nodded toward the patio at the far side of the building, where I'd squeezed in all our small wrought-iron tables and chairs for now. There wasn't room inside or on the front sidewalk for them at the moment, with the people circulating through the stores.

"Fine." I preceded him toward that area. A few people sat at the tables chatting, most with dogs lying on the cement beside them. I quickly checked to make sure our outdoor water bowls near the entry into the Barkery didn't need replenishing. They weren't completely full, but any thirsty pup could at least take a few slurps.

There was an empty table at the far corner of the patio and I headed there. "I can really only chat briefly because I have to say my farewells in"—I pulled my phone from my pocket and checked the time—"ten minutes." I sat down at the side of the table where I could continue to watch the dwindling crowd, and Jack Loroco took a seat across from me.

He leaned toward me. "I can tell you what I want in less time than that, although I can't give details. Right now I just want to seduce you."

"What?" I felt my eyes widen. The guy wasn't bad to look at— maybe six feet tall, wearing khaki shorts and a white knit shirt that suggested a muscular physique beneath. His arms and legs were tanned and sported sparse hair a few shades lighter than the ample crop on his head. He had a prominent, straight nose, wide mouth, and slightly concave cheeks, which all looked good together.

Nice looking, sure. But I didn't like his too-forthright attitude. Although it had been a while since I'd seduced, or been seduced by, anyone ...

He laughed and leaned back in his chair. "I just wanted to get your attention," he said. "I'm actually here to seduce your business."

"What do you mean?"

"Well, I'm an executive with VimPets. Have you ever heard of it?"

Anyone who worked with pets for a living, or owned pets, or breathed, had probably heard of VimPets. It was one of the largest and best regarded pet food manufacturers.

"Yes," I acknowledged. "I even feed my dog Biscuit VimHealth kibble along with her canned food. But I'm only selling my home-made dog treats in Barkery and Biscuits." I figured he intended to turn this into a sales call. I wasn't sure if Harris Ethman was still around—maybe I should aim this Jack Loroco toward him. As far as I recalled, Harris did not carry VimPets products at the Emporium.

"Great," he said. "I won't keep you much longer, but here's what I want you to think about. In addition to checking out your shop, I've been watching your customers visit for the past couple of hours and feed samples to their dogs, who all seemed to like them. A lot. I've even tasted some myself."

I blinked at him. "Really? You ate the pet treats rather than the bakery treats?"

"I admit to trying those too. I like what you're doing here, Carrie." He gestured toward the store. "And what I want you to consider is whether you'd like to make a lot of money by selling your recipes to VimPets. We'd also hire you to help promote your healthy, homemade products. They'd be mass produced, of course, but with the greatest of care, right in our L.A. factory. With your supervision, of course."

I shook my head, my mind boggled. "And you're willing to offer all that to me on the basis of how this opening-day party is going?"

"There'd be a lot of details to work out," he said. "And this isn't a full-fledged offer. I'd still have to get my employer's okay. And then we'd need to check out your recipes and the kinds of ingredients and all that. But this would be unique in the industry, the way I visualize it. There's a lot for both of us to learn and negotiate, but … well, think about it. We can talk more later, okay?"

"Well …" I had no intention of committing to anything except running my own little store—stores—here and now. Preferably forever. Depending on how things went, though, I might be willing to consider a portion of what Jack was saying. Some kind of expansion on my own terms. Someday. In the future.

"We can talk," I told him slowly, "but I'm not sure it'll lead to anything."

"I get it. And I can't promise it'll lead to anything from the Vim-Pets perspective either. But I'm impressed enough to think it will. I'll be in town for another couple of days. I live in L.A. and visit Knob-cone Heights often to engage in some of my favorite pastimes—water skiing and snow skiing. Here's my card. I'll be in touch."

I accepted his card, then reached toward my pocket for one of mine—but I didn't have any with me.

"Don't worry about it," he said. "I picked up one of the Barkery brochures inside. As well as some samples for my own dog Rigsley. He's a rescue, a midsize gray whatever who's my great pal. My family member. I bring him to Knobcone Heights some of the time, but not this trip. I'll take him some of your treats as a payoff for staying home."

"He sounds cute," I said, meaning it. I wasn't too sure what the guy was—or wasn't—offering with respect to my Barkery products, but I liked his attitude about his dog.

"Anyway, I'd better run. Got dinner plans."

A date? Why did that make my heart sink? I'd just met him. He had a business proposal to discuss, nothing social.

"Okay." I rose. "Thanks for the suggestion. I'll think about it."

"And I'll definitely be in touch."

I started toward the door into the Barkery, seeing him leave out of the corner of my eye. By then, the crowd had thinned considerably. Good. I wouldn't have to throw anyone out.

Neal was still there with Biscuit, of course. My little dog was on her leash, and there was room for her to walk without being stepped on.

Neal approached right away. "Those fool Ethmans are still here," he said quietly. "This is one of those times I'd like to ream my boss. Myra's been making all kinds of noises about how awful this store and its products are—loud enough for everyone to hear. I know she wants Harris's store to continue to do well, but she's being a jerk about it."

Sure enough, notwithstanding my invitation for Myra and Harris to leave, the conclave still stood in the corner talking: the three Ethmans. Billi Matlock had left, though.

Judy remained behind the counter. She looked exhausted, but she was smiling bravely as she discussed our treats with people who were looking at the few rows of products remaining in the display case and asking questions.

I'd definitely acknowledge her help later.

I started to circulate through the room again. It was a lot easier than before. I said hi to the people who were there—avoiding the Ethmans for now.

But Myra apparently had no intention of avoiding me. She drew away from the others and approached. "So do you really think that people will come back for your shoddy products when you're not giving them away for free?"

I knew that the attention of those who were still in the store had been captured by the volume of her voice. I couldn't help it. I was tired. And, I admit it, I was worried that people might think there was some validity to what she said just because of who she was and the fact that she'd said it. And I still couldn't help wondering why she was being so miserable about everything. Was her—Harris's—store in trouble? Or did she just enjoy being a regal Ethman and resent someone choosing not to pay attention to her royal commands?

Rather than just telling her again to leave, I snapped, "Shoddy? Oh, you mean the customer service at your resort?" Except for my brother's, of course, but I didn't want to mention Neal and have her come down hard on him. "Or, more likely, the horrible mass-produced products your husband sells in his pet store?" I paused.

"Look, I don't mean any of that. Why don't we just call a truce here? You don't like my store. I don't like your attitude. Why don't we both just live with it?"

"Live with it? Oh no, my dear. You can't just compete with the Knob Hill Pet Emporium and expect to survive. Right, Harris?"

Her husband took a step forward. "Right." But he didn't sound quite as convinced as his wife.

"I mean, you're going to do all you can to make sure this little venture is seen for what it is, aren't you?" Myra had turned and seemed to be confronting Harris now. "That's what we discussed. It's why we're still here. You're the number one, superior pet-product supplier in this town and that's that. You need to show her, show everyone, that you're tops."

Neal had already told me he'd heard that Harris had been living off his family trust until Myra stepped in and bought the store to keep him busy and give him a way to make a living of his own. But she apparently wasn't pleased with how he was doing it.

I also gathered, from the steely glint in Harris's expression, that he didn't like her criticism. "Of course I'm tops," he said through gritted teeth.

It was time for Les to step in—a good thing, since my remaining customers were staring at the Ethmans. And me. As if they expected my retort. Which I swallowed as Les said, "Knobcone Heights is a wonderful town. It's my town. And I say there's room for more than one pet supplier here. I mean, what's right here in town is definitely the best. The chain store on the highway is a nice one, but the stuff that's carried here, and at the Emporium, really rocks." He grinned a political smile at everyone who might be his constituents, including his family members and me.

"We'll see about that," Myra said. Then she looked at me. "This place is toast, Ms. Kennersly. And I don't mean nice baked bread. I'll make sure you're out of business in no time." She aimed an angry glance at her employee Neal and, finally, flounced out of my shop.

"I'll bet her resort did a whole lot better this afternoon without her," I said to no one in particular as her husband followed her. "But it'd have been even better if she'd stayed there and not come to my shops."

"I get your point," Les said. "Myra can be a little … off-putting at times." His down-turned eyes looked particularly sad, and I felt a little sorry for the politician for having to put up with those family members.

"Off-putting doesn't quite cover it," I said. "Anyway, Barkery and Biscuits, you're open now and you're here to stay." I twirled on my toes, raising my arms in salute to my store. Everyone clapped, and I took several exaggerated bows.

"Here, here." That was a man I'd never seen before.

"Thanks," I said.

"But what will you do if those nasty people try to make you go out of business?" That was a woman I recognized, with a Pekingese in her arms—a local, although I couldn't remember her name offhand. "I mean, they've already threatened you. I love your stuff and so does little Phaedra here." She gestured toward her pup.

"Thanks," I said. "And don't worry. They're not the only ones who can threaten—and do something about it." I smiled grimly. "Myra Ethman did enough damage today with her criticism, but she'd better stop. Immediately. She may not realize it, but I'll do anything in my power to make sure that Barkery and Biscuits will survive, and that means finding a way to keep her quiet."

Could I get her fired from the resort by telling her bosses what a jerk she was? Unlikely, since at least some of her bosses were other Ethmans. But I'd think of some way to make her stop insulting my shop and endangering my new business. I just didn't know what it was yet.

I said goodbye to the rest of our guests, and then Judy, Dinah, Neal, and I—and even poor, sad Brenda—cleaned things up to prepare for tomorrow's early morning baking.

I made it a point to have Judy and Dinah work in different areas—one in the Barkery and the other in Icing—since this evening was apparently not a good time to work on their truce. They'd started sniping at one another almost immediately when they began cleaning different parts of the kitchen.

Soon, we all were ready to go. I watched as my new assistants retrieved their purses from a closed cabinet at the kitchen's rear; this was easier to get to than where I stashed my own purse in the small back office. Judy and Dinah left at the same time, acting amazingly civil toward one another now that their working day was finally over.

At the back door of the kitchen, which led out to our parking lot, I hugged Brenda once more before locking up. "You're off down the hill tomorrow to go to your mother's?"

"Tonight, actually." Tears ran down Brenda's cheeks. "But I'm going to miss it here. I'll miss Icing on the Cake. I'll miss you, Carrie."

My eyes were filled too by then. "I'll miss you too, Brenda."

"I'll be back to visit whenever I can," she said. "And someday, maybe I'll move back here."

"You're always welcome," I said, realizing without even hearing her sobs that she was anticipating the loss of her mother in that "someday."

And then everyone but Neal and Biscuit were gone. They piled into my old white Toyota and I headed toward the home we shared.

————

I'd set my alarm for four a.m. the next morning, and I came fully awake as it went off. Time to get up, shower, get dressed, then go to work baking all kinds of treats. As much as I'd miss Brenda, the Barkery and Icing were all mine now, and they were officially open for business today.

Biscuit was immediately at my side. I let her outside into the dog run, then went to wash my face. To keep my mind awake, I turned on the television in my bedroom, keeping the sound low so I wouldn't wake Neal. He didn't have to get up for another couple of hours.

I'd listened to newscasts before at this hour, but they were generally repeats of whatever had been broadcast at eleven p.m. the night before. Not today, though. There was a breaking news story. Curious, I stopped in front of the TV to hear what it was.

Someone had been murdered. I gasped as I saw a familiar face plastered on the screen.

It was Myra Ethman.

I didn't like the woman, but still... she had a family. Friends. She'd be missed, I felt sure, even though she and I weren't exactly buddies.

It was definitely a shame. In fact, I felt awful for everyone involved. Losing someone you cared about was always so hard.

But then my mind focused on the last thing I'd said about her threats to my business. In public. Right there in my Barkery.

Surely no one would think...

Well, I couldn't be the only one she'd been nasty to. Certainly, she'd had friends and family. But she must also have had real enemies. The cops probably already had a suspect. I'd be fine.

But I nevertheless regretted my words: *I'll do anything in my power to make sure that Barkery and Biscuits will survive, and that means finding a way to keep her quiet.*

FOUR

I HEARD BISCUIT BARK. I wasn't sure how long I'd left her outside, but I hurried back down the hall and into the kitchen. I opened the door quickly, dashed onto the back patio and tweaked the end of the dog-run fence to open it and let her in, hoping she hadn't disturbed the neighbors at this early hour. Or Neal, for that matter, although maybe talking to him would help my distressed state of mind.

Or not.

It was still dark outside. I had to get to my bakery/barkery right away and start creating the day's products. My shift at the veterinary clinic wasn't till late afternoon, and my assistants would both be at work long before that.

But despite all my attempts to focus on those things, on my life, my mind kept returning to what I'd heard on TV.

Myra was dead.

I hadn't been particularly fond of her, but still…

I'd seen her yesterday. Argued with her. Said words, though not to her face, that could be interpreted as threatening.

I now regretted that. Even, surprisingly, felt some sorrow.

The news story had said murder. Did they have the culprit in custody? That hadn't been clear, so my assumption was no.

If the cops were still looking … well, surely they wouldn't consider me because of our disagreement. I hoped.

"This is terrible, girl," I whispered to Biscuit, who now sat on the wood-grained kitchen floor looking up at me, waiting patiently for the treat I always gave her when she came inside after a bathroom outing. I knelt first and gave her a hug, as much for myself as for her. Then I rose and went to the area beside my metal sink, where I kept a cookie jar shaped like a doghouse on the multicolored stone counter.

I liked my kitchen. I liked my house. I wanted to stay here and let my concerns revolve solely around whether my new business venture would be successful. Yet as I led Biscuit back to my bedroom so I could get dressed, I half listened for my smartphone to ring. Or for a knock at the door.

Forty minutes later, though, I was in the kitchen of my shops. I'd driven Biscuit and me here from home and parked in the small lot behind the stores. I'd fed Biscuit breakfast at home before we left, and right now she was shut into the Barkery while I got things started in the kitchen. It was Sunday morning, and I'd asked Judy to arrive about an hour from now.

First things first. In the Icing section of the kitchen, I washed my hands carefully and started putting the ingredients together for scones, since they were often breakfast food. Blueberry scones this morning. Yum, my own favorite. I then placed the first batch on the cookie sheets, ready to bake. When I put them into the oven it was time to prepare some people-biscuits, also popular early in the day.

The aroma of sweet pastry filled the air and I inhaled often as I worked, smiling, enjoying the smell and the feel of working in my own kitchen, ready to face my first real day as the owner of a retail business. *Make them sweet and make them good.* That was Brenda's edict regarding Icing, and I would follow it.

And that was all I would think about. *Could* think about, since I had to concentrate. Or so I told myself, as my mind continued to return to that announcement on the TV news…

Over the next half hour, I focused on Icing's products. I got a lot of breakfast goods baked first. I loved the aroma. I loved doing this—and especially looked forward to starting on the Barkery's treats of the day.

Judy soon entered through the kitchen's back door. I'd made sure that both she and Dinah still had the keys given to them by Brenda.

"Good morning," I said, glad I sounded cheerful.

"Hi." The older of my two assistants yawned. "I enjoyed my break from getting up this early while you were remodeling, and I was glad you had Dinah come in first yesterday morning. But I'm ready to go now."

We baked, facing each other, for maybe ninety minutes, wearing aprons over our store-promoting shirts and jeans. It was getting close to seven a.m. by now—near opening time. Judy stayed on the Icing side of the long, narrow set of waist-high shelves that divided the two parts of the kitchen, and I moved over to the Barkery side. We concentrated on mixing our respective kinds of batter and cutting or forming them into the appropriate shapes for the treats we were making, washing our hands often.

When we were quiet, which was most of the time, my mind kept returning to that awful bit of news. Did Judy know? Probably not, or she'd have mentioned it.

Or she could have been like me, wishing on some level that, if she said nothing about it, it couldn't possibly be true.

But she hadn't argued with Myra. She might have known her, since most people in town were at least aware of the most elite families. And she'd at least seen her yesterday. But she might not care, at least not much.

We removed things from the ovens, and when they were cool we took them into the appropriate parts of the shops and arranged them in the glass-fronted display cases. I went into the Barkery the most, where I patted a still-loose Biscuit a lot before washing my hands again. One of the things I'd designed for the Barkery was an area for Biscuit, which featured a large crate with a removable top and a leash-hitch for my dog when she wasn't inside the crate. I wanted Biscuit to be near me as much as possible during each business day.

Eventually we didn't have much left to bake, but some of our ingredients were getting low—flour and milk, mostly. I didn't want to leave, so I asked Judy to go to the nearest supermarket and pick some up, along with a few other items we'd need such as fresh apples, lemons, and yams.

"Sure." Judy seemed happy for the break. From a locked desk drawer in the tiny rear office, I retrieved the special credit card I used now for purchases and handed it to her, and then she left. There would be time for her to brew coffee for Icing on her return. I went back to baking.

About five minutes later my phone rang. Had Judy forgotten something? Did she have some questions?

I pulled my phone from my pocket. Caller ID told me it wasn't Judy but Neal. I'd thought his shift at the resort wasn't supposed to start till the afternoon, and Neal hated to get up this early if he didn't have to, unless it was for a tourist outing.

"Hi," I said. "What's—"

"The cops were here a little while ago, Carrie. I wasn't exactly awake and...well, I am now. They want to talk to you about—"

He didn't get to finish before I heard the banging from the other room, probably on Icing's front door. "Police," came the muffled voice. "Open up please, Ms. Kennersly."

Biscuit barked. She was still locked by herself in the Barkery, running loose there rather than confined in her open-topped crate, and her presence made it impossible for me to pretend I wasn't here.

"They're here," I rasped quietly back at Neal. "What did they tell you? What did you tell them?"

"Nothing much, either way. I only said I didn't know for sure where you were, but probably at the bakery."

Thanks a lot, I thought. But what else could he have done? "I'll call you back later and let you know what happens." And then I pushed the button to hang up.

I opened the door into Icing and maneuvered my way behind the display case. I stopped there for just a moment, beyond where I could be seen through the front door's glass, trying to quiet my irregular breathing and slow my heart rate.

But another knock, which sounded much louder this time, only accelerated both. "Police!" The voice was curt now, not a request but a demand. "Open the door."

Trembling, I obeyed.

I recognized one of the two people who stood there. Her name was Bridget Morana, and her cat's name was Butterball. Butterball was a patient at the Knobcone Veterinary Clinic. I doubted she was here about her cat, though. She wore a light blouse and dark skirt and a frown on her middle-aged face.

41

"Hello, Carrie," she said. "I'm Detective Bridget Morana of the Knobcone Heights PD. This is Detective Wayne Crunoll. I know you and I have met at the veterinary hospital, but Detective Crunoll and I are here to ask you a few questions. May we come in?"

I didn't think I had a choice. And by now, poor, ignored Biscuit was barking herself into a frenzy. "If you don't mind, let's go next door."

Apparently they didn't mind. After they stepped inside, I locked Icing's outside door behind them and motioned for them to follow me through the shop and into the Barkery. Biscuit hurled herself toward me when I opened the inside door, and after removing my apron I knelt and hugged my furry friend.

I needed that probably even more than she did.

"Can we sit down?" That was Wayne Crunoll. He appeared to be in his mid-twenties, his hair dark and short, with a hint of shadow on his pudgy face. Like his companion, he wore a white shirt, but his trousers were gray, not black like her skirt.

"Sure," I said and rearranged the chairs around one of the small tables set on top of the bone decoration on the floor of the Barkery. We all sat down, including Biscuit by my feet. I looked at each of cops before they began, attempting to appear both friendly and oblivious. "What's going on?" I asked.

"You had a party here yesterday?" Bridget began. Since she was older, I assumed she was the senior detective. Or maybe she was just starting the conversation off because we had a relationship of sorts—as tenuous as it was.

"I'm sorry if it got too loud." I again attempted to seem naive. "Did some of my neighbors complain? I invited anyone interested to come, but—"

"Carrie, one of your guests from yesterday appears to be the victim of a homicide that occurred last night." Bridget looked straight at me, her light brown eyes serious beneath straight, somewhat bushy eyebrows. Her hair was short and the same nondescript shade of brown as her brows.

I drew in my breath sharply, as if this was the first inkling I had of such a terrible occurrence. "Oh, no. Who? What happened?"

"We're hoping you can help us figure it out," she said, apparently responding only to my second question.

"Me? How?" Okay, maybe I was trying too hard to sound unaware. Or maybe I was reading skepticism in Wayne Crunoll's too-blank stare.

"Did you have a … disagreement with someone at your party?" he asked.

"I assume, since you're asking, that the … deceased person is Myra Ethman." I swallowed, trying to interpret their expressions, but nothing changed on either of their faces; there was no acknowledgment of my brilliant deduction or anything. And I'd "guessed" Myra and not Harris, with whom I'd also argued, so they probably knew I'd heard something. I decided to continue, weighing my words. "She and I did snipe at each other a bit, yes. She wasn't happy about my opening the Barkery." I waved my hand toward the display case.

The gesture got Biscuit's attention. She'd been lying at my feet, and now she stood and looked at me closely, wagging her tail as if she knew something was wrong and wanted to make it better for me.

If only she could.

"So you argued about it." That was Bridget.

"I wouldn't call it an argument," I contradicted. "I tried to make her see reason, that my new business wouldn't directly compete with

43

the Emporium. They sell different kinds of food from what I make here."

"Can you describe the whole discussion for us?" Bridget asked.

I hesitated, then shook my head. "I'm a veterinary technician, as you know, and a new business owner. I have a feeling you're asking me these questions because you want me to be a suspect in your investigation. I didn't do anything to Myra. But I think I'd better stop answering your questions now."

"Are you going to hire a lawyer?" Detective Crunoll sounded disgusted, but his expression remained blank.

"Do you advise me to exercise my legal rights?" I asked, then made myself smile. "In case you can't guess, I sometimes watch cop shows on TV. But this is all new to me. I assume you're just starting your investigation, and since you haven't read me my Fifth Amendment rights, I'll just wait and see for now. But let me repeat this. I didn't harm Myra, not in any way. And I hope that if it was in fact a murder you figure out who did it really fast. And—"

The front door to the shop burst open. Biscuit stood up and leaped toward it, barking.

Neal barged in. "Don't say anything, Carrie. I've met some lawyers at the resort and we'll hire one for you. No way can they arrest you for just fighting back when that bitch insulted you."

I closed my eyes for a second, and when I opened them I just looked at the ceiling. I knew my brother was trying to help—but had he given these cops motivation to arrest me right now?

———

Never mind how Neal's attitude had appeared when he stormed in and made an apparent attempt to protect me. He'd even disturbed

44

poor Biscuit, who'd stood up and looked from my brother to me and back again as if trying to figure out whether there was something really wrong with her pack.

There was, but I didn't want her worried about it. She was generally a sweet, calm little girl. Even though I'd had an urge to either yell back at my brother or run away, I didn't want her to sense it and do something to incur the authorities' wrath.

Now, it was ten minutes later. Neal had quieted down almost immediately and was currently smiling at the two cops who'd stood up and glared when he'd barged in. Biscuit was fine now too, lying at Neal's feet.

The detectives had started asking Neal questions, as if they also considered him a person of interest—or did now, after his outburst. But at least they'd all sat down after Neal brought another chair over. I remained off to one side while the cops and Neal talked.

An interrogation? Of sorts, but it was reciprocal. The two of them answered as many of Neal's questions as he responded to theirs. For the moment, I was out of it. I felt relieved yet antsy. I needed to open the shops soon.

While listening, I looked around the Barkery, seeing it from the cops' perspective. It would be all new to them since neither had attended the party yesterday. Along with the muted aroma wafting in from the kitchen, there was now a good supply of today's doggy treats in the glass display case. But I suspected that Bridget and Wayne didn't notice them. Since Bridget's pet was a cat, she probably wasn't even interested in perusing the display.

No blood was on anything, of course. This place contained no clues to the murder they were investigating.

Blood? That was just an assumption, since Myra had apparently been murdered. But perhaps there wasn't blood.

How had Myra been killed?

Maybe I'd find a way to ask. Maybe I'd find a way for *Neal* to ask. I wanted to hug him. After his initial onslaught, he'd been the most engaging and personable guy imaginable, just smiling and saying he didn't know anything and neither did his sister. He hinted that we were each other's alibis, since we'd slept in the same house, as usual, last night. But fortunately he wasn't asked to vouch for me specifically, and neither was I asked to vouch for him.

But I knew what made Neal one heck of a good tourist guide. He was popular, and people loved the hikes he led along the local trails beneath the knobcone pines, his boating expeditions on Knobcone Lake, and the skiing outings he organized on the slopes in winter. He was sweet. He was personable. And somehow, he seemed to be winning over Bridget and Wayne. Yes, he was on a first-name basis with both of them.

"So you used to work for the Los Angeles Police Department?" he asked. "Both of you?" He leaned forward, grasping his hands between his knees as he looked from one to the other and back with his intense blue eyes, appearing the picture of earnestness. "It's really great that you came to Knobcone Heights. I'd have thought that working for the San Bernardino County Sheriff's Department would be the big thing around here."

"In a way, yes," said Bridget. The frown I'd noticed on her before had been replaced by a look I couldn't quite read, except that it appeared mildly amused as well as somewhat predatory, as if she was just humoring this overly enthusiastic young man, waiting for the right time to leap in for the kill. "I got some good training in L.A. and could have stayed there, but I enjoy the San Bernardino Mountains. The Sheriff's Department would have been a good choice, but I liked the people here, the location, and, honestly, the fact I could probably get promoted more quickly."

I was a bit surprised she was being so forthright—or at least I was till she continued.

"So now I'm a detective with a lot of seniority. If I determine someone's a prime suspect, a lot of people jump in to help me find all the evidence needed to arrest them."

Why wasn't I surprised when her gaze moved from my brother to me? My feeling that she was preparing herself for the kill was probably correct—but she'd aimed it at me, not Neal.

It was my turn to smile at the senior detective, although a lot more weakly than my brother had. "Gee, and I thought you came here because you wanted to try some of my baked goods, Bridget. In fact, I need to check on the scones my assistant put into the oven a little while ago. If they're ready, I'll bring some nice warm ones out to both of you."

"I'll go with you," Wayne said in a hurry, after receiving a glance from Bridget. He stood at the same moment I did.

"You must really be hungry," I said, trying to continue joking—because if I didn't, I might cry.

"A bit," he said. "But in case you were going to use the opportunity to run, don't even think about it."

He, too, had been trained by the LAPD. He hadn't said why he'd chosen to work for the Knobcone Heights Police Department, but he probably had a similar response to Bridget's—yet he was one of the people who jumped to do her bidding.

I looked into his face and clenched my fists, but only for a second. "I didn't think about that till you mentioned it. And, no, I'm not about to leave my store just because you two are barking up the wrong tree." I paused. "That's a joke of sorts. You know that I sell doggy products here."

He nodded. "I have a couple of dogs at home. They're more my wife's than mine—little guys, both dachshund mixes. She got them from a shelter."

"That's wonderful," I said, entering the kitchen. "Mountaintop Rescue?"

"That's right."

Using thick oven mitts, I got the tray of scones out of the oven, then glanced at the clock on the wall. I needed to open the shops. I needed help.

As if they'd heard my thoughts, the kitchen was suddenly filled with both of my assistants. "What's going on?" Dinah asked immediately, looking stricken. Her medium brown hair was already pulled back from her face, and she was clearly ready to begin work.

"I've brought the extra ingredients." That was Judy, and she lifted the grocery bags she held in each hand, then put them on top of the long counter separating the two parts of the kitchen. "Aren't we ready to open?" There was a frown on her long face and she appeared confused.

"I hope to, very soon," I said. "But … Dinah, Judy, something terrible has happened and Detective Crunoll is here with Detective Morana, who's in the Barkery with my brother right now. They had some questions for me."

I half expected one or both of them to mention the murder, since it had already been in the news. But neither appeared to know what I was talking about. And of course I hadn't mentioned it to Judy earlier.

"What's happened?" Dinah asked.

"Myra Ethman—" I began, but Wayne interrupted.

"Ms. Ethman has passed away," he said, looking at me warningly. "It was sudden, so we are looking into it."

Both of my assistants looked shocked.

"Was she murdered?" Dinah asked.

"Why else would the cops be looking into it?" said Judy, her tone suggesting that she didn't consider Dinah very bright. Dinah glared at her.

"That's a premature assumption," Wayne said. "And—"

I was afraid he was about to tell my staff why he was here investigating. They might figure it out anyway; they both knew I'd argued with Myra, for one thing. But it was my turn to interrupt him.

"I'm so glad you're both here," I said. "Please just check out the displays to make sure they look good for when customers arrive, okay? Start with Icing."

"Sure, but—" Dinah began.

"Great. Now, Wayne, let's go back to the others, okay?" I used napkins with Icing's logo on them to pick out some scones, then headed toward the door back into the Barkery.

When we returned, Neal and Bridget were both standing. I handed the scones to our two unwelcome guests. I'd get one for my brother later.

"I've been asking Bridget about what we can do to help figure out what really happened," my brother said. "To make it clear we're both sorry but had nothing to do with it."

Bridget's face was unreadable, but she shot a glance toward Wayne, then nodded slightly, taking a small bite of scone without even thanking me for it.

Wayne kept his scone in the napkin and put it on a chair. Then he pulled a phone from his pocket. "We're going to keep things as confidential as we can as long as we can," he said. "But you know how the media is. They're going to push till they learn how Ms. Ethman died."

I gulped. Was he going to show us a picture of her body?

But no. Instead, the photo he pulled up turned out to be one of a dog leash.

"One that looked just like this was wrapped around her neck," he said. "Do you happen to have one like it?"

It was beige, and made of woven mesh. I had a similar one for Biscuit—the one I kept at the Barkery, in fact—but it was black. And that kind of leash was very common anyway.

"I definitely don't have a beige one like that," I said firmly, "but I can't swear that the black one I have for Biscuit isn't similar, maybe even from the same manufacturer. And I think I've seen ones like it in the Ethmans' pet store—the Knob Hill Pet Emporium."

I glanced toward Neal, and he nodded. He'd been there too, to buy dog food for Biscuit. Biscuit currently sat on the floor at our feet, looking from one human to another.

"That's quite possible," Bridget said. "That leash is a fairly popular style, and we're still checking out possible sources."

"Is that what killed her?" I asked. Could she really have been strangled with a leash like that?

"It's still under investigation, but the leash is believed to be a factor," Bridget said. "And there's something else."

Once more, I caught her nod to her colleague. He brought up another picture. "This was found near Ms. Ethman," he said.

He passed the phone to me, and I tried not to gasp.

It might not be true, of course. They could just be attempting to rattle me. To trap me into a confession—one that would be false, of course.

But the item found near Myra's body did look familiar. Too familiar. It appeared to be a large portion of one of the dog treats from the Barkery: bone-shaped, with a stylized B&B that I'd etched into the dough to promote my new venture.

It had apparently come from right here, in my shop.

FIVE

My mind began swirling like an expanding vortex. Could I possibly recall everyone who'd gotten one of these treats for their dogs? Unlikely. I'd passed out a bunch of our products, but so had my assistants and even Neal, and some treats had just been left on trays for people to pick up.

"There were a lot of these given out yesterday," I managed to say, snapping off all attempts at remembering specifics and turning to face both detectives. It wasn't easy. My knees threatened to buckle, especially under their chilly stares. Fortunately, I remained standing. "It doesn't matter that they were baked here. Anyone who came to our party could have gotten one and left it at ... at the site." Wherever the murder site was. I still wasn't sure, but the TV news had suggested Myra was found outside her garage, on the edge of some nearby woods. If my flimsy reciprocal alibi with Neal wasn't enough to remove me from their suspect list, I couldn't claim innocence based on having no idea where Myra had lived. She was an Ethman by marriage. Everyone in town knew where they lived.

"You could have too," Bridget said.

She'd seemed to be such a caring person when I'd met her at the veterinary clinic. At least she loved her cat. But that affection clearly didn't spill over onto an acquaintance she apparently considered a murder suspect.

"So what's your opinion about why the biscuit found there was broken?" Wayne asked.

What was he looking for? I hesitated briefly, considering how to respond. "I don't know," I finally said. "All I know is that I didn't leave it there and have no idea who did." I looked from one of them to the other. "I know I'm a convenient suspect. I argued with Myra, I admit that, but it wasn't that huge a disagreement. Even if it had been … You don't know me very well, but I can assure you I'm not stupid enough to argue with someone in public and then kill them."

"She's not," Neal confirmed. "In fact, my sis is pretty smart."

"Then she'd be smart enough to plant a clue against herself so she could claim later that she's being framed." A snide grin bisected Wayne's wide face.

"I can't believe you're zeroing in on me," I said softly. My fear must have been obvious to poor Biscuit, who sat leaning against my leg looking up at me. I bent to pat her, wishing I felt secure enough to reassure her.

"They're probably just trying to trap you and doing the same thing with everyone else they consider a suspect," Neal said, also drawing closer. I appreciated the protective presence of my brother, especially when he maneuvered around Biscuit and put his arm around my shoulder.

"Including you," Wayne said casually to Neal, and I felt Neal stiffen.

"But I didn't—" he began.

53

"Argue with her?" Bridget cut in. "No matter. You undoubtedly heard your sister arguing, and protecting a family member is a good enough motive." Neal released me and opened his mouth to reply, but Bridget continued. "Look, we know neither of you is going to step right up and admit today that you killed Myra. It's time for us to go. But you can be sure the whole Knobcone Heights Police Department will continue to investigate this homicide and collect evidence a whole lot better and more efficiently than those unreal clowns you see portrayed on TV shows. Then we'll arrest the person who murdered Ms. Ethman and make sure the charges stick. Goodbye, Neal. And bye, Carrie. I hope the next time I see you is at the veterinary clinic when I pick up some vitamins for Butterball—but I wouldn't count on it. It's more likely to be when we have more questions for you."

With that, both detectives strode out of the Barkery—and it was a good thing, too. A couple of customers were waiting outside the front door since it was a few minutes past seven a.m. The man and woman glanced curiously toward the two cops, but hopefully they didn't know that's what they were. At least the detectives hadn't been in uniform.

I noticed then that Judy was just inside the doorway to the kitchen. She stepped into the Barkery quickly to greet the customers but shot a glance over her shoulder toward me. Her expression was blank, all except for a look in her eyes that I couldn't quite interpret. Fear? Accusation? My imagination? I wasn't sure, but her face appeared paler than I was used to seeing it.

She must have been listening in.

"It'll be okay, Carrie." That was Neal. He was still standing beside me. "But I'd better get to work now. You call me if they come back, okay?"

"Okay," I said.

He gave me a hug and Biscuit a pat, and then he left. And despite the customers who stood by the full display case, I felt completely alone. Even Judy had disappeared into the kitchen after greeting the visitors.

I put Biscuit into her large, open-topped crate, then approached our guests, but before I could do more than say hi Judy returned, carrying one of our trays. This one was covered with a layer of dog cookies shaped like spaniel faces with long ears.

It wasn't the kind of biscuit in the photo relating to Myra…

"Thanks," I told Judy. I went behind the counter and just watched, smiling while she waited on the customers, who seemed happy to buy a dozen of the newly baked dog treats.

"We'll want more later," said the lady. "Other kinds, too. I left our little Missy at the resort and will probably bring her here a time or two before we leave. We'll be around for another week, so that should work well."

"That would be delightful," I said. Judy had already packed the order into a decorative bag, and I impulsively grabbed another biscuit from the tray. "Let's make it a baker's dozen today."

Both the lady and the man with her smiled, said thanks, then left.

"That was nice." Judy remained beside me behind the display case. She was smiling too, although her long face didn't look particularly cheerful.

"It's always a good thing to make a customer happy," I said, "and since we opened a few minutes late, it didn't hurt to add a little extra to encourage them to return." I sounded as if I'd been running a store for a long time rather than just trusting my instincts as a new retailer—instincts derived from my own experiences as a customer.

Judy didn't look impressed. "You'll need to give us instructions on when to add that little extra to an order." She paused. "Brenda never wanted us to do that."

I didn't want to say anything against my friend, but I wondered if Icing on the Cake would have been more successful if Brenda had been a little more impulsive that way.

"I may regret it," I said, "but let's give it a try."

"Okay." Judy turned slightly, as if preparing to return to the kitchen, then stopped and looked back at me again with her soft blue eyes. They appeared sad. "Those detectives. Do they... I mean, they were asking Neal and you questions, right? About Myra. And... um, do you know how she was killed?"

"I... well, the cops indicated she was strangled," I told her. "With a dog leash. But they indicated there might have been more to it, too."

"And the police think you did it?" Then Judy bit her narrow lips as if she regretted saying it.

I lowered my head for a moment, resting my gaze on Biscuit. "I gather that, yes, I'm on their suspect list. But I didn't do it, and they're sure to figure that out soon."

"Who do you think did it?" Dinah had just entered the Barkery from the kitchen behind us.

Both my assistants stared at me, as if waiting for a huge revelation that would make them feel a whole lot better about the situation. But even if I'd hazarded a guess, I had no idea if it would have any potential validity. Even so, I needed to reassure them that all around here was fine. That I'd be around and able to keep this shop open and maintain their jobs.

"I didn't know Myra well enough to say who would have wanted to hurt her," I told them. "She seemed rather... domineering to me."

And officious and nasty and over-the-top for no reason. "And not everyone likes that." Like me. But it still hadn't driven me to murder her. "The natural guess would be her closest friends and family, maybe one of the other Ethmans. But I've met several of them, including her husband Harris, and my initial reaction isn't to point fingers at him or any of the rest." I paused. "Do you two have any ideas?"

Both pairs of eyes opened wide. "Me? Oh, I didn't know her much either," Judy said.

"Me neither," Dinah added.

"But you're right, Carrie." Judy nodded. "Books and TV shows and all would indicate that the people who knew her best would make the most likely suspects. I just hope the police do a good job of investigating and finding out the truth."

"Me too," I said fervently. "Now let's go back into the kitchen. I want to see what you've started baking for both shops and help decide what should come next."

———

A couple of hours later, I felt better. A little, at least. I hadn't heard again from Neal, so I assumed he'd gone to work at the resort.

Since Myra had been the executive manager, I wondered who was in charge now. I didn't believe they'd shut down the whole resort in mourning, but I was curious about how things were being handled there today. Myra had been an important member of the family even though she wasn't born an Ethman.

I'd talk to Neal later. Right now I was working at Icing, finishing up with some new customers—three women I recognized from seeing them in a store or somewhere else in town. But I didn't really know them, so I assumed they didn't have any pets to bring to the veterinary clinic. They'd bought some people-cupcakes for a lunch that their book club was holding at one of their homes. I thanked them and gave them an extra treat too, hoping they'd mention it to the others in their group.

When they left, I realized my mind hadn't really settled down yet. I needed a break. It wasn't time for me to head to the vet clinic, though. Did I feel comfortable just leaving for a while?

Why not? After our initial difficulties with getting started that morning—and the discussion about who might have killed Myra—Dinah and Judy had been hard at work, apparently enjoying trading off which one staffed which store, and fortunately their interaction remained peaceful. We'd finished baking today's people and dog treats unless we got low on something and had to bake some more, and even though we had a steady stream of customers, neither of my assistants appeared to need help.

I decided to take advantage of all this and head to Cuppa-Joe's, a family restaurant owned by a pair of dear friends of mine, Joe and Irma Nash. And, yes, they served good coffee.

I gave my assistants my instructions and my thanks. They both had my cell phone number, and I told them to call if any questions arose, no matter how insignificant. I assured them I'd be back for an hour or so before heading to my other job.

Then I went into the Barkery, where I'd left Biscuit in her comfortable open-air crate, and she and I left.

Cuppa-Joe's was on Peak Road at the far side of the town square. It was a sprawling one-story structure with several different dining areas inside, as well as a couple of patios. One patio was in the center of the small complex, accessible by a path between the buildings. That was where Biscuit and I headed.

For the moment, my dog was the only canine there. It was a little early for lunch, and some people appeared to prefer the other patio. I didn't think Biscuit would mind. There were quite a few customers around and she might get extra attention.

I sat at one of my favorite tables. I came here as often as I could, partly because I enjoyed the family-style food and the attentive service. But I also visited often because I was so fond of the owners.

"Hi, Carrie," said Kit, who then knelt and said, "Hi, Biscuit," but without patting my dog. She was, after all, part of the restaurant's wait staff, so if she petted visiting animals a lot she'd be washing her hands constantly. She rose again and grinned at me.

Kit was around twenty-five years old, with curly blond hair shorter than my wavy mop. She had pink cheeks and a huge, toothy smile. Like the other wait staff members, she wore a knit shirt with buttons and a collar, which had a steaming coffee cup logo on the pocket. The staff all wore different colors. Today, Kit's shirt was orange.

"Hi," I responded. "I just want a quick, early lunch—tuna salad sandwich on wheat bread, lettuce and tomato, and some low-fat chips on the side. Oh, and joe, of course. Black."

"You got it." She wrote it down on a small pad of paper, then said, "I'll let the Joes know you're here," and took off.

The staff, and others—including me sometimes—referred to Joe and Irma Nash collectively as "the Joes," since this place was Cuppa-Joe's, and it was theirs.

Joe and Irma came out onto the crowded patio a couple of minutes later, pulled up chairs, and sat down with us—after each gave me a big kiss on the cheek and patted Biscuit's head. They weren't serving food, so they wouldn't need to wash their hands right away. They had, however, each brought a cup of coffee to the table with them. Good. That meant they intended to stay awhile.

59

"Great to see you, Carrie." Irma was in her sixties but looked much younger, with stylishly cut and highlighted brown hair framing a face made up as well as any model's. And she hadn't resorted to Botox or anything artificial.

"Ditto," said Joe. "But what brings you here on the day after you opened your new shop?" Unlike his wife, Joe looked his age, partly thanks to the grayness of his hair beyond his receding hairline. He also had deep divots on either side of his mouth, which only seemed to frame his frequent smiles.

They'd both popped in at the party, separately and briefly. They had their own business to run, of course, and their limited participation hadn't hurt my feelings. I knew they'd been with me in spirit.

"Oh, well…"

"Spit it out," Joe insisted.

"And don't pretend," said Irma. "We heard about Myra Ethman, along with some rumors that you and she had a bit of a falling out at your party."

"More than that," I said. "But it wasn't enough for me to have killed her, as the police seem to think."

"Oh no." Irma rose and came over to hug me. "I was afraid of something like that when I heard those rumors."

"Who—" I began.

"Some of our early morning customers who like to talk too much," Joe interrupted. "We made it clear we'd be glad to serve them food but we don't allow gossip around here."

"Thanks." The word spilled from me in a throaty sigh. "You two are the best."

In fact, Joe and Irma were like family. No, they were better than family—at least, better than Neal's and mine.

Neal and I had been brought up by our family in nearby Riverside, California—two sort-of misnomers. First, although the northern part of Riverside is actually beside the Santa Ana River, most of the town doesn't exactly front the water. Second, except for each other, Neal and I don't have much of a family. Our parents divorced years ago, and both remarried and had other kids. Those younger stepsiblings were all-important to each of them.

Neal and me? Not so much.

The Nashes had been here forever. The restaurant had been started by Joe's parents when they were younger than me, or so I gathered. Joe and Irma's own kids were grown, and their daughter remained in Knobcone Heights. She and her husband helped to run this place and apparently were teaching their two daughters how important it was. Their son had become a lawyer and moved to L.A. but visited often with his own family.

Yes, the Nashes believed in family, their own and those they'd adopted into the fold. Like Neal and me.

Kit soon served my sandwich, and I shared my chips with Joe and Irma. Everything was delicious—particularly the charming conversation about some Hollywood types who'd recently come to town and visited Cuppa.

I was about to take the last bite of tuna when I saw two people stroll onto the patio from the front of the restaurant—two people I'd prefer to never see again, and definitely not this soon. The detectives.

Joe and Irma followed my gaze as I put the sandwich down. "Them?" Joe asked.

I nodded. "They've been asking me questions."

"We know they're cops. They eat here a lot, usually inside. But I'll be glad to throw them out."

"No need," I said. They'd probably seen me and decided to take the opportunity to silently harass me. Maybe make me so nervous that I'd run right over to them and confess.

Not.

"But honey," Irma began.

"It's okay. Really. I'm pretty much finished, and I have to head back to my shops for a while before going to my other job."

"You're still working as a vet tech too." Joe didn't make it a question, since he knew the answer. "You're really something, Carrie."

Yeah. Something. A new business owner, a veterinary technician—and a murder suspect.

I waved Kit over and requested my check. The Joes had offered to let me eat free, especially now when I was starting a new venture, but I insisted that I'd continue to pay my own way.

"Believe me," I told them both quietly. "If I hadn't been finished, I wouldn't be leaving now. I wouldn't let them scare me, honest." I began to stand, and Biscuit immediately rose to her feet too and shook her curly golden fur. I patted her, then managed a small smile that I shot first to Irma, then Joe. "But if you happen to overhear any of your customers confessing to killing Myra, please let me know."

SIX

BISCUIT AND I WALKED back to the Barkery and went inside. Judy was there but no customers were. "Everything okay here?" I asked.

She gave me a rundown of who'd stopped in. Fortunately, it didn't include any cops, or at least none she'd identified. Instead, it sounded mostly like a bunch of Knobcone Heights residents who hadn't been at the party yesterday and came to scope out the new section of the store and buy some of our products.

Dinah came in and said that nearly the same had held true for Icing. We'd had a lot of foot traffic, although the place hadn't gotten especially crowded at any time.

"Great. Let's see how we do for the next hour before I head to the vet clinic," I said.

The day continued pretty much as Judy had described and Dinah had seconded. There was a nearly steady flow of customers, not overwhelming but definitely encouraging.

I—we—might really make a go at this new venture, I thought. Of course it was still the weekend, but even so ...

I felt pretty jazzed by the time I had to leave for the veterinary hospital. Especially since Dinah and Judy appeared to be getting along okay today.

Because I owed the clinic a lot and always wanted the best for its patients, I loaded a sack with dog treats. I'd leave them with the clinic's greeters to pass out in the reception area to dogs who'd been cleared to nibble on wholesome snacks. I didn't have anything prepared for dogs with particular dietary issues, since I'd only do that if I was made aware of a pet with special needs.

Then I opened Biscuit's crate door and clipped her leash to her collar. She'd accompany me there. The Knobcone Veterinary Clinic also had a doggy daycare facility, so I'd always been able to bring my dog to work after I'd adopted her. Biscuit had been an injured stray, brought in as a puppy two years ago. I'd fallen in love with her as I'd helped her heal, and, after futilely attempting to find her careless prior owner, I delightedly adopted her as soon as she was well enough to leave the clinic.

The doggy daycare part was separate enough from the rest of the hospital that I didn't worry about any of the patients' health issues affecting Biscuit, or else I'd have found someplace else to care for my best friend when I couldn't be there for her. She'd gone through enough trauma as a pup. She didn't need any more now.

The walk to the clinic wasn't far. It was located close enough to the town center to be convenient for the area's most privileged families, just a block behind the town square. Mountaintop Rescue was a block beyond that, so I particularly liked this neighborhood.

The veterinary hospital had been designed to be as stylish as a lot of the places in Knobcone. Like some of the mansions owned by the town's elite, including members of the Ethman family, it had the look of a Swiss chalet. It was only one story high but had a tall, sloped roof, an inviting front porch where people and pets waiting for appointments could hang out in good weather, and multiple paned windows. Its exterior walls were of textured blue.

Biscuit and I didn't worry about going past the animals and their owners on the porch, which was crowded since the weather today was good. I wondered how many others were inside in the waiting area.

I had a feeling this would be a busy afternoon for a certain veterinary technician, which could be a good thing. It might keep my mind off the situation that had never come close to evaporating from my consciousness that day, even when I was busy waiting on customers at my shops.

Using the path at the side of the hospital, we walked to the back parking lot. I opened a rear door and let Biscuit lead me into the familiar hallway to the daycare area, which was one large room with a gleaming, beige linoleum floor—easy enough to clean if any of their charges had an accident. Along the walls were crates of various sizes, in case any of the visitors did not play well with others. We had a special staff dedicated to the daycare, who got groups of compatible dogs together for learning and playing and having as great a time as possible.

I sometimes dropped in unexpectedly when Biscuit was here, just to make sure thing were going well for her, and they always were. She was smart, she was friendly, and she was one of the staff's favorites.

"Hi, Faye," I said to the chief caretaker, a forty-something woman whose thinness I attributed at least partly to the energy she used in caring for and playing with her charges. Her dark hair resembled that of the many terriers she helped to watch here—short, kinky, and in disarray. "Here's my baby. She'll be here for the next couple of hours."

"And you know I'll take good care of her," Faye responded with a huge smile. "*We'll* take care of her," she amended as a couple of other staff members approached, both part-timers who were college kids deciding whether they were interested in becoming veterinarians. They both wore T-shirts that said "Knobcone Vets Rock" over jeans.

"We sure will," said one of the boys, Charlie. He reached for Biscuit's leash and I handed it over.

"Hey, Biscuit," said the other one, Al. "Let's dance." He reached into his pocket, pulled out a small doggy treat—not one of mine—and encouraged Biscuit onto her rear paws and into a spin.

I laughed. "Better watch out or she'll start training you." I touched my baby on her head. "See you soon," I told her.

I walked through a different door, the one that led into the hospital. I left my bag of treats with the receptionist on duty and she promised to put it in the spot designated to hold items to give out to the patients. Then I went into the rear dressing room, opened my locker, and changed into my well-worn blue vet tech uniform shirt and matching pants.

When I exited into the main hallway, one of the other techs was walking by, holding a squirming little Shih Tzu. "Teeth cleaning," Yolanda explained. I nodded and followed her back to the general treatment area, where other dogs under observation were confined in different-sized crates along the wall. She handed me the dog. "Her teeth are in good condition so we don't have to turn this into major dental care, sedate her or anything like that."

"Good." I watched while she prepared the toothbrush and special canine toothpaste. Her blue uniform shirt looked a lot newer and crisper than mine. Her black hair was pulled back into a bun at her neck, which as always emphasized the sharpness of her dark-complected face. Even so, she was an attractive lady about my age—and as skilled a veterinary technician as I was.

Holding the pup steady on the metal-topped table in the middle of the room while Yolanda did the brushing, I helped to steady him and adjust his jowls for easier access.

"Ouch," I said in sympathy when he squealed and tried to jump out of my arms. I had a good grip, so his attempt to flee was futile.

I sensed the malaise of the other dogs around, and even saw a couple of them stand up in their crates. I was sure they felt some kind of sympathy—as well as relief that, at least this time, it wasn't them.

"You want to take him back out to his folks?" Yolanda asked. "Room 6. I need to get some flea repellent ready for them to take home."

"Sure." I snuggled the little guy—his name, according to the tag on his collar, was Shammy—and headed down the hall with him.

I entered Room 6 and found Arvie there with Shammy's people. He held out his arms for the dog. "All set?" he asked.

"Yes, teeth nice and clean. Yolanda asked me to bring him back while she got the flea meds ready." I smiled at the young, Hispanic-looking couple who apparently belonged to Shammy.

"Great," Arvie said to me. To them, he added, "You can wait out front while Yolanda gets your supplies."

And pay your bill, I thought, but I didn't say that.

As they left, Arvie turned to me. "You okay, Carrie?" he asked softly.

I looked into his light brown eyes and felt my own tearing up. Like the Nashes, Arvie was dear to me, almost family, and I knew he gave a damn.

I also knew from his question, and from his caring expression, that he'd heard not only about Myra, but he was probably also aware that I was a suspect in her murder. I'd managed to stay calm when I was with Joe and Irma, but I wasn't so successful right now.

"I ... I guess so," I said, but the tears that ran down my cheeks told him I wasn't doing so well after all.

He came over, pushed up the sleeves of his white medical jacket, and took me into his arms. Arvie might look a bit frail with his increasing age, but he was definitely strong—a result, no doubt, of having to wrestle with pit bulls and dobies and Rottweilers and such while examining them.

"It'll be all right, Carrie," he said softly.

I pulled back and looked into his caring eyes. "Not sure you know the whole story," I said. "I assume you heard about Myra Ethman, right?"

He nodded.

"As if a murder in my favorite town wasn't enough ... Well, it doesn't matter that we weren't best friends. I hate the idea that she's dead." I paused. "And are you aware that the police seem to think I killed her?"

"Yes, I do know that." He moved a little to rest his back against the metal examination table in the middle of the room. "The word's out there." He shook his head while pursing his thin lips. "People love to gossip."

"I wish they'd just gossip about good stuff regarding my new Barkery and Icing venture," I grumbled.

He laughed. "Don't worry. I'm hearing about that too."

Dear Arvie. I knew he was on my side. For one thing, he wanted my venture to succeed because of the money he'd loaned to me. And I had no doubt he trusted me not to have killed Myra.

Just as I trusted him that way. I recalled, as I stood there, the argument they'd had a couple of months ago. Myra had accused Arvie of misdiagnosing Davinia with ticks. It was impossible for Davinia to have ticks, she claimed. They sold only the highest quality repellents at the Emporium, and of course they'd used them on Davinia. But Arvie had already treated Davinia for ticks, and, at her next examination, she'd been tick-free—surprise, surprise.

Even so, Myra had bad-mouthed Arvie publicly for his supposedly vile and erroneous claims. Had she done so recently enough to make him a suspect in her murder?

I really hoped not.

A knock sounded on the examination room door and it opened. Yolanda stood there. "Oh, sorry," she said. "Just wanted to find out if you're available, Doc, to examine a cat that got into a fight with a neighbor and may need stitches."

He was available. So was I, to help out—I held the cat during the exam as her nervous, worried owner looked on. I was careful to make sure her paws never got close to Arvie or me, since cat scratches can be downright nasty.

Yolanda helped me shave the wounded areas and inoculate them with a numbing agent. Then Arvie cleaned the spot even more thoroughly and stitched the unhappy cat.

"She'll be fine," Arvie assured the owner, who hurried over to the table to hug her unhappy, newly sewn baby. I knew the kitty would get some prescribed antibiotics to avoid infection.

My day continued after that with helping to bring a batch of prescription weight-control food out for a dachshund whose tummy was large enough to touch the ground. Then I was called into another examination room, where Dr. Reed Storme was working with a Maltese mix with fleas. He needed me to bring in the pills and spray we recommended for that.

When the owner took that dog out, I scratched at my arm. "Yick, fleas."

Reed laughed. I liked the sound of his deep voice as much as I enjoyed looking at him. But as much as I'd started to enjoy flirting with him, I didn't feel much like doing so now. Grinning at him, I pivoted to leave the room.

"Wait, Carrie," he called. I turned back. He wasn't smiling now. "I heard about what happened last night. About Myra Ethman, I mean. And I also heard—"

"That I'm a major suspect," I said in a sing-song voice. "I know." I didn't intend to sound so sarcastic, but I still preferred that with Reed instead of crying the way I had with Arvie.

"I thought our police force was more intelligent than that," he said. His words brought my smile back. "So did I."

He walked toward me and took my hands, looking down with his deep brown eyes. I willed myself to stay calm and not tear up despite how my eyes burned under his sympathetic stare. I started to pull away.

"Hey, you know what? I want to hear how they've been harassing you, but we won't really have time here. How about joining me for dinner?"

I immediately thought of a dozen reasons why not to—and then realized it was something I actually wanted to do. In fact, I knew where I wanted to eat: at the Knobcone Heights Resort's restaurant. While there, I could ask a few questions and even eavesdrop to hear which of Myra's friends and relatives might have been likely to strangle her.

"I'd love to," I said warmly. And when I told Reed where I wanted to dine, he laughed again.

SEVEN

WHEN MY SHIFT WAS up at the clinic I retrieved Biscuit from doggy daycare, thanked Faye and her helpers, and headed back to my stores, which would still be open for another two hours—till six p.m. I hung out there with my staff, who were waiting on customers as they trickled in and out.

"You're still okay with being alone again when you come in tomorrow morning?" Judy asked. We stood in the Barkery as closing time approached.

"Of course. Although either or both of you are always welcome to join me at five a.m. whenever you feel like it." And, yes, I was feeling a little tired, but I was okay for now with my very long hours.

"How about . . . never?" That was Dinah. She'd just joined us, and she was smiling. She erased her words with a wave of both her hands. "You know I'm kidding. Just say the word and we'll come in at five or whatever."

"Hey, I was just going to say that." Judy's voice sounded grumpy, but she was smiling. Sort of.

"Great," I said. "Thank you both." Though tomorrow was Monday, no longer the weekend, I still had both of them scheduled to come in; I would start alternating them soon. I myself would be working seven days a week, sometimes at two jobs each day, but I wouldn't ask anything like that from them.

I turned then and went back into the kitchen, leaving the two of them alone together—and my ears perked to eavesdrop on any argument.

But all was silent in the Barkery except for noises suggesting that one of them was playing with Biscuit outside her crate and the other was reorganizing the remaining goods in the display case. No conversation, but no yelling either. I started breathing again while examining both sets of multi-row ovens to make sure they'd been cleaned, so I wouldn't have to scrub them before starting to bake in the morning.

I'd walked into this whole situation fully aware of the tension between my assistants. I was determined to be firm but kind. So far, we'd all gotten along reasonably well despite snipes now and then between my helpers. As long as things stayed that way, I'd keep them both on, especially since I needed more than one person's backup to maintain my part-time job. If I needed to hire someone else as well, fine. I'd do all I could to afford it.

But I would make sure nothing got in the way of my two stores' success.

Nothing … except my potential arrest for the murder of Myra Ethman.

I couldn't let that happen. But my mind roiled once more about that situation as I finished cleaning—as if it had ever stopped.

With determination not to let it get me down, I removed the apron I'd donned and went into Icing. Dinah was there now and I said goodbye, then watched as she left. "Thanks," I called. I locked the front door behind her, then slid into the Barkery, where Judy was also getting ready to go. I thanked her too as I retrieved Biscuit and the three of us walked out together.

My car had stayed all day in the small lot behind the store. It was a bit of a trek along winding streets if Biscuit and I walked between our home and the stores, so I'd started driving here when the stores were under construction, just as I always had to the veterinary clinic. It was even better to do so now, when we had to arrive so early in the morning.

But right now we were going home. I needed to change clothes for my date with Reed tonight.

My very important date at the resort, where I'd be enjoying the company... while subtly seeking information.

At home, I fed Biscuit her regular, wholesome food in a reasonably sized portion. I'd been careful, both at Barkery and Biscuits and in what I'd instructed Faye about treats, to make sure Biscuit didn't overeat, even on the wonderful stuff we were now preparing at the Barkery. Biscuit was part of my family, and I wanted her to stay fit and trim and healthy.

Did she get more than she should some of the time? Probably. I'd just have to keep an eye on her—and on myself when I gave her treats.

"You're on your own here tonight," I told her a little while later. After letting her into the dog run for a brief post-meal romp, I'd donned a lacy white top over a deep green skirt and traded my slip-on athletic shoes for heels. Neal was working late and I'd probably see him at the resort while I was there.

I'd turned on the TV to watch some news and learned that the speculation now was that Myra had merely been rendered unconscious by the leash found wrapped around her neck. Though it hadn't

74

yet been officially substantiated to the media, the further speculation was that Myra had then been bashed on the head with a rock.

I could never have done that. Any of it. But someone apparently did.

Weren't the police checking for fingerprints or other evidence? If so, they would surely stop focusing on me.

I hoped.

I quickly turned the TV back off.

Feeling a little guilty about leaving Biscuit alone—and needing some positive attention myself—I knelt on the kitchen floor and hugged her, running my fingers through her curly golden hair. Seeing her mournful expression, I relented enough to give her a small piece of a treat I'd brought home from the Barkery.

"I won't be late," I assured her. Not if I intended to stay awake for my entire date tonight—and wake up early again tomorrow. I slipped through the door to the garage.

Reed had offered to pick me up, but he lived in the more elite hillside area of town, closer to the lake on whose shores the resort was located. Plus, his schedule at the clinic ran as late tonight as mine did at my stores. It was easier, and saved time, for me just to meet him there.

The roads to the resort were twisty, as were most streets up here on the mountain. I drove down the hill, then onto Summit Avenue to follow its curving course to where it ended near Knobcone Lake. I arrived in about fifteen minutes.

The resort was a bit north along the lake's shore. It was a sprawling facility, each building two stories high with sloping slate roofs over thick white walls and dark wood-framed windows. The main reception building looked similar, including in its height, and inside the ceilings were tall and slanted with a couple of large stone fireplaces venting through them.

At the rear, facing the lake, was the main restaurant, a highly popular locale not only for its view of the water but also because the food was excellent. That was where I was to meet Reed.

The parking lot in front was, as usual, nearly full, but I found a spot near the entrance gate. It wasn't cheap to park there, but I'd get my ticket validated at the restaurant. I pushed the button to lock my aging white Toyota sedan and headed toward the main door—me and a half dozen other people. Were they guests here, or had they come for dinner too? Or both?

In any case, life apparently was continuing on here despite the death of the facility's manager. I entered and saw a line at the long wooden registration desk off to the right. I also saw my brother behind it.

That was a shame. I wanted to talk to him, learn whether he'd talked about Myra's death with anyone at the resort or heard anything potentially useful about what had happened to her. Was the method of her death under discussion? But I didn't want to bother him. He was talking with a middle-aged couple as I walked by, and I stood there just long enough to catch his eye and wave my head toward the restaurant to indicate where I was going.

I passed beneath the thick, decorative wooden beams in the crowded lobby and glanced upward as if utterly captivated by them. My real purpose, though, was to casually meander around, eavesdropping on multiple conversations. Some were about how nice this resort was, how there were so many things to do here even now, in summer, with no snow on the ground. In fact, there were lots of recreational activities to do on the lake: boating, water skiing, kayaking, swimming, and whatever else people enjoyed doing around clean, appealing waterways.

Interesting. I was glad to hear what was being said, since the more tourists were around, the better that retailers—like I now was—were likely to do. Plus, some of the people had their dogs leashed beside them since this was a pet-friendly place.

Both sides of my shop could take advantage. Additionally, Neal might get scheduled for more tourist expedition gigs.

But those weren't my primary motivations for eavesdropping. I listened in on multiple and mostly hushed conversations about what had happened last night, and how the murder victim had been affiliated with this place. I even heard a bit of speculation about who had killed her. An "unidentified local resident" was the main suspect, someone the victim had argued with last night.

I felt my shoulders sag more each time that was said. But what else had I expected? Gossip always grew exponentially as it was repeated.

Had I really thought someone here actually knew who'd murdered Myra and would let all lobby visitors know that bit of truth? Hah.

I stopped circling the lobby and strode toward the restaurant. As I passed the front door, Reed entered. He saw me at the same time I spotted him and came toward me.

"You okay?" he asked immediately, his dark eyes looking concerned.

I nodded. "I'm fine. Just hungry." That was a lie. I wasn't sure if I'd be able to force myself to eat. But I didn't want anyone to know how upset and, yes, frightened I was, so I'd do all I could to act normal.

"Okay." But his voice sounded dubious.

I looked him up and down. He either kept a major wardrobe change at the clinic or he, too, had gone home. He wore a dark suit, a white tie, and a blue necktie printed with black doggy paw prints. He looked great, and I liked it. I liked him. Determinedly, I grabbed his arm, shared a smile with him, and strode toward the arched doorway to the restaurant.

"What the hell are you doing here?" demanded a voice from behind us before we reached the entrance.

Without slowing our pace, I closed my eyes for an instant, feeling all my muscles clench. I recognized the voice, of course. I'd heard it yesterday, mocking me in tandem with his wife.

Harris Ethman, the new widower.

Reed stopped, though, and since I was still holding onto him I had to cease walking. He turned back first. Then I did too. I didn't want to look at all guilty, and my avoiding Harris might do just that.

Before either of the men could say anything, I approached Harris and gave him the briefest of hugs. "I'm very sorry for your loss," I told him, meaning it for many reasons. I backed away again.

His eyes, which always looked a bit sad to me since they were turned down at the ends, blazed. "No you're not," he spat. "You killed her."

I felt, as much as saw from the corner of my eyes, the people nearest us stop their own conversations and stare.

"Now, Harris," Reed began, but I raised my hand.

"I can understand your being upset, Harris," I said, proud of how calm I sounded. "And everyone's aware that Myra and I weren't exactly on the best of terms yesterday. But you can be sure I didn't do anything to harm her."

I watched his gaunt face, his dark brows dipping down at the ends, like his eyes, beneath a receding hairline. He glared, and his fists clenched beside his scruffy jeans as if he was barely restraining himself from punching me.

But it could all be an act. Who was more likely to murder a person than her spouse? And Myra had clearly been an overbearing, critical wife who'd told Harris what to do—like how to run the Knob Hill Pet Emporium. Did Harris even like pets? The fact they owned a dog and a cat didn't prove anything.

And what had he really thought of his wife?

Now wasn't the time to accuse him, though. I was merely speculating. I hadn't a shred of evidence... yet.

"So you say," he growled. "But—"

"Please excuse us," I said. "We're here to have dinner." I pulled at Reed's arm and he began walking alongside me again.

"You're not welcome here." Harris had hurried to place himself in front of us.

I opened my mouth to respond, but before I could, Neal joined us. "Harris, I'm sorry to interrupt, but your parents have just arrived. They're by the registration desk. I assume you'd like them to get the best suite available, right?"

"Of course." Harris glared at me again for an instant, then hurried away toward the desk. I glanced in that direction and saw a senior couple off to the side. I hadn't met the elder Ethmans but had a ridiculous urge to go thank them for their perfect timing.

I knew whom I should really thank, though: Neal. I didn't know how long the Ethmans had been there, so it was actually my brother's timing that had been perfect—and from his both sympathetic and slightly amused glance, I recognized he knew it.

"I get a break in fifteen minutes," he said in a low voice. "I'll grab a cup of coffee with you then." He followed Harris back toward registration.

Reed looked down at me. "Ready for dinner?"

"Absolutely, as long as I also get a glass of wine."

Though the restaurant was crowded, we were seated immediately and couldn't have requested a better table. It was near the huge windows looking out over the lake. The sun was setting, and a brilliant pink glow outlined the homes and hotels on the far side of the water.

This almost made the turbulence so far feel worth it. Now, if only I could somehow glean further information about Myra's death, and who, besides Harris, might have had a motive.

For now, though, I scanned the menu, then ordered a salad and grilled bass. Had the bass been caught in this lake? Possibly, since it was one of the kinds of fish that were plentiful here, along with trout, catfish, and more—some of which were stocked by the local lake association to encourage tourists.

Reed was on the same fishy wavelength, since he ordered trout. He got a beer, though, while I chose a glass of imported Pinot Grigio. I could always order a second if I needed it for fortification—although the fact that I had driven here might nix that idea.

When our drinks arrived, Reed lifted his glass in a toast. I looked into his smiling brown eyes and felt pleased that not only was I here, but I was in wonderful company.

I took a sip of my wine.

But before I could take a second, I saw three figures suddenly loom around our table.

"Have you no shame?" demanded the woman.

"What are you doing here?" asked the older of the two men.

The other man was Harris, and though I hadn't paid much attention to what they looked like clear across the lobby, I figured that the couple with him was his parents, the senior Ethmans. The ones who owned this resort. I'd heard they didn't live in Knobcone Heights right now.

"I'm here to have dinner," I responded as cordially as I could muster. "Apparently you're the ones with no shame, since you're causing a scene for no reason. As I told Harris, I'm sorry for your loss. All of you. Now, if you'll please leave us alone, I want to enjoy my meal."

They looked ready to scream, but just then another couple joined us.

"Mom, Dad, I don't think it's the right time or place for this," said the woman, who looked around Harris's age. His sister? "Please, let's go to your room now, okay? Harris, why don't you show them which one they'll have for tonight?"

Without another word, the older couple and Harris left. I looked at the newcomers with a sense of relief.

"Thank you," I said. "That was rather … uncomfortable."

"Well, don't get comfortable yet," the woman snapped. "I was just trying to defuse this situation for the sake of Harris and this resort. I'm his sister Elise, and I know who you are, Carrie. Go ahead and stay for dinner, since you're here. But in case you don't know it, I'm in charge here now, at least in the interim till a decision is made about who'll manage this resort. So I can tell you— when you're done with your meal, don't ever come back."

EIGHT

I FELT AS THOUGH Elise had first hugged me, then slapped me in the face. Even if I knew her, I wouldn't have wanted either from her.

But I did like eating here at the resort now and then. And the fact I'd been uninvited wouldn't stop me.

In fact, I now felt even more like returning soon. Very soon.

Maybe Elise didn't want me here because she was hiding something … like the fact she was the one who'd killed her sister-in-law.

As I watched both couples and Harris stomp away, I realized that Reed was talking. " … We could just leave now, and I wouldn't mind stiffing them with the bill under these circumstances. That was entirely uncalled for."

I looked at him. His great-looking face was twisted into an angry scowl on my behalf, and I had an urge to run to his side of the table and kiss him. But he might misunderstand that. I definitely was attracted to him and appreciated his concern, and I was interested in seeing where our new relationship—if it was a relationship—might lead.

I didn't really need a champion, though—a man who'd slay dragons on my behalf. If I ran into any dragon that needed slaying, I'd take care of it. Although, as a vet tech, I might instead choose to find the appropriate anti-anxiety med to calm the creature without permanently harming it.

Since Reed was a Doctor of Veterinary Medicine, I could even ask him to prescribe the drug.

"It's okay," I said quietly, giving him as big a smile as I could muster, although I had a feeling it appeared sad. "I don't want to give her or any of them the satisfaction of my leaving."

He didn't argue with me. In fact, he gave a decisive nod. "I'm with you, Carrie, all the way."

I turned my head to see which nearby diners might be watching us, but most were looking studiously down at their plates or at who-ever sat across from them. Good. They were polite, even if their hosts weren't.

Our food had just been served when someone else came over to our table, the man who had arrived with Elise. He was wearing a plaid shirt, jeans, and an uncomfortable look on his mustached face. "Carrie?" he asked.

I nodded as I braced myself for another onslaught, holding my hand up slightly when I saw that Reed was about to rise and face the guy.

"I'm Walt Hainner. Elise's husband. I want to apologize on her behalf, and on behalf of the rest of the Ethmans. No one should have acted that way with you. Not unless, or until, the police arrest you for . . . well, you know." His smile was weak, as if he'd tried unsuccess-fully to crack a joke.

I knew that name. He was the contractor that Myra said I should have hired to do the work to separate my shops. Since I'd had no need of a contractor for anything previously, and I certainly didn't socialize with the likes of the Ethmans, I had never met him before.

I stood to look up at him. He was tall. As far as I could tell despite the looseness of his shirt, he was muscular—not surprising for a man who built things for a living. He could easily have wielded a murderous leash around Myra's throat and been strong enough to beat her to death with a rock...

But he'd been kind enough to come over to apologize for his wife and in-laws. I certainly wasn't going to accuse him—unless and until he was arrested for the murder. But did he have a motive? Most likely, since he'd known the not-very-nice woman.

"Thank you, Walt," I said softly. Reed had stood when I did and remained beside his chair, watching and listening but not doing anything other than sending me supportive looks. "I appreciate what you've said and hope your family doesn't give you a hard time about it." I paused, then made myself continue. "I'm sure they're feeling terrible about what happened to Myra and are lashing out to try to ease themselves through this difficult time. My condolences to all of you."

His thick brown eyebrows rose. "Thanks." He looked down at the table. "I'll leave you to your meal now. And in case you're wondering, you're always welcome back."

For a price, was my first thought. *And do you really have the authority to say that?* was my second. But I just thanked him, and Reed and I resumed our seats as he walked away.

"Maybe that was a nice thing for Walt to do," Reed said as he took a bite of his trout, "but it shouldn't have been necessary in the first place."

I placed my fork into my salad and stabbed it around a little until I had a few pieces of lettuce on it. Could I force myself to eat?

Heck, yes. I put the lettuce in my mouth. The dressing was a tangy honey mustard, and it tasted good. I chewed and swallowed and then scooped up some of the bass. It was delicious.

I had an appetite despite what had gone on here, and I continued to eat while sweet Reed asked me questions about my two new businesses and how I was doing with them. It really did help me keep my mind off what I didn't want to be thinking about here. And soon, as promised, Neal joined us for coffee as we finished eating.

No introductions were needed. Reed and Neal had met before.

"Hey, you doing okay?" Neal asked as he sat down at my right. The Knobcone Heights Resort shirt he wore that day was light brown, another color that looked good on my handsome younger brother. But at the moment I wasn't thrilled about his promoting this place, even though he worked here. "I saw a whole kettle of the vultures in charge of this place stomping in and then out of here," he finished.

I looked sideways at him. "Kettle?" Was he suggesting stewing them for dinner?

"Well, sure." He looked proud of himself. "That's a group of vultures while they're flying. They're referred to as a committee when they're just roosting in trees. I think there are more terms for that, too. But I learn a lot here while staffing the reception desk—and even more when I'm out and about giving hiking tours and all."

"A bit pretentious, aren't you?" I rolled my eyes until they met Reed's. He was apparently trying to keep himself from laughing aloud.

"You got the vulture part right anyway," Reed agreed. I nodded. But Reed's expression grew more serious. "I had the impression they were ganging up on your sister—all except Walt. Maybe. But if that—what? committee?—groups together to protect one of their own who *really* killed Myra, it might be hard to prove what's true."

The server returned then. I'd barely noticed the attractive young lady before except to note her dark hair and friendly demeanor. But now she aimed a huge smile at Neal. "Can I bring you something?" The words weren't exactly suggestive, but her teasing tone suggested they knew each other and perhaps had some kind of flirtation going.

Neal confirmed this by saying, "You can bring me anything you want, Gwen," and winking at her. "But for now, I'd like a cup of coffee."

"Cream?" I'd never heard that word said so suggestively before, and I blinked as I looked at Neal to get his reaction.

"Oh yes," was all he said.

"Anything else I can get for you?" Her tone was normal now, and her gaze turned away from Neal toward Reed, then me.

"We're fine," I said. But when she left for Neal's coffee I asked him, "What's going on between you two?"

"Not really anything ... yet," he said. "We're just having fun."

"I bet." Reed's tone was amused.

"But I think she'd be a good resource for asking about ... well, you know," Neal continued. "I hear a lot of things at the front desk, but because Myra was our boss it wasn't considered a smart thing to gossip about her, at least not much. But I know that some of the wait staff here not only take care of the Ethmans when they eat at the restaurant but also bring food orders to the resort's offices for them. Even though they've retired from the resort, they still pretty much own it and act like they're in charge while they're around— maybe especially now since their chosen manager Myra is gone. Anyway, let's talk to Gwen."

"Fine." I leaned toward my brother. Quietly, I asked, "Is the gossip ban still on now? I'd think that, under the circumstances, everyone would be talking about Myra and what happened ... and maybe even speculating how it happened."

"They are, to some extent." Neal also kept his voice low, and Reed leaned over the table so he could hear. "Today everyone's acting like they're in shock, and not many of us are even hinting that we won't miss the b—er, witch."

"She wielded a heavy broomstick?" I speculated, my half-grin wry. "I'll say."

Gwen returned then and put a beige pottery mug in front of Neal. She poured coffee into it from a metal pitcher and set a small container of cream on the table. She then looked at him. "Just let me know if you'd like anything else." She was still flirting, but I was glad to see that the look Neal leveled on her was serious.

"Actually, there is something." He crooked his finger to draw her closer. She frowned a little, as if she realized that this would go beyond their friendly banter. "Gwen, that's Reed over there, and this is my sister, Carrie." He pointed to me.

"Hi, Reed. Hi, Carrie." Her expression was wary. "Good to meet you both."

"And, Carrie and Reed, this is Gwen."

"Hi," I repeated, as did Reed.

"Gwen," Neal said, "I'm sure you saw and heard what our ... let's call them 'superiors' since they like that word, even though they aren't. What our *superiors* said and did around Carrie before."

Her face froze. "Yes, but—"

I thought I understood what Neal was doing and decided to help, keeping my voice very low. "Gwen, I'm sorry to hear about what happened to Myra Ethman, even though, as you may have heard, I argued with her. It wasn't much of an argument but now I'm a suspect. To protect myself, well—"

"We, of all people, know there were plenty of people around here with motives to hurt Myra," Neal said, taking over. "Not that we would have. But are you aware of anyone who might have been particularly angry? Maybe someone who got fired recently. Or even was just chewed out."

Gwen looked around, as if worried that all the patrons around us were eavesdropping. I didn't think they could hear but understood her concern.

"I did wonder about it," she admitted, even as she stood taller for a moment and picked up her coffee pitcher. "This was just freshly brewed, but if you don't think it's hot enough I'll bring you some more right away," she said loud enough for others to hear. But before she left, she leaned down again and whispered, "A chef got fired recently for not getting a meal ready fast enough for those … superiors. And for not obeying their cooking orders. He was really mad."

"I hadn't heard that was the reason he left," Neal said. "That was Manfred, right?"

"It was," she said. "Be right back with your coffee," she called over her shoulder as she hurried toward the kitchen.

"That's Manfred Indor," Neal explained when she was gone. "He was actually a pretty good chef. Trained at the CIA."

"What?" I stared at Neal, confused. "Was he a government agent?"

"Nope. Like I said, he was a chef trained at the CIA: Culinary Institute of America. It's in New York City."

I gave my brother a gentle punch on the shoulder. "Drat. I was starting to get all excited about the possibilities. An angry government agent would probably be able to kill someone and frame another person fairly easily."

Both my table companions laughed. I just smiled weakly.

"If she'd been poisoned," Neal said, "I'd definitely consider Manfred the perfect suspect."

Well, even if Manfred wasn't with the CIA that most people thought of when hearing those initials, he'd still apparently been an angry guy.

I wasn't planning on trying to prove who'd killed Myra, of course. That was for the police. But if the authorities kept considering me as a suspect, I'd need to be able to suggest some other logical possibilities, preferably with more than just names and claims of who'd not adored Myra.

And I already knew I wasn't the only person who'd argued with her lately.

I wondered where Manfred was now.

NINE

Neal had to return to the registration desk, and soon afterward Reed and I finished our meal.

He handled our bill. I'm not an old-fashioned wimpy woman who insists on being treated on dates. But practicality counts, so although we'd only gone out for coffee a few times since we'd met, I'd let Reed pay since he'd asked to. He's a full-fledged, well-paid vet, while I'm a vet tech—not paid badly, but I certainly bring home less than he does. I also foot some of Neal's bills, since I make more money than him.

And now, especially, with my new business venture, every penny counted to me, even after my generous loan from Arvie. Plus, this was our first dinner date, and Reed had invited me—not that I'd even considered playing coy about it. I'd wanted to go out with him.

I'd wanted to come here.

I did, however, insist on leaving the tip, and since I appreciated Gwen's potential clue I was even more liberal in the amount than I usually am—and I'm not particularly stingy.

"Do you want to head out of here?" Reed asked as we strolled into the lobby. There weren't many people around now, but Neal was still behind the registration counter.

I took Reed's hand and headed in Neal's direction. We passed a couple of open doors to offices, and I noticed that the Ethmans were all gathered in one of them.

Well, not really all the Ethmans. I hadn't thought about him earlier, but there was one missing who was actually fairly nice, or at least I thought so: Les Ethman, the City Councilman who'd come to my opening party... was it just yesterday? Too bad he wasn't here making his family members act somewhat polite, even if their mind sets were nasty.

Mrs. Ethman—Susan, I thought her name was, Harris's and Elise's mother—spotted me and glared. I simply smiled and kept going, but the event helped me decide how to respond to Reed's question about leaving. "Not yet," I said. "Why don't we take a walk on the beach?"

Although it was getting late, there were lights on near the water, I'd noticed, so it wouldn't be too dark there. I wasn't sure if the Ethmans would notice us, but I at least would know that I was defying them, or maybe all of them but Walt Hainner. Before we were out of view, though, Susan's husband also saw me. His name, I believed, was Trask. His glare was similar to his wife's.

I was good friends with quite a few senior people: Arvie and the Nashes in particular. But these Ethman seniors were anything but buddies of mine. Aging apparently didn't always make people grow nice and kind and civil. With some, maybe, the opposite occurred.

I knew they saw that I'd ignored their statement that I wasn't welcome here. To rub it in further, I spoke loudly enough for them to hear. "I think the beach outside will be a great place to walk this evening."

I felt Reed's slight tug on my hand and looked at him. His grin was sideways, his expression amused. He knew what I was doing. And, sweet guy that he was, he went along with me.

"Right," he said, also loudly. "I really enjoy walking along the beach at this resort."

I laughed and used the leverage caused by our clasped hands to swing our arms as we walked out one of the lobby's rear doors and down the concrete stairs to the beach.

The lights illuminating the vicinity were attached to the upper areas of the building. The sand was a wide path, leading to the edge of water that sparkled under the artificial radiance. We were far from being the only people there. Some were walking. Others lay on blankets or towels on the sand, mostly fully clothed. A few hardy souls in bathing suits waded into the lake despite the coolness of the late spring evening.

"Want to take off your shoes?" Reed asked. I looked down at my low tan heels and considered it.

"Why not? Although I don't want to get into the water."

We walked slowly along the sand, and I felt its grittiness on my soles and between my toes. We talked not about what had brought us here, but about animals we'd been treating at the clinic.

Eventually, I said, "I'm really enjoying myself, but I think we'd better go. I have to be at my shops at five o'clock tomorrow morning."

"Really? Every day?" We'd stopped, and Reed looked down at me. I enjoyed the concern and amazement in his shining brown eyes.

"Yes, at least for now, till I get things started. My assistants may help me in that way, too, soon, but I have to get into a routine with them and make sure I trust them to do everything necessary at that hour before I'll let either or both of them get things started in the morning."

"You could also hire someone else," he said.

I nodded. "That's another possibility I'm considering, but it would mean paying another salary, so that's in the future as well."

Reed's eyes had changed a bit while we looked at each other. Now there was fondness and more in his gaze.

So, yes, right there on the beach, all the world—or at least as much of it as was on the Knobcone Heights Resort's beach at this hour—got to see us share a really nice, warm kiss.

We walked back to the stairway. Still smiling, I brushed the sand from my feet and put on my shoes, and then we went up into the lobby again.

We were crossing it when Reed's phone chimed. He pulled it from his pocket and looked at the screen. "The clinic." He answered immediately.

It was soon apparent that he was talking to one of the techs staying there overnight, who had a complicated question about a new patient's overnight treatment. I knew which dog they were discussing, a Portuguese water dog named Riff who had had a fight with an even larger dog. The patient had been badly bitten but should be fine, although for right now his injuries needed to be treated very carefully. Reed walked to a corner of the lobby. I didn't stay with him. There was nothing I could do at the moment.

I considered baiting my new enemies, but when I walked by the door where I'd seen them before, it was closed.

I figured I'd just write a note to Reed and hand it to him, thanking him and letting him know I'd see him soon at the clinic but I needed to go home to sleep. I headed to the desk, where Neal was talking with someone, to request a piece of paper to write on.

I recognized that someone right away—Jack Loroco, the guy who'd not only come to my party but suggested I might want to sell some of my dog treats nationally as a VimPets product.

"Hi," I said somewhat hesitantly. It was too soon for me to approach that kind of marketing, even if I eventually wanted to. But just in case, I needed to be friendly.

"Carrie, hi," he said. "Remember me from yesterday?"

"I do, Jack," I replied. I looked at Neal. "May I have a piece of paper? I need to leave Reed a note since he's on the phone. I unfortunately need to get home now."

"Yep, sis, you do." Neal looked at Jack. "Since you're in the business—we were just talking about your store and VimPets, Carrie—you must know, Jack, how early someone who runs a bakery needs to get started in the morning."

"Definitely," Jack replied.

"I'll give Reed your good night," Neal said. "I'll still be here for another half hour or so. He's bound to be off the phone by then."

I liked the idea that Reed would get the reminder personally. "Great. Thanks. And he can call me on my way home—as long as it's no later than about ten minutes from now."

"Got it."

I turned to say goodbye to Jack, but he said, "I'm staying here but I'll walk you to your car. Got a couple of ideas."

I sucked in my breath. Did I want to talk any kind of business with him now?

But he fortunately said, "I'll be here for another day or so before heading back to L.A. We should make arrangements to talk when it's not getting so late."

"Good idea," I said.

We decided that coffee tomorrow afternoon might work, and I gave him my phone number to call and confirm it.

"Now," he said as we reached my car in the crowded parking lot and I pushed the button on my key fob to open it. "You know I was there when that Myra woman gave you a hard time about baking things that compete with her husband's pet emporium."

I held my breath for a moment. Was he going to accuse me of murdering her too?

"I heard that she was killed last night," Jack continued.

"Yes," I said. "It's a shame." I reached for my car's door handle but he beat me to it, opening the door for me.

I slid in quickly and waited for him to make a comment about the rumors—or worse, about my guilt. Which he did, but not exactly as I'd braced myself for.

"She was a silly woman," he said. "Competition can be good. And her ridiculous attitude still wouldn't have given you reason to harm her. So, all I've heard around here today? I know it's untrue. In some ways, I had more reason to kill her than you did—and I didn't do it either, Carrie. Good night. I'll look forward to our talk tomorrow."

He bent down and unexpectedly kissed me on the forehead, then closed the door.

———

I had a lot to ponder on my drive home on the curving, hilly, and artificially lighted streets of Knobcone Heights. At the top of the list was why Jack Loroco thought he was a more logical suspect in Myra Ethman's murder than I was.

Had he argued with her too? Had anyone heard it?

Most of all, *had* he killed her?

If it wasn't Jack, then what about Chef Manfred Indor? He'd been fired by Myra. To most people, that isn't a horrible enough event to lead to murder, but I didn't know Manfred. Maybe he'd flipped out because of the insult, or the way she'd handled it, or... who knew?

Most important, were the cops aware of Jack or Manfred or anyone else who had an motive, arguably, to kill Myra—assuming Jack actually had a motive?

Sure, the detectives were harassing me, but I couldn't be the only one—could I?

And would I be able to sleep for my few available hours that night?

I'd started to pull into my driveway when my phone rang. It was hooked up to the car while I was driving, and the sound startled me. I stopped and pushed the button, figuring I knew who it was.

I was right. "Hi, Carrie. It's Reed. Sorry I got distracted by the call, but—"

"It's perfectly all right," I told him. "Riff's care is much more important than our saying good night."

"Yes and no," he said. "Anyway, I assume I'll see you at your shift tomorrow afternoon."

"Sure," I said. But my smile faded when I pushed the button to hang up and finished driving into my garage. I could have added, but didn't, *As long as I'm not in jail.*

I didn't have to say it, though. Just thinking it—again—made me quiver. I was scared. But I couldn't let myself focus on it.

Even so, I was so glad that Biscuit was waiting when I went into the house. Her exuberant greeting helped my state of mind. "I missed you too, girl," I told her with a hug, then took her out for a brief walk under the neighborhood's streetlights.

And, yes, I did somehow get some sleep that night, since I was awakened by my alarm when it went off again at four a.m.

———

"Oh, no," I whispered around five o'clock in the morning. I barely heard my own words over Biscuit's barking in—where else?—the Barkery. I was in the part of the kitchen right behind the Barkery, since I'd already gotten the human breakfast treats started and was about to commence the doggies'.

I wasn't sure which door I'd heard someone knocking on—and calling "Police!" from outside. Couldn't they at least wait until I'd gotten all my initial products ready, so I could open the shops on time? Or maybe till six a.m. when Judy was due to arrive?

Maybe I could buy them off with a couple of scones. They'd seemed to enjoy them before. Or ... I looked down at the dough I had just been preparing for the first round of dog biscuits, ones that contained fresh apple slivers. Maybe the police would like these better? All my doggy treats were good enough to be eaten by people.

I heard the knock again and realized I'd better move. I quickly rinsed the dough off my hands and hurried through the door into the shop. I grabbed Biscuit's leash and attached her to the crate. Then, taking a deep breath, I opened the Barkery door.

The two detectives stood there under the lights. "Can we come in, Ms. Kennersly?" Detective Bridget Morana demanded.

"Do I have a choice?" I hadn't had one last time. And I'd no reason to think that Neal would join us again, since as far as I knew he'd been sound asleep when Biscuit and I had left this morning—and I wasn't aware of any visits he'd had from these cops.

Wayne Crunoll and Bridget both came in as I stood aside. My heart was thumping erratically. Were they here to arrest me? If so, why?

What evidence had they found that they thought implicated me?

As it turned out, they were here more to harass me than anything—although I forbore accusing them of it. I already had a horrible relationship with them. Why make it worse? They disguised it, though, in a way they probably thought would make me feel like one of them—at least till they could put the cuffs on me.

"Sorry for coming here at such an early hour, Carrie," Bridget said, "but we knew you'd be here and we have a couple of things to run by you."

That sounded totally odd, so I rearranged three chairs on the Barkery's floor to fit around one of the small round tables so we'd have somewhere to sit while we talked.

I couldn't completely hate Wayne, since he knelt even in his dressy detective clothes to gently roughhouse with Biscuit while Bridget watched me. But I couldn't exactly like him, either.

"You know," Bridget said, her pale brown eyes tired but intent, "we don't get many murders here in Knobcone Heights, which is a good thing. But that means Wayne and I, as two of the main detectives on our small police force, have to work twice as hard as if we did it all the time."

"As a person now following two careers at the same time, I understand," I lied. I offered them scones, which both said they'd love. Leaving Biscuit there, I went into the kitchen to fetch a couple of my baked goods, Wayne at my heels. When I returned to the Barkery, I handed them their treats. Then I settled into the chair I'd set up for myself.

I did understand their having to work hard, but I did not understand at all why they were here. Maybe I shouldn't be so generous with the treats. It might encourage them to visit even more.

Bridget sat down too, crossing her legs in her dressy slacks. "Let me be honest with you," she said. As if I believed that. "You still seem like the most obvious suspect, given your argument with Ms. Ethman that night. But to do our job right, we have to look at all angles, all possibilities."

What was this about—especially at this hour? Was she trying to put me off guard so I'd say something that would lead to whatever evidence they thought they were looking for?

"I'm glad," was my wary response.

"So... do you have any ideas who else we should look at? You've now had a day to try to work out your own defense. Not that we want you to try to figure out who committed the murder—assuming you didn't do it. In fact, it's best if you stay far out of it. But since you might want to aim our attention toward someone else—well, who would you try to aim it at now, after a day's reflection?"

This was weird. I still thought they were trying to put me off guard, but what if they were serious? Was this some new way of detectives investigating a murder case? Based on some odd TV show with pseudo-psychics or whatever?

"All I really know is that it wasn't me," I said cautiously. "Or my brother Neal. But... " Ah. It occurred to me that they might have received a call from Harris, or his parents or sister, or even Walt Hainner, letting them know I'd been taunting them by hanging out at their resort's restaurant. "But as I think you might know, I did spend a little bit of time last night at the Knobcone Heights Resort having dinner with a friend."

"Well, yes, we did hear that." Wayne was now sitting in the third chair I'd put out for us, eating his scone. "Were you sounding any of the Ethmans out about whether they could have killed Myra?"

I stifled my ironic laugh. "No, although most of them made it clear I wasn't welcome there for dinner, even as a paying customer." I didn't need to mention I'd only paid the tip. "Walt Hainner, Elise's husband, was a lot kinder than the rest of them."

"And would you like to point your finger at one or all of them, to get ours pointed away from you?" Bridget smiled as if she intended this to be a joke, but I knew better.

Would they then use my theoretically pointed finger to take my theoretical fingerprint and compare it against ones they found on Myra? But joking with myself didn't make me feel any better. Besides, I was sure that if they actually wanted my prints they'd ask or get a warrant or whatever cops did.

"Honestly? I don't trust any of them—not even Walt, not entirely. But I can't tell you which of them might have murdered Myra. Maybe they all colluded. It wouldn't hurt for you to check into that."

"Of course," Bridget said, but I suspected she wouldn't really look too deeply into any of them. "Thanks for your suggestion. And for us to check things out—could you give us the name of the friend you were with last night?"

I hesitated. They'd probably find out anyway if they didn't know already, but I didn't want to sic them on Reed. "I don't think so. He's one of my bosses and I don't want to get him involved in this."

"Okay," Bridget said, so I felt certain she already knew.

I considered mentioning Jack Loroco instead, since he'd hinted at some kind of motive to harm Myra, but I also didn't want to send these detectives after him until I knew if he was joking or if there was actually a reason to question him.

"Well, if you hear anything about the Ethmans that we should know, I'm sure you'll tell us." Bridget paused. "Oh, and by the way, do you happen to have any of that kind of dog treat you made the first day—the kind that was found near Ms. Ethman's body?"

Ah-hah. I wasn't sure why, but this could be the real reason for their visit. I doubted they actually wanted me to point to an elite Ethman and make accusations—although I would, of course, if I had any evidence to support it.

But as to the biscuits? "Sorry, no," I said. "The ones we didn't give away were all sold yesterday. I'll make some again soon. I know you have a cat, Bridget, and these are dog treats. Does Wayne want some for his wife's dachshunds?" I tried to sound innocent, as if I didn't believe this was some kind of trap they were setting up.

"Sure," Wayne said. "Or any others of your treats. I'm sure my dogs would love 'em."

"I'm sure they would," I returned with a smile.

"But he especially said he wanted to give his dogs those particular treats," Bridget said, sending what looked like a warning glance to her partner.

"Absolutely," Wayne said. It only underscored the fact that they wanted more of these particular biscuits for some reason, although how they'd be able to use a new batch to prove I supposedly killed Myra, I had no idea.

"When I make more, I'll save some for you," I said. Which meant I probably shouldn't make any more of that particular kind of treat until Myra's killer had been found and arrested. Too bad. I really liked that recipe.

"Well, thanks," Bridget said. "We'd better be going now. I'd imagine you have other treats to bake—both for dogs and people. Maybe even that special kind of biscuit."

She was pushing it too hard, but I wasn't about to tell her so. On the other hand, if I could get them sniffing in a different direction...

"There is one thing I did want to mention, although it might mean nothing," I said. "Did you know that Myra recently fired one of the resort's best chefs? From what I heard, he was really resentful. Whether he'd have killed her, I don't know, but it wouldn't hurt to ask him."

"We're still looking for him," Wayne admitted as they reached the door, earning him another evil look from his partner.

"Well, if I happen to run into Chef Manfred Indor, I'll be sure to let you know," I said. Not that I'd recognize him. But if I could set these two on another, much more likely suspect, I'd be delighted.

TEN

I BREATHED A DEEP sigh of relief when the cops finally left. But that relief didn't last long. I had lots of treats to finish baking before the day at the shops could begin, although Judy would arrive soon. I'd asked both my assistants to help out today. Staggered days would begin later this week.

Fortunately, I hadn't left anything in the oven, so I wouldn't face a burned batch of baked goods. I checked that Biscuit's leash was still attached to her crate, gave my fuzzy golden girl a big hug to comfort myself more than her, and hurried back into the kitchen. I washed my hands for a long time, as I always did as a vet tech and now as a baker. Only then did I start grabbing the ingredients for the next batch of dog biscuits and begin to mix them.

I lost myself in the process for a while, trying to concentrate on mixing and baking and my stores. How business might be today. How I'd shift from working at the Barkery to Icing and back again.

But not unexpectedly, my thoughts eventually started heading toward my cop visit. Their insinuations and questions. My vulnerability.

My fear, that I couldn't suppress all the time. Like now.

What was I really going to do? Not just wait and see what happened. I had to take control of something, at least.

I was beginning to feel like I was trapped in one of the mysteries I loved reading. I enjoyed a lot of books, in fact, and even had an e-reader. I particularly liked to read about animals since I'd devoted my life to them, and I especially enjoyed mysteries with amateur sleuths. I'd always thought it was fun to see what mischief might befall an oblivious protagonist who suddenly finds herself in a position to help solve a murder. Silly, yes. Fiction, yes. Or so I'd always believed.

So how had *I* gotten into that position?

But here I was. And—

The back door opened behind me and I jumped, nearly skidding on the clean tile floor. When I turned, I wasn't surprised to see that Judy had just entered the Barkery side of the kitchen.

"Good morning, Carrie." She had a skeptical grin on her face as she scanned the almost empty counters. "So, are you ready for us to come in earlier to help you start baking?"

"Soon," I said.

"I'm not sure you can wait. I think you need help. Did you sleep in this morning? There aren't a lot of trays with product to put into the cases outside here. And they all seem to be Icing goods."

"You're right. But at least there are several trays of scones and croissants and things that you can fill the Icing display case with. And as to your question—" I hesitated. Should I tell her what had happened earlier—about the return of my unwelcome visitors?

Well, why not? Judy knew I was a suspect. And I might have to rely on her and Dinah's help even more till this situation was resolved—assuming it ever was.

"I was here on time, but I had an early visit from the detectives looking into Myra Ethman's murder," I finished. But I really didn't want to burden Judy with the fear I had about possibly getting arrested. Nor did I want to concentrate on it myself. "They wanted my opinion about who might be viable suspects in the case."

"Really? They wanted your opinion?" She'd started putting on her apron but now stopped, turning back toward me. Doubt shadowed her light blue eyes, and no wonder. But I'd told her the truth.

"That's what they said, although I didn't really believe them. The thing is, I'm not sure exactly what they were looking for." I paused. "I did manage to suggest other people they might want to check out, like Myra's relatives. And there was also a chef Myra fired recently, who I heard about while I was at the resort for dinner last night."

Judy laughed, her broad smile bisecting her long face. Shaking her head as she reached behind her to tie the plain white apron's strings, she said, "Maybe they really did want your opinion. You seem to have a lot of them."

"Yeah," I said, "and the most important is that whoever killed Myra, it wasn't me."

To my surprise, Judy approached and gave me a hug. I hugged her back. She'd been reasonably friendly to me since my taking over the bakery, but a bit reserved, too—at least more so than Dinah.

I thought frequently about how she'd said, from the first day I'd taken over Icing, that she hoped to open her own bakery someday, perhaps become a rival. But at the moment, she could probably still teach me more about human baked goods than I could teach her—and she seemed inclined to do so.

She was thin, especially for someone who'd worked in a bakery for a while. Her hug was strong, but she released me fairly quickly, as I did her.

"I believe you, Carrie." She stepped back to look me in the eye. "I know you didn't kill Myra. Maybe the cops will figure that out too."

"Amen," I said. Then, feeling as if we'd gotten too serious, I turned back to the batter I'd been preparing. "Now, let's get busy before customers start coming in."

———

Dinah arrived a short while later. We only had a few customers at first, but business started picking up as the day progressed. About mid-morning, I was behind the display case at the Barkery checking our inventory when the door opened and Billi Matlock walked in.

She wasn't the only customer present, and I wasn't the only person serving customers at the time. But Dinah was helping a young woman who'd carried her Yorkie in, trying to determine the best treats for such a small, energetic pup. We had a great selection available by then, so it was just a matter of the customer making up her mind. Dinah was definitely busy.

So I was especially pleased to be able to wait not only on a member of Knobcone Heights's other most-esteemed family, but on a member of City Council. Not to mention her role at Mountaintop Rescue. I'd always appreciated how she and her staff often brought rescued animals to my vet clinic for their checkups, treatment, and shots. Fortunately, the Mountaintop shelter was fairly well endowed both by the Matlock family and by other local residents. There was no doubt around here that animals were welcome members of the community.

"Hi, Carrie." Billi walked up to me. Not surprisingly, she was in workout clothes—expensive-looking ones. In addition to her work with the shelter and on City Council, she owned and ran a very posh day spa and fitness club, the Robust Retreat. It was on Summit Avenue but a few blocks in the more elite direction, toward the lake. Again not surprisingly, she was slender and looked good in her outfit. Her hair was long and loose now, dark with golden highlights. Her eyes were deep brown, and her face was … well, lovely. I was surprised she wasn't always followed by a herd of men trying to get her attention. But as attractive as she was, she wasn't married, and I'd never heard about anyone she was dating. That could be because she was discreet. Or maybe men were afraid of her, thanks to her powerful position on the council.

Was I jealous of her looks? No. I was okay-looking, and certainly didn't want to stand out in a crowd as she did. But since she was a politician, attracting attention was undoubtedly second nature to her.

"I want to buy an assortment of your dog treats to bring home to my Fanny and Flip to try out," Billi said. Fanny was her beagle mix, and Flip was her black Lab. "Then I'll want to buy a bunch of what they like best for the shelter."

"Of course," I said. "I'm sure they'll love everything. But—well, this is only our second full day of business and we're running low on everything. I intend to donate any leftovers to Mountaintop Rescue anyway." I'd also continue to bring some to the veterinary clinic.

"Really? That's fantastic. But we'll buy some from you too. I want to make sure you're really successful—and that way you'll be able to keep those donations coming."

I smiled and led her to the glass display case to pick out what she wanted, which was a smattering of everything.

I handed her the nearly filled box when we were done and she paid for her order. By that time, Dinah had finished with her customers too and had gone into the kitchen. Billi walked to the side of the room, where Biscuit slept on her soft bed in the crate near the wall. She knelt and petted my dog, who wriggled with pleasure.

When Billi stood, she came back to where I remained near the counter. "Look, Carrie. I've heard … well, I know some people may think your stupid little argument with Myra led you to kill her." I opened my mouth to assure her of my innocence but I didn't have to. She put her hand up to keep me from talking, then said, "I know you didn't do it. So do most people. But you're a convenient suspect, so the cops are after you."

I nodded ruefully. "That's for sure. In fact … " I told her briefly about my two visits from them.

"Well, don't you worry." She leveled her dark, attractively made-up eyes on me. "City Council can't do everything. I can't do everything. But anything we can do to get behind you and get the authorities looking for who really did it? You can be sure that's what we'll be doing."

"Thanks," I said gratefully. And for the second time that day, I shared a hug with someone, this time a friend.

———

Billi left soon afterward and I returned to the kitchen, this time sending Judy out to staff the Barkery. I wanted to start other dog treats baking, planning in advance to have leftovers to give to the rescue organization.

I rather lost track of time, but when I heard a bunch of voices in the Barkery and hurried back in to help Judy wait on customers,

I realized that Biscuit and I had to head to the veterinary clinic for my shift. I packed up a box of the treats we'd baked, since I'd decided to create a lot today. And I made sure there were plenty of extras so I'd have some to give to Billi later. While I was at it, I decided to bring some extras to the clinic to share with the dogs at daycare with Biscuit that day.

It was always good for promotion to give out freebies now and then, and I placed a sticker for the Barkery on the box. I'd tell Faye, and also let Charlie and Al know, that it wouldn't hurt for them to mention to owners of the day care dogs just where the delicious dog biscuits had come from.

"Of course we'll let people know," Faye asserted after I handed the box to her at the check-in counter. Her grin beneath her terrier-rough dark hair was huge. "I've already mentioned to a few people how one of our wonderful vet techs has opened a shop that includes the sale of healthy hand-baked dog treats. Now they'll get to sample it. Rather, their dogs will."

Her eyes scanned the large room full of dogs of various sizes, most of whom were chasing balls being rolled along the linoleum floor by Charlie and Al. My gaze followed hers. I hadn't brought enough for everyone, but at least some of those pups would get a taste. Maybe their owners too.

"People could also try it if they want," I said to Faye. "We use only the best ingredients both for the dog treats and the people baked goods next door. Or is this too much promotional information?"

"Never!" Faye's smile grew even wider. Giving a quick nod, she reached into the box and pulled out a bone-shaped biscuit. She pulled off one end and put it into her mouth. "Delicious! Although do I dare ask what's in it?"

It was one of the ones I thought might become a favorite. "Apple slivers, for one thing. And—"

A dog owner I knew from seeing her at the daycare before came over. "I want to pick Pete up," she said, then looked down at the box sitting on the narrow counter. "What's that?"

I explained, and before I was through, another biscuit was gone—after she, too, had tasted an end.

"I'll be visiting your shop really soon," the lady said, then reached out for the little black dog Al handed her. "With Pete."

I laughed, thanked Faye, patted Biscuit—who'd remained at my feet during all this—and then hurried through the door into the veterinary clinic. I went to the dressing room to change into my usual scrubs, then entered the back room to learn my first assignment of the day.

I didn't have to wait long. Arvie needed a tech with him to hold onto a young Weimaraner who'd gotten something stuck at the back of his mouth. He didn't have to wait until one of the male techs was available; I was strong enough to help.

The owner, a motherly woman who was biting her lips nervously, said she didn't know what the dog, named Kato, had gotten into. It turned out that he'd bitten the wrong way into one of the thick manufactured treats that were supposed to be excellent for dogs' teeth. It had broken and gotten stuck. This didn't happen often, and poor Kato hadn't been able to dislodge it.

Arvie removed it as I held Kato. The dog's mother was extremely grateful and thanked us both over and over.

So did Kato, with a few licks.

The next patient I helped was a Shih Tzu there for shots. I brought the necessities into the room where Reed had been examining her.

The rest of my shift progressed equally well, with nothing particularly noteworthy, which meant it was a good day. No truly ill or injured animals, no life-and-death situations.

When it was over, I went into the back room to change again. My phone was ringing as I grabbed my purse from my locker. I looked at the ID and didn't recognize the number. But I figured out who it had to be.

I had a sort-of date scheduled for this afternoon.

Sure enough, it was Jack Loroco. "I went to your shop to see you and Judy told me when you got off work at the vet hospital. I'm here in the waiting room now."

"I'll be out in a minute," I said.

I wondered if I should thank or scold Judy for giving out somewhat personal information like when I got off duty as a vet tech.

But I'd given Jack my phone number, which was even more personal. And I'd looked forward to getting together with him—partly to find out what he was looking for in VimPets products, although I had mixed emotions about that possibility. Mainly, I wanted to extract from him an explanation of his strange comment about having a motive to kill Myra Ethman.

The rest of this afternoon might be very interesting.

ELEVEN

JACK WAS SITTING ON one of the long benches along the wall in the waiting room, between a woman holding a cat carrier and a guy with a dachshund on his lap. He seemed engrossed in conversation with the doxie guy, but as soon as I stepped into the room he must have noticed, since he rose and strode toward me.

He reached out to grasp my arms and give me a brief hug. It seemed a bit off to me as a greeting here, but I let him … until my gaze stopped at the large open window in the wall into the reception area. Reed was standing there, looking at us with an expression I couldn't interpret.

Surely he didn't think I was flirting with this guy. And even if I was, he and I had no exclusivity pact—not even an actual relationship. Not yet, at least.

Besides, I didn't exactly know why Jack had hugged me. Had he noticed Reed—whom he'd also seen at my store-opening event— and decided to play a nasty trick? Did he genuinely feel glad to see me? Did he think we were now somehow closer since he'd given me a platonic kiss on the forehead when he'd said good night? Or was the gesture designed to encourage me to do business with him?

In any event, I felt rather discombobulated and, though smiling, stepped back. "Hi," I said to Jack. "Thanks for coming." That was partially for Reed, in case he thought I'd been ambushed by Jack's appearance.

I glanced again toward Reed. He had some papers in his hand, yet his gaze remained on me.

I realized how stupid I was being—both professionally and personally. I pulled away from Jack. "Just a sec." I went toward the reception area. "Jack's visitor," I told Reed, ignoring the interest on the faces of the receptionists behind the desks. "He works for VimPets and wants to know more about my Barkery products. I'm a bit jazzed, since he might convince them to create a line of products based on my recipes."

"I think you'd better watch what he tries to convince you of," Reed said, but his expression lightened a bit.

Good. I certainly didn't want to burn any bridges with Reed. But neither did I want to turn Jack off—not till I'd talked to him not only about VimPets, but also about Myra. I gave a brief goodbye to Reed, then returned to Jack.

"Where would you like to go?" he asked.

"Around back first," I said, "to our doggy daycare area. I need to get Biscuit. Then … how about Cuppa-Joe's? It's my favorite coffee hangout in town, and I know Biscuit's welcome there."

"Fine." Jack said a quick goodbye to the dachshund man, then moved ahead to open the waiting room's door. We walked around the building to the daycare facility, and he opened that door for me too.

Faye must have been watching for me. She knew my schedule at the clinic, and as we entered she hurried toward me. I glanced around and saw that Biscuit had seen me, too. She'd been snoozing in a corner on some doggy blankets, but now she hurried in my direction.

I bent to pick her up as she reached me, then stood again to look Faye in the eye. "How was she today?"

"Perfect as usual. And in case you're interested, all the treats you brought are gone. I let the owners know where they came from, of course. I suspect you'll get a bunch of business from them."

"Thanks, Faye—for everything!"

I didn't introduce Jack. No need, and Faye was immediately distracted by some growls as a couple of dogs that Al was watching started arguing over the same toy.

As we walked out, Jack said, "That sounded like an excellent testimonial. I'll add it to the report I'm sending to my employer about you and your products."

I felt my face flush, as if he'd complimented me on my good looks. He had, though, said nice things about something even more important to me.

"We can walk to Cuppa-Joe's," I told him. "It's only a few blocks." It still took some maneuvering on the town's twisting streets, but we got there in about five minutes.

"Cute little place," Jack remarked as we arrived on the sidewalk in front of the coffee shop.

"Not really so little," I told him. "Lots of inside space and patio areas."

I led him into the main room, holding Biscuit in my arms. I waved at Joe and Irma as I led the way to my favorite patio, one where Biscuit would feel right at home. I lowered my pup to the concrete surface, then sat down on a metal chair at a small, round table. Jack took the seat across from me.

Irma, rather than Kit, was there immediately to take our orders. "The usual?" she asked me, then gave a brief quizzical look toward Jack that added more lines temporarily to the sides of her brown eyes.

"Maybe," I said. "First I'd like you to meet Jack Loroco. He's a visitor to town and has some business ideas for the Barkery part of my shops."

"Oh." Irma drew out the word, as though she was saying *that explains why you're not with Reed*. Maybe she was being too maternal to me. I'd probably have to talk to her one of these days. "What can I get for you, Jack?"

"Brewed coffee, lots of room for cream," he said.

Although that was my usual coffee choice, I told Irma I'd decided on a treat today: mocha, heavy on the dark chocolate.

While we waited, I bent to pat Biscuit's head while she settled down. I knew Irma would bring her a bowl of water. Then I straightened in my chair and said to Jack, just to make conversation, "So what do you think about Knobcone Heights?"

"Enjoyable place. I often come here with staff members who report to me. We use it as a retreat where we can talk business and still have fun. I think I told you before that I come here for boating and skiing, and they're at different times of the year."

"You leave your pets at home?" I smiled to show I intended no criticism, but he made his living from pets and presumably liked them.

"Just one pet, Rigsley. I mentioned him to you before—a wonderful rescue dog. Sometimes I bring him, but not always. I didn't last time, or this time either."

115

"I'd love to meet him sometime. But if you get to town often, I'm actually glad I haven't met him yet since that would probably mean you had to bring him to our veterinary hospital."

Jack laughed. "Yeah, fortunately Rigsley is a healthy pup. I'd guess he's about three years old." He bent down and patted Biscuit again. My little girl looked up and wagged her tail.

Irma brought our drinks then, in disposable cups we could take with us when we left. I took a sip of my mocha, closed my eyes for a second, and smiled. "Perfect," I said.

Jack poured cream into his coffee, then tasted it. "Good stuff," he said to Irma.

"I'll have one of the girls bring some water over for Biscuit," Irma said, then left.

Okay. It was time to talk business. Or at least about one of the two topics I wanted to address with Jack. And the easiest one to start with was VimPets.

"So, what's your title at VimPets?" I asked.

"Senior Product Manager. I'm always looking for new stuff that fits our high-quality inventory."

Jack appeared professional today. The first couple of times I'd seen him—at my shop and at the resort—he'd been dressed more casually. But now, in his beige button-down shirt and brown trousers, with a calculating expression in his coffee-with-cream-colored eyes, I could see the executive side of him.

Which made me just a little uncomfortable, since I was the one he was evaluating. This was, at least somewhat, an official meeting.

But, heck, I didn't have to do business with him even if he made me a great offer. I would need to feel comfortable before selling anything, even ideas, to him, let alone the recipes I'd been perfecting. For now, we'd chat and I'd see how I wound up feeling.

"From what I know about VimPets," I said, "that 'stuff' in your inventory includes food, treats, toys—"

"Yes, a lot of variety." He nodded, the afternoon sunlight brightening the soft brown of his ample hair. "We get into different kinds of pet products, although mostly the edible or chewable kind, not clothes or fluffy toys or that kind of thing. Not that there's anything wrong with them." He paused. "And in case you're curious, I've visited the Knob Hill Pet Emporium on most of my visits here and they still don't carry VimPets items."

I felt my eyes light up and immediately focused on my coffee cup so he wouldn't notice, necessarily. Had he done that on purpose—changed our conversation topic so I could easily bring up Myra Ethman and his potential motive to be her killer? Apparently he had.

"Then," I began as casually as I could, "you've met Harris before this trip."

"And Myra."

I looked straight into his eyes and saw an expression I couldn't quite read: regret? Challenge? Amusement?

"I wanted to get this out into the open before we do more talking," he continued. "As I told you before, I may have had as much motive to kill Myra as you did—which wasn't very much, by the way. And I don't consider your supposed motive viable either, at least not from what I've heard about it."

I inhaled slowly before continuing. "The cops seem interested in me thanks to the disagreement I had with Myra about my products at my opening party. I suppose it's because our argument was public and happened on the evening of the night she was killed."

"Probably. I've half been expecting them to come to question me—although my disagreement with her wasn't so out in the open. Harris knew about it, of course, and so did the sales help at their store, but maybe no one else. Plus, in case you're wondering, it's a long-term disagreement, but I poured some salt into that particular wound on the day of your opening party, when I stopped in at the Emporium in the morning. She was there and we argued, as we have before—although it consisted more of jabs than an outright fight."

I sipped some more of my coffee, which was getting cooler. Cuppa-Joe's kept a microwave oven inside for its guests to warm their drinks, and I often took advantage of it when my server was slow in bringing a refill pot of regular coffee. But I didn't want to do anything to interrupt this conversation.

At least not anything major. Instead, I looked around. Cuppa employee Kit had just brought out a tray; she laid Biscuit's water bowl beside us, then served some drinks to patrons at another table. I noticed then how busy this patio was getting. Under other circumstances, I'd have attempted to leave soon so as not to take up space that Irma and Joe could use for other paying customers. But at the moment, I wasn't moving. And Kit had seen my glance and came over again. "Everything all right here?"

"Yes," I said, "although I'd love it if you'd warm my drink with some coffee. You too, Jack?"

He nodded. "Thanks."

"Oh, and please bring us each a cup of yogurt—peach for me. What kind would you like, Jack? My treat."

He looked at me oddly. "Strawberry for me. Thanks."

When Kit left I said, "I tend to feel guilty for overstaying my welcome at a place I like, and I certainly didn't want to order a pastry that competes with my better stuff."

"I get it." Jack grinned.

I liked the grin on his handsome, angular face. I reminded myself this wasn't a date—not exactly. And I really didn't need another guy in my life in an indefinable relationship, as I'd sort of started with Reed. No, this was strictly business—with a hint of interrogation thrown in.

"So tell me, while we're waiting," I said. "When did you first come here to Knobcone Heights—and when did you start visiting the Pet Emporium?" I decided some background would be helpful before I grilled Jack even more on his disagreements with Myra.

His grin shifted into something more sardonic, then disappeared. "The first time I came up here was about three years ago, strictly on a whim. I was with an old buddy from college who'd told me how fun Knobcone Heights is in winter, so we drove up in the worst mountain conditions to ski—and had a blast. And when I noticed the Emporium, I had to stop in to see if they carried VimPets products."

"Did they then?"

"No, although they did sell other manufacturers' items that are considered to be of similar quality—though of course nothing really compares with VimPets." He smiled again, and I smiled back. "I immediately said I wanted to talk to the owner—and the sales clerk who'd come over to assist me introduced me to Harris Ethman. I didn't quite get it when he said he couldn't make a decision on the spot about what items they sold in the store, so I kept coming back on that trip and others—and a few visits ago I hit the jackpot... or not. Myra was there, and Harris, who recognized me and probably thought me a bit of a pushy jerk, introduced us."

I got it then. "So even though Harris was the genuine Ethman and in charge of the shop, he had to check with his wife before adding another manufacturer's goods into the inventory."

"Exactly."

Kit returned then with a coffee pot and filled our cups to the brim. She also had a small foil pack of rich cocoa for me to add to mine. Plus, she had our yogurt on her tray. I'd not only pay for our treats, but I'd give her a nice, healthy tip.

When she'd left again, I picked up the thread of the conversation, looking down at my yogurt first as I took a bite of the creamy, delicious stuff, then back up at Jack. "And I take it that they didn't agree to carry VimPets."

"No, although I got their cards and email addresses and corresponded with them—both of them—for months. It didn't take me long to realize that Myra was looking for more than excellent products at a reasonable wholesale price for them to jack up when they sold at retail."

"What did she want?"

"We never did come to an agreement, but I gathered she wanted an even more substantial discount—maybe free products, at least at first. Even more important, she wanted VimPets to talk up Knob Hill Pet Emporium in all of its promotional materials, say what a wonderful town Knobcone Heights was and how its only pet store exemplified perfection … whatever."

Which would have helped to promote the town where she managed the primary resort, as well. I could understand that—to a point. "Do the manufacturers of all the other things they carry do that?" I asked.

"She never told me for certain. Maybe they do. Or maybe she'd simply decided that VimPets should—or she disliked me enough to hold out for something she wanted that could be to my detriment. She never said anything about the other manufacturers, and I'll never hear it from her now. And I suspect that Harris, if he even knows, won't reveal it."

"So, like me, you argued with her that day and she died." I didn't believe Jack had had anything to do with it. On the other hand, he'd brought this subject up.

"Yes, like you."

I took that to mean that he wasn't confessing anymore than I was. I knew the reason I wasn't: innocence. The way he'd described things, the same went for him, too. Probably.

He reached across the table and touched my arm. "Look, Carrie. I got a call earlier today, and I have to go back home tomorrow for an important meeting. I'll be back here as soon as I can, and we can discuss then the possibility of VimPets buying some of your recipes. But I'd like to bring more samples back with me than I got last time, including different products."

My inclination, still, was to refuse. I wanted to think about this more. And I would really have preferred saving all my remaining dog treats to donate to my veterinary clinic and Mountaintop Rescue, but until I knew more about VimPets and any offer it might make—and had time to consider that offer—I wouldn't do anything to turn Jack away. In fact, I'd encourage him … for now, at least. Plus, I did need to get back to my shops now, so I agreed.

We finished our yogurt. Biscuit rose as soon as we did. She'd drunk a little of her water and now seemed full of energy.

I insisted on paying and leaving the tip. Unlike Reed, Jack didn't seem to mind. That actually gave him a boost up in my estimation, even though we were here ostensibly discussing his business.

But at the back—no, front—of my mind were a lot of questions. Why had Jack bothered telling me about his disagreement with Myra? Should I consider him a suspect? He should at least be on the same suspect level as I was, in official eyes. Should I therefore mention his revelation to the detectives next time I saw them?

I was, unfortunately, sure that I would see them again.

Holding what remained of our cups of coffee, we walked along the sidewalks of Knobcone's streets around the town square until we reached my shops, with Biscuit sniffing at our feet—and occasionally relieving herself, too, but fortunately nothing that required a pickup.

When we reached my shops, I was glad to peer in the front windows and see groups of customers in both stores.

"Looks busy," Jack observed.

"Yeah," I said happily. I headed for the Barkery, both to put Biscuit inside and to collect a few samples for Jack.

Dinah was in charge there at the moment, and she looked a little harried. "Sorry," I told her. "I'll help out in a minute." But first, after fastening Biscuit's leash to her crate, I used tongs to put just one sample each of the six different treats we had available today into a box and handed it to Jack.

"Thanks," he said. "I'll be back here soon, and I'll be in touch in the meantime. I assume I can reach you by phone, or, by email via your website?"

I had, in fact, had the Icing on the Cake website redesigned to include Barkery and Biscuits as part of my remodel of the stores. "Yes," I said.

He took the box from me and bent down for an instant, giving me a quick kiss on the cheek. Which made me blush. I felt the redness creeping up my face and hoped that Dinah hadn't seen anything.

When I glanced at her, though, she looked away quickly, back toward her customers. Of course she had seen it.

I sighed. And wondered, at least for an instant as Jack left the store, if I should have tried to detain him here, in town, until those detectives of mine had had an opportunity to question him as they'd been doing with me.

TWELVE

Neal got home early that evening from the resort. He'd had an early shift that day and still, unfortunately, no hiking, boating, or water skiing expeditions planned for a while, so we were able to eat dinner together.

I'd spent a few hours at my bake shops after my coffee outing, then closed for the day and returned home with Biscuit before my brother arrived. Neal brought us a good roast chicken dinner from a local fast food place. The idea not only sounded delicious to me, but the actuality tasted good, too.

Even Biscuit—as always, "Bug" to Neal—was impressed, keeping her little nose sniffing into the air as she sat beside me on the floor by the kitchen table while my brother and I ate. I admit that I did give her a couple of small tastes of chicken after checking carefully to make sure there were no bones. But mostly she ate her usual dinner of highest quality dog food. I wanted what was best for her health. That was the only way to treat my customers as well.

Because Neal had brought dinner in, I was the one to clean up. If I cooked or brought stuff in, Neal generally took over cleanup duty. That was our deal.

Even though I pretty much paid for it all.

Biscuit hung out with me in the kitchen, partly because she was my baby but also because it gave her more opportunity to beg. When I finished rinsing our dishes in my gleaming metal sink and put them all into the dishwasher, I purposefully took our bag of chicken bones outside to the trash to make sure Biscuit didn't try to dig into the kitchen garbage container, even though it had a pretty solid lid. I put her on her leash to join me outside.

We live in a very nice neighborhood in a relatively flat area several blocks south of Summit Avenue. It's filled with houses that were built over the course of many decades. Our home is probably twenty years old, single story, its exterior an attractive wood siding stained a cedar shade, with several small wings with sloped roofs. I'd bought it soon after moving to Knobcone Heights about five years ago, when I'd interviewed for and gotten my vet tech job.

It hadn't hurt that I'd received my degree from Pierce College, which was recognized for having a good program for vet techs, or that I'd gotten my first job in L.A.'s affluent Westside, where I'd worked for an animal hospital frequented by upscale residents and even a few film and TV stars. After a relationship gone bad, I'd decided I didn't want to stay there any longer.

I'd grown up in Riverside and considered returning there, but chose to avoid it—and our remarried parents with their second families. I'd looked online for jobs available in the field, saw the Knobcone Heights Veterinary Clinic opening, and contacted them for an interview; the rest was history. And Neal, who had majored in liberal arts and had no aspirations for a career beyond what he was doing now, had soon followed me up into the mountains.

It was twilight now, and Biscuit and I walked along the side of our winding road, passing neighbors' homes of similar architecture to ours—attractive but not garish like some of the huge estates in the hills overlooking the lake. I loved it here. This was my home.

As a couple of cars drove slowly by, my phone rang, and I pulled it out of my pocket. It was Brenda.

I hoped she wasn't calling with bad news about her mother.

"Hi, Brenda," I said. "How're things down below?" I braced myself for her answer.

"Fine," she said. "My mom even recognizes me—most of the time. And she's getting along reasonably well with her walker although her heart's still pretty weak. So how are you doing, Carrie? Everything okay there?"

There was something in her tone that suggested she was aware that things weren't perfect here. Or maybe it was just that she hoped I'd tell her my shops couldn't get along without her.

"Sure," I lied. Well, it wasn't completely a lie since her interest would be centered on how the stores were doing, and the answer to that was definitely okay. Maybe even better than okay.

"Really?" she persisted.

I saw a neighbor, Bob, walk out the front door of his house with his Doberman on a leash, so I stopped to make sure my grip on Biscuit's was nice and tight. The two dogs usually liked to sniff noses, but occasionally the dobie—named Dog, of all things—acted like he wanted to sample my Biscuit for dinner.

I therefore hesitated a second before responding to Brenda. "Really," I said.

"I thought so. You're in the middle of it, aren't you? Carrie, what happened up there?"

"I said things are okay," I began, but she immediately chided me.

"No, you didn't answer right away. I know you. That means you aren't telling the truth. Now, spit it out."

I started to explain noticing Dog and his owner coming outside and having to check the leash and all the related blather I could think of … then stopped. Though I was telling the truth about that, I wasn't really responding to my close friend's real question.

I sighed, then pulled gently on Biscuit's leash to turn her around to head back to our place, in the opposite direction from where Dog and Bob were going.

"You're right," I said quietly, not necessarily wanting Brenda to hear me. "I know you left to go down to your mother's right after my party. That night … well, I know you heard my disagreement with Myra Ethman, didn't you?"

"Yes," she said, "I did. And the news media here is full of the fact that a member of one of the most noteworthy families of Knobcone Heights, the manager of its major resort, was found murdered that night."

At least I didn't have to tell her. And I wasn't really surprised that the media down the mountain had picked up on the story and were reporting it. But I worried why Brenda had called me about it. I had an awful suspicion I knew the answer.

"Unfortunately, that's true," I said. "What else are the media saying about it?"

"Mostly that the police aren't giving any details but are looking into reports that Ms. Ethman was arguing publicly with someone the night she was killed. Is it you they're talking about? Are the police going to arrest you?"

"They visited me and asked some questions," I said, stumbling as Biscuit pulled sideways to sniff a bush near the curb. I quickly stabilized myself, realizing I was stumbling also because of the emotions welling up inside me yet again. Fear, anger, determination, whatever. I had to beat this.

Yet even the media might be against me. Even though they hadn't identified who I was. Maybe.

My mind stumbled around the possibilities. Brenda had been at my party, had heard me argue with Myra. Had left town in a hurry. For a good reason? Yes.

But what if she'd had something against Myra too? She had a perfect excuse for fleeing.

Could she have killed Myra?

Surely not. And yet … Why had she called me?

Because she's your friend, my mind shot back at me. *She's worried about you.*

Even so …

"I'm very sorry about what happened to Myra," I said, still standing in the same spot while Biscuit squatted to add her own odor to whatever she'd been sniffing. "In many ways, she wasn't a very nice person. I didn't like her attitude. I admit that to you, my friend, and I admitted it to the cops too. But I'm sorry she died. And I didn't kill her." I paused. "Did you know her very well? Did you know anyone who didn't like her?"

I waited many long seconds for Brenda's answer. "I'd met her before. She sometimes came into Icing and ordered huge cakes for events at the resort. She … you're right. She wasn't a nice person. She always tried to get me to cut my price, usually after the cake was finished. She'd always find something wrong with the color of the icing or the decorations or whatever. But in case anyone asks you about me—well, for one thing, I was already at my mom's at the time they said she was probably killed. For another, I didn't hate her enough to kill her."

"Same goes for me, Brenda," I said. "If nothing else, you can believe that."

"I do, Carrie. Really. When I heard, though … well, I was worried about you."

"Thanks, but really, you don't need to be." I was worried enough about myself.

"I can't help it." Brenda paused. "Are you going to Myra's memorial? The media said the whole town was invited by her family."

"What memorial?"

"Oh … then maybe some people in town weren't invited." Brenda sounded contrite. "Although it sounded, from what I heard on the news, that the event was intended to be a huge celebration of her life. The Ethmans are going to pull out all the stops and show how they felt about her, as if she'd been a blood relative. That kind of thing."

"How did they invite people?" And why hadn't I heard about it—even if I wasn't on their guest list?

"I don't know—word of mouth, maybe."

I hadn't talked to anyone whose ears had been near those mouths, I supposed.

"Do you know when and where it'll be?" I asked.

"Why? Do you think you'll go?"

"I'll have to decide, but I at least want to know enough about it to make a rational decision."

At this point, depending on where, when, and whether I could find out who else would be there, I had an immediate suspicion that I would attend—and listen to any and all discussions about Myra and how much she'd be missed.

Maybe, just maybe, someone would let something slip about how much she *wouldn't* be missed, and why.

And who might have done something about it.

THIRTEEN

It was Saturday—the day of Myra Ethman's memorial.

I'd first spoken with Brenda about it on Monday. Had it really been five days ago? Time had gone quickly since then, and a lot had happened—including a couple more conversations with my dear friend.

She was clearly worried about me, and also sounded sorry that (a) she'd inquired indirectly about whether I actually had been the one who'd killed Myra, and (b) she'd told me about the memorial. She mostly regretted the latter since I'd informed her that, yes, I was attending. And, no, she couldn't talk me out of it.

Right now I was in the kitchen of my shops decorating a large tray of people-cupcakes. I'd considered bringing some treats like these to the memorial but decided against it. I didn't know how the service would go nor if a reception with refreshments was planned.

Most of all, I had no idea how a gift from me would be regarded— let alone whether I'd be thrown out the moment I appeared.

I'd fight to be allowed to stay, though. To leave would encourage people to talk about me—and assume my guilt.

"How are you doing?" Judy had just entered the kitchen from the Barkery side. I'd rested my last batch of decorated people-cupcakes on top of the elongated set of shelves in the center of the kitchen. Judy stopped near them and eyed them assessingly. "Cute," she said. "I especially like the ones with the two Bs, where you play around with the shape and color of the letters."

"Thanks." I'd stopped using the B&B symbol that was on the biscuit found near Myra's body. No one had asked about this, but I was prepared to say that I thought it looked too much like a logo for a bed and breakfast.

"You're welcome." Judy hesitated as if she had something else on her mind, and although her gaze met mine for an instant, she looked away quickly. She rubbed her hands along the sides of the plain, white-bibbed apron that was quickly becoming our uniform over our regular clothes.

"Everything okay?" I asked.

"Well ... are you aware of the memorial this afternoon for Myra Ethman?"

"Yes," I said. "Are you planning on going?" I hadn't discussed it with my employees but had been pondering what to do about it. Should I close the store so we all could attend?

"Yes, and I talked to Dinah about it too. We'd both like to go. But we hate to leave you here without either of us to help."

"No problem." I made a quick executive decision. "I'm going too, so we'll just close the store for an hour or so. I'll prepare a couple of signs, one for each door, telling people why we're not open and when we'll be back."

Judy's eyes widened. "Really? You're going to go?"

"Are you?" Dinah had entered from the Icing side. I suspected she'd heard our voices and discerned what we were talking about. "But Carrie—well, we know you didn't hurt Myra, but her family…"

"All the more reason for me to attend," I said firmly. "I'll take Biscuit to my vet clinic's doggy daycare before we go, but my mind is made up. I'll be there."

———

Since I was the shops' proprietor and sometimes wanted to impress customers with more than Barkery and/or Icing T-shirts, I kept a change of clothes in my small office at the rear of the kitchen. My office was on the Icing side, and a similar enclosed area behind the Barkery was our restroom, where I now went with my outfit to change.

I was ready to go.

I sent Dinah and Judy on their way to the memorial. Biscuit and I were going in a different direction.

But I would be joining them. Soon.

———

By design, Knobcone Heights didn't have an actual church or other facility established by members of a single religion. There were many of these in towns within easy driving distance, at least when we weren't in the thick of a winter snowfall. For years, our City Council had supported the idea that there be just one large, lovely, multi-denominational chapel.

The Knobcone House of Celebration was along the lake, a half mile or so from the Knobcone Heights Resort. I wasn't sure what its style was—modern, maybe, even though it had been there for twenty years or so. It was a couple stories high, but actually only contained one floor. The outside was long and slanted and windowed and streamlined. The inside was pretty much only one huge room that could be segregated into several if the event inside required it. There was an office off to one side, and a large stage area that could be used as a worship center or whatever. The walls were of silvery, matte metal peppered by all those windows. The floors were all of gleaming wood. And one whole wall of windows looked out over the lake.

I'd been there only once before, when the owner of an elderly English Sheepdog who'd needed to be euthanized because of a bad heart condition had rented the place to hold a memorial for her lost pet. I thought it sweet, if a bit over the top. A contingent had been sent from the veterinary clinic, including Arvie and me. It was before Reed had started working there. A local choir had been brought in to sing some sorrowful chants for the poor dog, and my eyes had teared up more than once.

Of course my eyes always teared up if we had to put a patient down, even though it was only done to prevent further suffering. But it also meant the beginning of further suffering for most of the owners—those with hearts, who'd actually considered their animals more than pieces of property.

After dropping Biscuit off, I hurried back to my shops and then drove to the House of Celebration. The parking lot there was nearly full. I figured the facility would be crowded too—possibly more because of who the Ethmans were in this area than because of how much Myra had been loved or even admired.

As I got out of the car, I steeled myself as much as possible for what would follow. This wasn't about me. I had to remind myself of that. But I would hopefully be able to use the event as a research vehicle of sorts—not that I expected people who'd disliked Myra to even hint at it here.

I certainly wouldn't. In fact, I truly did feel bad that she had died, especially given how it had happened, and no matter that I wished I wasn't a suspect. Death was so sad. So final.

There was a bit of a line at the tall front door, which was as angular as the rest of the place. I recognized some of the people who were also waiting to get in—primarily members of the town's most elite families whom I knew only if they happened to have pets they brought to our clinic. I felt the stares of a few of them as they noticed me, but I didn't respond.

Also in line was kitten owner Cece Young, with some other men and women I assumed were friends or associates of hers, perhaps other teachers. I wondered if she'd told any of them about being at my grand opening celebration and receiving some Icing treat samples for herself.

As I neared the entry, I glanced beyond some of the group to scan the inside. Among those occupying the nearby rows of seats I saw both Arvie and Reed. Great! I just hoped they had a chair near them that I could plant myself on. They'd probably come just to be nice and pay their respects; they'd need to get back to the clinic soon.

Fortunately, I didn't have a shift there today. But I did want to get back to my shops.

I also saw two other vets from the clinic: Dr. Paul Jensin and Dr. Angela Regles. They sat a few rows away. Neither were quite as senior as Arvie, but they'd also helped to found the Knobcone Veterinary Clinic.

I wondered where Dinah and Judy were sitting. I might not get them to come back to the stores with me after the memorial, but I'd just have to see how things went.

Finally, I reached the door. A row of people I didn't know—probably Ethmans—extended in a greeting line inside. I felt a faint tinge of relief that the first person was someone I was actually friends with: Les Ethman.

"Thank you for coming, Carrie," the sweet City Councilman said as I reached him. "I'm sure it wasn't especially ... easy." Though the edges of his eyes always turned down, the rest of his expression today added to his morose look. I felt for him. I didn't know what he'd thought of Myra, but he was definitely grieving now.

"No," I admitted. "But I wanted to pay my respects. And in case you're wondering—"

"I trust you, Carrie." He clasped my hand in both of his and pulled me close enough to give me a hug.

When he released me, he gave me a sad smile, then turned to the person behind me in the line.

I didn't know the next few greeters but assumed they were family members. They were not Harris, Elise, or their parents, thank heavens, nor even the less-antagonistic Walt Hainner. Once I'd gotten through the line, I was able to breathe again.

Although I now saw Dinah and Judy sitting in the middle of a row near the front, I approached Arvie and Reed. Fortunately, they had an empty seat near them.

As I sat down, people began walking onto the stage. I saw Les Ethman move down the side aisle and take a seat near other City Council members, including Billi Matlock. Some of Billi's upper-echelon family members sat in front of them.

I assumed that anyone who was anybody from this town was here, no matter what they'd actually thought about Myra. Too bad I couldn't take a poll as to who really cared that she wasn't around any longer and who was there just to score points with other elite Knob-cone Heights residents.

"Hello, everyone." The female voice was raspy over the loud-speaker system. Elise Hainner, dressed in a slinky black dress, held a microphone in her black-gloved hand. Her husband Walt was right beside her, also dressed in black—a button-down shirt and trousers. On the stage now were Harris and his parents, all in black too and staring sad-faced toward their audience.

"Thank you for coming," Elise announced. "In case you're wondering what we're planning, it will be a celebration of the life of Myra Landrum Ethman, my dear sister-in-law."

I wondered if any of Myra's blood relatives were here—and, in any event, what they'd thought of her. But if none had been in town at the time of the murder, I couldn't consider them as possible suspects.

"We're going to make this fairly informal," Elise continued. "I've already got a list of people who will come up here and talk, but feel free to join us—though we'll have to cut it off if the service gets too long."

Elise seemed right at home up there in front of everyone. I wondered what she'd done for a living before taking over at the resort. Her husband was a contractor. Had she designed homes? Sold them?

Presented memorial services?

Or had she done nothing, the way her brother Harris had until his wife had bought him a pet store to manage?

Elise next launched into her sister-in-law's life history, as if she'd seen it all.

Had they really been that close? Maybe so.

My mind, and eyes, wandered as she spoke. I wasn't surprised to see that my newest best friends, those detectives, were among the people seated in the audience. Like me, they must have been there to observe the show—and see if they could glean any antagonism against Myra among the mourners. I certainly didn't object to that. Maybe they'd be convinced to aim their suspicions in a different direction.

Unless they'd spotted me, too, and were waiting for me to say or do something to provide irrefutable evidence of my guilt.

For the next half hour, I watched and listened as person after person walked out on the stage area, took the microphone, and described his or her relationship with Myra, all in the most eloquent and sorrowful language. Music was piped in from somewhere, kept low but possibly representing some of Myra's favorites songs, everything from current pop to music from Broadway shows.

It was an amazing presentation, all the more astounding because it had been put together so quickly.

Plus, there were so many folks who had nothing but nice things to say about Myra.

Apparently Myra had gotten a degree in tourism management and had held jobs in L.A. and San Diego at various hotels before winding up here in the San Bernardino Mountains. She'd started at the reception desk at the Knobcone Heights Resort and worked her way up to manager.

Neal wasn't here. I'd called him on my way over, in case he had some interest in coming. He'd called me back and said he'd requested the time off but was told that although his caring was appreciated, he could do more in support of Myra's memory if he just stayed at the resort and did his job.

Too bad. I'd have liked to have had his company. Plus, it might have been a good thing for Neal to hear this part, at least. His main goal these days was to head as many outdoor escapades as possible, since he considered boating, hiking, and skiing to be his bliss.

But lately that hadn't been working out. Maybe hearing Myra's story would ignite some other interest in him.

Or not.

I was listening to it, though. And I admitted to myself, although I wouldn't to anyone else, that Myra's story got to me. She might have been nasty to me, but there were obviously a lot of people she'd gotten along with just fine. More than fine. She'd been cared for by some, both family members and friends. She'd inspired others as she had worked her way up at the resort and caught the Ethman family's attention, especially Harris's. From the descriptions of those who had reported to her, she had been an inspirational leader, even though she hadn't put up with any mistakes. Maybe that was because she never made any.

Or at least, no one who was given time off work to attend the service had ever noted any on her part.

Sitting among all the other mourners, I heard whispers and sighs and even a wail now and then. When I looked around, people tended to be staring raptly at whoever was speaking or down into their own laps, perhaps hiding tears—or disbelief.

I sometimes looked out the large side windows toward the lake, just to escape momentarily from the room's emotions.

I glanced often toward Arvie, whose expression was solemn but didn't seem to convey great sorrow. And every time I looked toward Reed, he looked back at me, his dark brown eyes questioning and caring. I had the sense that he'd come here more for me than to mourn Myra, and I appreciated it.

Among those who spoke were Harris, of course, and both of his parents. Apparently Myra had fit their version of an elite Ethman. The two children of Harris and Myra both said something brief and tearful. The daughter must have come back from college to mourn her mother, but the high school age boy appeared to grieve even more.

My odd, caring, sad mood seemed to carry me away, and at one point I had an urge to go and stand in front of everyone and take that microphone, relate the story of my non-relationship with Myra, explain how I regretted her death for many reasons—and tell everyone here that I'd had nothing to do with it despite our argument.

But that wasn't exactly in keeping with the spirit of the day. And my doing so was unlikely to convince anyone of my veracity anyway. They'd probably consider it self-serving and entirely inappropriate for today's memorial.

So I just sat there.

After about an hour, at least a dozen people, maybe more, had expressed their sorrow, and Elise again took the microphone.

I could see even from here that her eyes were damp. "Thank you all for coming. And our particular thanks to all of you who got up here to talk about our Myra. We don't have her back yet to bury her, and that ceremony will be a private family affair."

And then it was over.

Which was a good thing. I hadn't intended to stay away from my shops this long, but there'd been no graceful way to depart.

Everyone started leaving the House of Celebration. I heard laughter, as if some people needed to change the subject fast to keep from crying. I heard others talking about Myra.

"You all right?" Reed took my arm as we waited for a break in the crowd so we could leave our row.

"More or less. I think this was a lovely thing to do, and it was handled well. But—"

"You did come. We thought maybe you wouldn't," Dinah said. She and Judy stood near the end of our row, holding the crowd back so we could leave. Arvie was first, followed by Reed, then me.

"Thanks," I told my assistants. "Are you going back to the stores now?" Fortunately, they were.

When all of us finally made it outside, I saw that the crowd was mostly dispersing. But as I started to thank Reed and head toward my car, I saw Billi Matlock looking in my direction. She gestured for me to join her on a tree-shaded path along the vast lawn on the inland side of the building.

I didn't like the idea since she was with some fellow council members, including Les Ethman. But my friendship with Billi seemed to be growing, and I figured it would be in my best interests to learn what she wanted.

As I got nearer I had an urge to ignore Billi and dash in the opposite direction, since others had joined the group. Some I believed were Billi's relatives. And some I knew were Les's. Many had spoken about Myra at the service.

But even if it could be a bad idea to join them, I had nothing to be ashamed of and I wanted everyone to know it.

"I need to talk to Billi," I told Reed, who was still at my side.

"Okay, then I will too," he said, earning him another brownie point or two in my estimation.

I was especially glad he was still with me since, as I approached the group, so did the two detectives. Harris Ethman was there now, and even Elise and Walt.

Walt saw me and broke away from the others. He stopped me before I reached them—by design? Was he protecting me too, as Reed was attempting to do?

"Thanks for coming, Carrie." His voice was hoarse, his eyes moist. "This was a very moving memorial, wasn't it?"

Interesting. Had he been that close to his sister-in-law, or was he just an emotional person?

I didn't get a chance to ask, since the two cops suddenly joined us.

"Hey," Detective Wayne Crunoll said. "Ms. Kennersly and Mr. Hainner, two of my favorite people. What did you think of the memorial?"

"Yeah," said Detective Bridget Morana. "Did it give either of you any urge to talk too ... to us?"

Was she implying that we were so upset we might confess?

We? No, most likely just one of us.

But she said "either of you." That wasn't only me.

Did Walt have enough of a motive to kill Myra that the authorities were pestering him about it, too?

FOURTEEN

INTERESTING, I THOUGHT. BUT now wasn't the time to ask those kinds of questions.

Maybe the detectives, who'd not exactly discouraged me before from trying to figure out who actually killed Myra, would be amused if I started asking questions now.

But I didn't trust them. They'd probably been teasing me, assuming I'd only dig a deeper hole for myself by attempting to find someone else to toss into it—a better suspect—when they seemed to believe that no one could be a better suspect than me.

So, although this wasn't a good time, I'd have to figure out when I could learn more about Walt and his possible motive.

Was that why he'd acted nice to me when so many people in his family were giving me a hard time? But if he actually was guilty, wouldn't he have encouraged them to think I was the killer?

"Is something wrong here, detectives?" Elise joined her husband and stuck her arm through his.

If I hadn't already known Elise was an Ethman, I'd have guessed it from the two detectives' behavior, since they immediately smiled and denied they were there for anything but being nice fellow citizens of Knobcone Heights who had come to mourn Myra and were now simply chatting like everyone else.

The gleam in Bridget's narrowed brown eyes as she glared at me suggested otherwise, though—it seemed she knew I was the guilty one but was willing to consider someone else, like Walt, until she had enough evidence to haul me in.

Okay, I was reading an awful lot into that snide look. It could have meant nothing at all. But it was time for me to go.

Like Elise, I had someone whose arm I could grab: Reed's. "Sorry," I said to the others as I stood close to him. "I need to get back to my stores. But I found the celebration very moving. I know you don't trust me or believe me, but I'm sorry that Myra is gone— and that's not because I had anything to do with her death. Honest."

I turned and was glad I didn't have to pull Reed to get him to stay with me. He walked at my side toward the large parking lot that was now nearly vacant of cars.

I heard mutters behind me but didn't know who said what. I assumed some might be calling me not only a killer but a liar, too.

I could possibly say the same about one of them and have it actually be true. But if so, which one?

If I had a choice it wouldn't be Walt, although I'd already figured that his niceness could be an act to turn my suspicion away from him.

Well, damn. I really needed to do some digging to figure out if he had a viable motive. Didn't I?

Oh, how I wished I didn't. That none of this affected me.

"Are you okay, Carrie?" Reed had slowed despite my efforts to nearly run away from the group behind us.

"Sure," I fibbed. It wasn't an out-and-out lie. I was sort of okay. And sort of upset.

Reed stopped altogether, which made me halt too, since I held his arm tightly. I gasped and looked up at him.

"No, you're not. You shouldn't have gone to Myra's memorial, but—"

"And you shouldn't tell me what I should or shouldn't do."

That came out much harsher than I'd intended, and I felt my free hand go up to my mouth as if I wanted to shove what I'd said back inside me. "Sorry," I whispered. "I didn't mean—"

He put one sturdy, warm finger over my mouth to stop me, a finger on a hand that had caressed and cared for more pets than I could possibly count. That perhaps someday might caress me. We had already kissed briefly. But that had been all ... so far.

We were standing in the parking lot now and I realized we were beside his nice black luxury car. Of course he had stopped. My own old white Toyota was only a row away.

I looked up at him. I hadn't paid a lot of attention before to what he was wearing that afternoon, but he'd put on a dark suit that looked great with his wavy black hair. He had a touch of the five-o'clock shadow that he tended to have at this time of day.

And he was looking back down at me with his caring dark eyes.

"I know you need to get back to your stores, Carrie. I need to get back to the clinic. But let's get together for dinner tonight, okay? And not at the resort. Someplace nice and neutral and unemotional."

"Sounds good to me." My tone was fervent. I considered inviting him to my house and cooking something, but decided that might sound like an invitation for more. "Let's talk in about an hour to figure out what to do."

"Okay." He kissed me on my forehead, then walked me to my car.

145

It was late when I returned to my shops. Fortunately, my assistants had gotten back faster than me and had both sides open. Only the Barkery had some business at the moment. And we'd only be open for another hour.

Dinah was staffing the Barkery side. I observed her waiting on our current customers, a young married couple who said they were both teachers at local schools. I wondered if they knew Cece, who'd also been at the memorial, but didn't interrupt to mention her.

Dinah asked the right questions about the dogs they had at home who deserved these wonderful treats: what their likes were, whether they had any health or allergy issues that would help in the decision. Then she encouraged them to buy a whole box of different kinds of treats for their two Chihuahua mixes.

I stayed out of her way as she finished by charging their credit card, then joined her as we both watched the apparently pleased customers leave the store.

"Good job," I told her. "I'll bet they'll be back."

"Me too," Dinah said with a smile. "As long as their pampered babies like at least some of those wonderful treats."

It was my turn to smile. But then I watched Dinah's pleasant expression morph into something I couldn't interpret.

"That was quite a memorial this afternoon," she said quietly. Her glistening blue eyes scanned my face, as if she was trying to determine whether I'd felt comfortable there or hated every minute.

And maybe as if she was trying to determine whether I was actually the one who'd killed Myra. Or was I just expecting everyone I knew to wonder that?

"Yes," I said. "It was. I'm sorry that Myra's dead, and that we had a disagreement before she died. A lot of people seemed to care for her and be genuinely grieving. Maybe if I'd gotten to know her better we would have made peace with one another, even gotten into a position where we'd both encourage customers to try stuff from each other's shops."

From Myra's initial reaction, and from the impression I'd gotten even from the people who'd eulogized her, compromise might not have been in her vocabulary, so I doubted it could have happened that way. But it sounded good. It even felt good, in a way.

What if it actually *had* occurred? I'd have liked to have had an ally in the pet retail business here in Knobcone Heights.

Maybe I still could—in Harris. But that could only happen if someone other than me was proven to have killed his wife... and if that person wasn't him.

"Heard you talking about Myra and her celebration." Judy had just walked through the door from Icing. "I... I was really moved by it. And I hardly knew her."

"She used to come in here—I mean, Icing—to order a lot of cakes for her big parties and other special occasions," Dinah said, coming out from behind the cash counter to look at Judy.

"Well, sure." Judy's long face was flushed and scowling, as if Dinah had accused her of killing Myra. "But that's all I knew her from—just taking her orders and helping to bake her cakes, and even sometimes delivering them."

The belligerence in Judy's tone made me step out too, to place myself between them. Even though most of the time my inherited assistants had been getting along just fine, I couldn't predict when they'd start confronting each other—like now.

"I get it," I said. "You'd met her—both of you—but you weren't her closest friends." I gave a wry smile. "I suspect those who were her closest friends had money, or something she wanted, or— Okay, I won't speak ill of the dead. I certainly didn't know her well either, but the fact that we didn't hit it off as buddies doesn't mean I couldn't eventually have gotten along with her."

"It doesn't mean you would have, either," Dinah pointed out.

I nodded, then intentionally moved my gaze from my assistants to the watch on my left wrist. "Know what? It's time to close up."

"Good. I'll get things in Icing ready." Judy quickly turned her back and went through the door once more.

"I didn't mean—" Dinah began.

"Me neither. Anyway, go home and relax and come back refreshed tomorrow," I said.

She helped me get the Barkery ready to close, then we both went into the kitchen. Judy was there giving a final scrub to the ovens, which I appreciated. Dinah did the same with the counters and I helped out, neither of my assistants looking at the other.

"Thanks to both of you," I said when we were done. "See you tomorrow." I watched as they both left together—fortunately talking civilly to each other. The crisis, such as it was, was over.

I got ready to leave too. Time to go get Biscuit from doggy daycare, then follow up on joining Reed for dinner. I went out through the front of Icing, leaving my car parked behind the building, and walked toward the veterinary hospital.

The more I thought about it, the better inviting Reed to my home for dinner sounded. Not that I had any intention of seducing him, or being seduced. But it could be a nice, pleasant, casual evening of just getting to know one another better.

It wouldn't involve figuring out which restaurant to try next. And I'd definitely get to treat, since I'd be the one to stop at the grocery store and to cook. Because of the growing lateness and my need to get some sleep that night, the meal would have to be something relatively quick and simple, but I already had a few ideas.

On impulse, I tried calling Neal to see if he was at home yet and whether he'd join us if Reed agreed to my proposed plan. When he didn't answer I assumed he was still working, and I didn't know when he'd get off. I didn't leave a message. No need.

I entered the clinic and waited till Reed was finished with a patient, then issued the invitation for him to come to my home for dinner. He seemed delighted by the idea. I then went into the day-care facility and hugged an excited Biscuit, but confirmed with Faye that it was all right for me to pick her up in about half an hour.

I hurried back to my car, drove to the nearest supermarket on the fringes of town, picked up the ingredients for the dinner I intended to cook, and then went back for my dog.

I was soon at home. After walking Biscuit briefly, then letting her out in the dog run for a few more minutes, I got busy creating my own version of a rich and creamy chicken Alfredo. When the doorbell rang, the meal was nearly ready.

I opened the front door to let Reed in. He stood there with a bottle of Chianti that looked of special vintage, although my expertise was limited. "Does this work for dinner?" he asked, holding it out to me as Biscuit, now in the house, jumped up on his legs. He was clad once again as he'd been at Myra's memorial, much dressier than at the clinic.

"Delightful," I said. I smiled as he bent down and gave me a brief kiss, then knelt to pat Biscuit's head.

"Mmm, delightful," he parroted, and I turned my back and hurried into the kitchen so he couldn't see my own happy grin.

Dinner went well. Neal joined us when we were about halfway done. I saw his gaze go from Reed to me and back as he said hi, as if assessing why I'd invited this man here and if he'd be a third wheel who should roll out of here for the night.

"Glad you made it for dinner," I told him, to assure him that he could stay.

At least this time...

The three of us talked mostly about the delights of our small town that provided something captivating for everyone's interests, and Neal invited Reed to come on any of the boat rides or ski outings he hosted, whenever. He said he did have a couple scheduled now and hoped for more. The two of them seemed to get along well, which was a good thing—in case my enjoyment of Reed's company actually did turn into some kind of real romantic relationship.

When we were done, my well-trained brother helped to clean up and so did Reed—another thing to add to the plus column about this good-looking, kind guy who saved animals' lives.

Then Neal excused himself and went to his room, probably to watch TV.

Reed and I sat down on the living room couch, although he said he couldn't stay long. As we talked, we finished the bottle of wine he'd brought.

When he prepared to leave, a little later, he kissed me good night at my front door and I savored the flavor of his warm, sexy lips.

"See you tomorrow afternoon, Carrie." He held me for a moment longer against his hard body.

"Yeah," I said. "Thanks, and good night."

I grinned the whole time as I walked Biscuit, then got ready for bed. I'd left my cell phone in my purse and got it out to charge overnight.

Only then did I see that I'd missed a couple of calls. One was from Jack Loroco. The thought of him and his business ideas—and his apparent interest in me—chilled my very warm thoughts of Reed just a little. I was glad it was so late, though. I wouldn't call Jack back until tomorrow.

The other call was from an unknown number, but when I checked voicemail I saw that I'd received a message from Walt Hainner, again thanking me for coming to Myra's memorial.

That really sent icy fingers up my spine. Why was he thanking me so much? Because my being a suspect in Myra's murder kept the authorities from looking too closely at him? Or was it something more innocent than that—he was just a nice guy who'd married into the Ethmans and knew that apologizing for their usual arrogance and condescension and accusations was a nice thing to do?

Whatever, it kept me awake, thinking, for much longer than I should have been that night.

FIFTEEN

SOMEHOW I SLEPT OKAY. Maybe I was just too exhausted to do otherwise.

The next morning I did what was becoming my usual: woke early, got dressed, put Biscuit in the dog run and then fed her, and headed for my shops with my dog beside me in the passenger seat of my car.

I managed not to think about Walt's phone message—at least not much.

When we arrived, I secured Biscuit in the Barkery and scanned the leftovers from the prior day. Some would be fresh enough to sell, but I preferred giving most away—some at the clinic and some at Billi's shelter. As for the Icing leftovers, I'd also sort them out later. Brenda had begun giving some to a homeless shelter down the mountain and had left me a way to reach the staff if I had any donations.

Then I got the baking for both sides started and was well on the way to being able to fill the display cases by the time either of my assistants arrived.

It was Sunday, and I knew weekends could be the busiest times in my shops if a lot of visitors came to Knobcone Heights between their work weeks. That's the way things had been for Icing, according to Brenda.

I was hoping both my stores' sales would surpass hers. Not that I'd ever tell her or rub it in.

Dinah was earliest to arrive that day. If I wasn't mistaken, my younger helper looked even more tired than I felt. In fact, her demeanor reminded me that she was older than she usually appeared. She entered by way of the kitchen just as I removed some dog treats from the oven, which wafted a delicious sent of meat and apples into the air.

"Good morning," I said cheerfully.

"Hi. Smells good."

"Yes, it does. Do you want to take over baking the dog treats for now?"

"Sure." She put her purse down in the usual place, on the bottom shelf of the closed supply cabinet at the back of the kitchen, and put on an apron.

I could tell I wasn't going to get a scintillating conversation going with her so I just asked, "Are you feeling okay?"

"Sure," she said again. She dragged her slightly chubby body in my direction and gave me a tired smile. "The thing is, I think I told you that my first love is writing, right?"

I nodded.

"For some reason, all that's been going on, including Myra's memorial yesterday, has triggered a story inside me and I stayed up much later than I should have to start writing it." She looked at me earnestly. "I like the way it's going, but I promise I won't do that again."

I laughed. "From what I've heard about writers, your inspiration may control the rest of your life. But do what's best for you—as long as you're here on time and able to work."

"Oh, yes, I am. I will be. I promise."

She made good on that promise, jumping right into baking, and then helped stock our two sets of display cases.

Judy arrived about an hour later. By then, most of the early baking had been completed and both displays were fairly full. I'd remained mostly in the kitchen, where I'd packed up some Barkery leftovers to take to the vet clinic and Mountaintop Rescue. I also called the homeless shelter down the mountain and discussed which leftover human treats to save for them, like cookies that wouldn't go stale.

Then I began playing around with one of my favorite dog biscuit recipes. It was one I particularly liked as it was, but I enjoyed experimenting with my creations for pets. I figured one of these days I might try playing with Icing's recipes too, but since I'd inherited those from Brenda, I didn't have as much knowledge about them—nor did I have as much of myself invested in them. I knew they were good and wasn't sure I could make them any better. With the Barkery products that might also have been true—but I also had a desire to find out.

I added some crushed yams to my favorite cheese-flavored biscuits. Hey, there were plenty of good sweet-potato-and-cheese recipes available for humans, and I liked the combo, so why not? I tasted the batter before I evened it out with a rolling pin and used biscuit-shaped cookie cutters to form the treats.

While they were in the oven, I visited first Icing, currently being run by Dinah, and then the Barkery, staffed by Judy. They both were sweeping floors and washing the insides of the windows. No customers.

In fact, so far that day we'd had only a few customers. The bells I'd had installed on both shop doors to let us know when someone came in hadn't rung often. I needed to think about how to promote both stores. An ad in a local paper or online? A contest of some kind?

Maybe some posters at the vet clinic, mostly promoting the Barkery but letting people know that they could treat themselves here too.

I liked that idea. I'd run it by Arvie soon. If he agreed, the other vets, Arvie's partners Angela and Paul, would have no problem with it. And I got along with them all just fine, so I wasn't too worried about obtaining their approval. And I knew Reed wouldn't mind. But in any case, he hadn't been there long enough to have a lot of say over administrative things like promotional stuff on the premises.

I returned to the kitchen a short while later to remove my new treats from the oven. I put the metal cookie sheet on the top of a counter so they could cool.

Judy soon entered the kitchen carrying some cleaning materials to return to the appropriate place—away from our cooking area. Good timing. I was eager to take charge at one of my shops, preferably the Barkery.

"Would you like a break now, Judy?" I asked as she removed the cleaning apron she'd donned—which was different from our sparkling white serving aprons.

"I'd love one."

She sounded almost relieved. Had I been overworking my staff? Maybe, but neither had complained. Not yet, at least. Even so, I'd try to be more observant and caring.

I'd learned from Brenda, though, what hours she'd scheduled her helpers for, and I didn't think I'd exceeded them. Maybe working in two shops at one time was more grueling for them, even though they'd initially said they wanted to handle sales on both sides.

It certainly was grueling for me, but highly exciting.

"I've got a request first," I told Judy. I asked her to take some of the leftover dog treats I'd packed up to the veterinary clinic and the rest to the shelter. Then she could do whatever she wanted for the remainder of her break.

She sounded fine with that and said she'd stop for a coffee treat at Cuppa-Joe's, since all we served here was brewed coffee, regular and decaf. I considered asking her to bring something more exciting back for me, but I didn't really need it. I instead suggested that she ask Dinah if she wanted anything—which she did. Dinah was working in Icing at the moment; I'd heard bells ring in both of the shops, and I knew I'd better get into the Barkery.

I decided to pay for drinks for both of them. They'd both be getting caffeine, after all. Maybe they'd have more energy then.

After handing some money from my wallet to Judy, I watched her exit out the back door. Then I went into the Barkery.

Every time I entered I paid some attention to my little Biscuit. I always at least said hi to her, and depending on whether I had time to wash my hands, I usually petted her, too. This time when I went in, Biscuit was still attached to her crate with a leash, having a sniff-fest with two dogs I hadn't met before—a couple of dachshund mixes. I noticed the dogs together immediately as I entered the room from the door behind the refrigerated display case and grinned as I approached them. Their entrance—or their owner's—must have rung the bell at the Barkery door. I was delighted to see them getting along so well.

As I moved out from behind the display case, I scanned the room to see what person belonged to these newcomer dogs—and almost skidded to a halt.

Detective Wayne Crunoll stood off to one side in front of the display case, looking at its contents. He also held the handles of the two extension leashes attached at the other end to the two visiting dogs.

He was more casual-looking today than I'd seen him before—an L.A. Dodgers T-shirt over jeans—and I doubted he'd shaved the dark hair on his face this morning. Sure, it was Sunday, but cops didn't necessarily have weekends free.

On the other hand, I knew this particular cop had been working long hours this week, investigating a case I happened to be somewhat familiar with.

He must have heard me, since he turned to face me. "Hello, Carrie," he said. "I'd like to introduce you to my dogs."

I recalled his saying he owned a couple of dogs but they were more his wife's than his. I'd never met them before, so maybe they were so healthy they never had to go to a vet's.

On the other hand, if they were going to stay that way, they'd need checkups and shots. Of course, there were other veterinary clinics not far away in the San Bernardino Mountains area—and those outside of Knobcone Heights might be less expensive.

"This is Blade." He stooped to touch the lighter brown pup on the head. "And this is Magnum." Magnum was mostly black, with an even longer muzzle than his buddy.

Interesting names. They sounded appropriate for a cop, even if this cop thought the family's dogs were closer to his wife.

"Hi, Blade and Magnum," I said. Since I'd been prepared to pet Biscuit anyway, I gave all three dogs some loving pats.

When I stood again, I faced Wayne. His raised brows over his light brown eyes and friendly smile looked absolutely guileless, and I was highly suspicious.

"So are you here to buy some treats for Blade and Magnum?" I asked. I doubted it—or if it was the case, that it was the only reason—but I'd play his game for now.

"You've got that right," he said. "But I'll bet you don't believe it."

"You've got that right," I repeated, hoping my smile looked as guileless as his.

He laughed. "Why don't you just pack up a couple of each of your treats so I can let my guys try them and decide which they like best? Then we'll come back for more."

"Sounds good," I said. "For starters, here's a couple that are a new recipe I've been experimenting with." I went behind the display case and removed three of my newest biscuits. I handed one to each of the dogs, including mine, since I certainly didn't want to slight my own Biscuit. They all seemed to enjoy them.

"Great. Well, add a couple extra of those to the package. And if you want to say anything about my investigation, feel free."

Ah. Here it was. He was acting friendly for a reason, and that reason was anything but friendly to me.

"Okay," I said. "I didn't do anything. That's all you need to know."

He laughed again, a louder, less credible-sounding than before. "Could be. But one thing you should know, Carrie, is that even though I'm fairly new here, I've been a cop for several years and a detective for a major part of that time. And you know what I've learned?"

He wasn't looking at me now but kneeling to play with all three dogs on the bone-decor portion of the tile floor. He might be attempting to appear casual and preoccupied, but I knew better.

"What's that?" I asked, still determined to play along—at least as long as I could without harming myself. I wondered if Bridget knew he was here and sanctioned this kind of casual conversation, which was instead just a different kind of interrogation.

"Well, I've seen in a lot of resolved cases that if someone appears at first to be a good suspect and not just a person of interest, she usually is a good suspect."

"You mean guilty."

He looked up and nodded, the broad smile on his pudgy face nearly making me throw up. But I'd never allow myself to throw up in my shops, either of them.

"Like I've told you, I'm not guilty." I kept my tone light but firm.

"You did have an argument with Myra," he said. "Other people heard it, and you apparently even threatened her."

"It wasn't like that." I raised my hands toward my mouth, wishing I'd said that in a calmer voice. "It wasn't like that," I repeated more slowly.

"Why don't you just tell me what you said, word for word if you can."

"I don't know that I can recall it that precisely. I know you're aware that Myra criticized my opening this Barkery." I gestured to incorporate the inside of my shop. "She said something like, 'Do you really think people will come in here for your inferior products when you're not giving them away for free?' I objected, talked about the less nutritious, less personal mass-produced stuff sold in her pet emporium, and we kind of agreed to disagree."

"You agreed on something?" Wayne was standing again now. "That's not the way I heard it. And what about your comment later that you'd do anything ... what was it?"

159

"I don't recall exactly, but I recognize, in retrospect, that it could have sounded threatening. All I meant was that I'd prove Myra was wrong in her assessment of the quality of my products." This conversation wasn't going anywhere—at least nowhere that could do me any good. I needed to get it aimed in a different direction. "You know, Wayne, I didn't know Myra well, but from all I've learned about her since... since she died, she wasn't only nasty toward me. Surely you've come across other people who argued with her. Maybe family members. Maybe other people."

Like Jack Loroco, but I wasn't about to mention him. His motivation to kill Myra was as trivial as mine. At least I hoped so.

"Could be. Anyway, I think my guys and I will get on our way. How much do I owe you?"

I considered exaggerating the price. Nothing could possibly compensate me for the anxiety I now felt but couldn't even hint at. I also thought about giving the dog treats to him for free, but I doubted that bribery would get me very far.

Instead, I tallied up the actual amount. "I hope Magnum and Blade love all of it."

Wayne paid by credit card, and I did all the regular mundane things like swiping it and making sure the receipt was accurate. I put the box I'd prepared into a plastic bag so he could carry it more easily while hanging on to the dog leashes.

I couldn't help it. As he got ready to go, I had to ask, "Wayne, did you really come here to get treats for your dogs, or did you think approaching me in a less official and threatening way would get me to blurt out a confession—not that there's anything to confess?"

"Honestly? A little of both, Carrie. I'd like to be able to erase you from our suspect list, but even this off-the-record stuff didn't actually convince me. I'll keep what you said in mind, and, yes, you can be sure we're still examining evidence and talking to other people who argued with Myra. She wasn't always the easiest person to get along with, is what we've learned. But even so ... "

He didn't finish his sentence. Instead, he pulled on the two leashes, and his dogs, who were again sniffing at Biscuit, hurried away and pranced ahead of him out of the store.

I was trembling when Dinah came in through the door from Icing. She was smiling—at least until she saw me.

"What's wrong, Carrie? I was just coming in to tell you I got a great order for an extra-large birthday cake for tomorrow. But you look awful."

I laughed. "You don't pull any punches, do you? But you're right. I'm not at my best right now. But that's wonderful. I hope you'll help me bake that cake."

"Absolutely."

We both heard Judy call from Icing, "Got your coffee, Dinah. Where are you?"

"Right here." Dinah hurried back the way she'd come, leaving me alone with Biscuit again, at least for the moment.

And with my roiling, frightened thoughts.

I didn't know why Wayne had really come. Interrogating me here for a third time, sure, and pretending not to? But why? He surely didn't really think I'd confess more easily under these circumstances.

Maybe the guy was a sadist who liked seeing suspects squirm. And he'd even used his poor dogs in his cruel mission this time.

Well, as awful as I felt, I wouldn't let him do it to me again. Should I hire a lawyer, as I'd wondered before, and refuse to talk to the cops at all, for any reason?

That might make me look even guiltier. But so what?

I'd already started asking questions, trying to figure out who really had a motive to kill Myra.

I realized now that I'd better do even more.

SIXTEEN

After making sure that Dinah was well ensconced in the Barkery, I stayed in the shop for a while too.

Though I played with my sweet little Biscuit as Dinah staffed the counter, my mind was doing somersaults. How could I survive this? Even if it resembled something straight out of fiction, like the mysteries I sometimes read, I really needed to do more to help myself, like find out who the real murderer was and then present evidence of it to the cops who were torturing—er, interrogating—me.

Were those mystery books just the result of people's imaginations? If not, maybe some of the authors were truly empathetic and put themselves inside the minds of real-life murder suspects who truly were innocent, and then fictionalized them in their stories.

Or maybe it *was* all fiction, and amateurs really couldn't solve mysteries even when falsely accused.

I was a veterinary technician. A baker. A store owner. Not a detective. What hope did I have?

Well, it was too soon to give up now.

I hugged Biscuit fiercely for another minute, then went back into the kitchen, gave my hands a good washing, donned gloves, and set myself to baking dog treats again... while my mind continued to go off on tangents of its own.

How could I learn the truth? Who should I talk to? How could I get them to talk?

And was this all completely irrational?

"Do we have any more red velvet cupcakes made?" Judy's voice barged into my thoughts, and I looked up to see that she'd just entered the kitchen from the Icing side. Of course. She wouldn't be asking about red velvet cupcakes for the Barkery. Liver cupcakes, maybe. I baked mostly biscuits for dogs now but had developed other kinds of recipes too—and I'd bought a separate set of baking dishes for them.

But this wasn't the time to start increasing our inventory.

"Not yet," I told her. "But I can start working on some next. Or, if you'd rather, I can handle Icing's customers once I put these treats in the oven, and you can do the baking."

"That sounds great to me." A smile bisected her long yet pretty face.

I wanted to hug her, since she was here for me. A steady resource, as was her counterpart Dinah.

Would they take care of running the shops for me if I was arrested?

Would they be able to get along well enough to do so, for an indeterminate period of time?

Brenda hadn't thought so...

I had to center my own thoughts on reality now. I needed to finish these trays of dog treats and go over to Icing.

Later, I'd head for the Knobcone Heights Resort.

Where had that thought come from? And then I realized. My own mind, my subconscious, was working on my problem. The place I needed to go—again—to try to figure out who'd killed Myra was the place she'd managed, the place her local family most often hung out.

The place she'd probably frequently been while arguing with people, including that fired chef.

Good thing my brother happened to work there. He'd be my excuse to visit. I wouldn't go there, of course, until after I'd finished up doing all I needed to here—the things that were my obvious responsibilities.

But my responsibilities to myself included keeping my businesses going, helping me keep my part-time vet tech job—and saving myself from worrying about being arrested. Or from actually getting arrested. I'd call Neal soon and warn him I'd be visiting him at the resort a little later.

———

I had a really enjoyable time taking over at Icing from Judy. A lot of customers came in, apparently a tour group whose guide had developed an affinity for the store's baked goods while Brenda had been in charge.

After they left, there weren't a lot of those goods left. But fortunately Judy came through and brought the red velvet cupcakes out to the display case, along with several dozen sugar cookies and chocolate chip cookies that she'd baked at the same time. I thanked her profusely when she appeared with them, and we spent some time organizing them behind the glass.

When we were done, I decided it was time. This was one Sunday when I didn't have a shift at the veterinary clinic. I'd leave my shops anyway for a while—but for an entirely different reason.

First, I went into the kitchen to call Neal while Judy and Dinah were still in the stores. He couldn't talk immediately but said he'd call me back. "As soon as you can," I told him before he hung up.

I didn't want to get back to baking just then, so I went into the office and booted up the computer, checking out sales figures but mostly staring at the screen. My stores were both doing okay, considering they'd been opened—or reopened—for just over a week.

Would that continue?

My cell phone rang. It was Neal. "What's up, Carrie?"

"I need an excuse to visit the resort today."

"Really? Why?" he asked. When I opened my mouth to respond, he said, "Oh, don't tell me. I think I can guess."

I smiled grimly. My brother might not have a lot of ambition, but that didn't mean he wasn't smart and intuitive.

"You probably can." I hesitated. "I had another visit from one of those detectives. It wasn't official—at least I don't think so. But I can't just wait to see what happens. So … good. Tell me how I can show up there and stay a while without getting tossed out."

"Not sure about the 'tossed out' part. You're not exactly the favorite person of any of my bosses. But … "

"Yes?"

"Hey, I know. We've got a lot of visiting dogs right now. A bunch of guests brought theirs along. Maybe you can bring some treats for them to taste."

"Good idea," I said, then stopped as I considered it further. "You think your bosses will be okay with it? In a way, it'll look like I'm flaunting that I'm competing with Harris Ethman's pet store."

"I know. But Harris isn't here, and Elise seems to still be running this place. She wants to earn brownie points with their parents, bring in a lot more tourists, make even more money than Myra did, so if you please a lot of those folks who brought their pets, she'll probably like it."

"Right. And I can always say it's a test, and it's something Harris might want to do too."

"Hey, right. Not a bad idea. So when will you get here?"

I glanced at the ovens on the Barkery side of the kitchen. Fortunately the treats I'd been working on before were nearly done. Yes, my Barkery shop could have used some more product—but now I had enough to give out a fair amount of samples at the resort. "About half an hour," I said.

————

I gathered up a generous sampling of the different kinds of the biscuits I'd made that morning, then put them into a couple of bags.

I treated them carefully. They would be my apparent excuse for hanging around the resort, so I wanted them to look good. And taste good. And garner a lot of attention, particularly from dogs ... so I would look as if I belonged there while I tossed some human inquiries around.

If the treats actually achieved the secondary purpose of introducing guests to my Barkery, all the better.

When I was ready, I said a temporary goodbye to my staff, then got Biscuit into the car. I didn't want my helpers to have to worry about her.

Even more, I didn't want to worry about her in the care of my helpers.

I dropped her off at her doggy daycare for an hour or two. Faye wasn't there but others I knew were, including Al. Then, I drove along the winding, busy streets to the resort. It was late morning and I wouldn't be able to spend a lot of time there.

I was also very aware that today, being Sunday, was the last day I'd have both helpers around for a while. Monday and Tuesday, respectively, were the days that Brenda had given her assistants off, since weekends were usually very busy. Last week, Dinah and Judy had both agreed to work both days, to get the two shops going, and I'd paid them a little extra—still thanks to Arvie's generous loan.

I needed to start staggering their weekdays off, though. Tomorrow was Monday again, and only Judy would be here. She'd seemed okay with the idea of my leaving for short periods, maybe an hour at a time, so I could do brief stints at the clinic. I wasn't sure if I was comfortable enough with anything longer, but I'd eventually have to get used to it, though not tomorrow. Tuesday was Dinah's turn to work at the shops, and again I could test leaving for short periods.

All the more reason to do what I was doing today—and hopefully get some results. Otherwise, I'd be hard-pressed to find time to conduct any investigation on my own over the next couple of days.

And if I was hauled off to jail... Well, I wouldn't even think about that. But when a hint of panic crossed my mind, I figured that, worst case scenario, I'd beg Judy and/or Dinah to give up some of their days off because of the emergency. Hopefully it wouldn't be for a long time... But in that kind of situation, I wouldn't have an opportunity to hire any additional employees to help them.

I reached the resort's parking lot, took a ticket to enter, found a spot, and retrieved the treat bags from the floor of the back seat behind me. After locking the car, I took a few deep breaths and walked first to the end of the lot so I could see the lake. There were quite a few boats visible on the quiet blue water today. I sort of envied those on board.

But I'd have envied them more if this lake hooked up to the Pacific somehow and I could have gotten onto a boat and just sailed away, not worried anymore about being considered a murder suspect.

That thought startled me and I erased it from my mind. I loved it here in Knobcone Heights. I enjoyed my job as a vet tech. And I was full of hope and ambition for my new venture as a baker for dogs and humans.

Squaring my shoulders after repositioning my purse and steadying the bags I held, I headed for the closest entrance to the resort's large lobby.

I pondered stopping by to say hi to Neal but decided against it. I didn't know how well my presence would be accepted, and although our relationship was known to his superiors, they might forgive him for his potentially over-assertive sister's presence if there was no indication he'd encouraged her. He wasn't paid much and his hours weren't always desirable, but it was a job, and his bringing some money in was better than none.

So instead, as I walked inside the spacious, crowded lobby, I headed toward the row of office doors near the registration desk. I wasn't sure which Ethman I'd run into first, nor which one, if I had a choice, was most likely to go along with my scheme—and perhaps deign to hold a conversation with me.

Given my druthers, I'd prefer talking to Les Ethman, but I doubted he'd be here. Next choice was Walt Hainner, but he was probably out building or remodeling something.

Harris Ethman? Even if he was here instead of at the Emporium, he was unlikely to give me permission to pass out treats let alone talk to me civilly.

His parents? Maybe they'd be best.

But instead of finding either Susan or Trask, when I peeked into the office I saw only Elise Ethman Hainner sitting there. She was on the phone, but she noticed me right away and scowled.

Maybe this had been a really bad idea after all. But I was here. I had to give it a try.

And I realized that, on some level, my mind had settled on Elise anyway. She might be the best one to talk to since she knew all the players—plus Neal had said she was in charge of running the resort, at least for now.

So instead of scowling back, or fleeing, I gave her a huge smile and lifted up the bags I was holding as if she'd requested them. I made a motion to let her know I'd be waiting right outside her door.

And that's what I did, making sure that though my back was to her she could see that I continued to stand there. I scoured the lobby and did, in fact, see a number of people with dogs on leashes, mostly small yapper types but a few medium-sized canines like Goldens and Lab mixes. I had an urge to approach one or two and start handing out my treats so I could demonstrate to Elise, when she emerged, exactly what my cover story here was, and show that it could garner a lot of interest from guests.

As it turned out, I didn't have to approach any of them. A person who looked familiar—I'd met her at the vet clinic, so she must have been a local—was drawn in my direction by a gold-colored Pekingese on a leash. The small dog had her nose in the air and seemed to be smelling the treats. I realized then that she looked just like one of the visitors to the Barkery at our opening party; if it was the same dog, she might recognize my scent and the treats' scent and be anticipating another handout.

"Hi," said the owner. "You're Carrie, aren't you? I met you at the Knobcone vet clinic, and you're also the lady who owns that Barkery, right? Phaedra remembers you."

"And I remember Phaedra," I said with a smile. I reached into one of the bags. "I brought some of my treats along today to see if I could introduce them to some other dogs here, but I'm delighted to share them with pups who've already had an opportunity to sample them."

Phaedra seemed happy with one of the small apple-flavored biscuits I'd brought, and her excitement drew the attention of some of the other dogs in the lobby, as well as their owners. By the time Elise emerged from her office a little while later, I seemed to be the most popular person in the large, well-populated room.

"What are you doing here, Carrie?" she demanded.

I grinned. "I think that's obvious. I brought some of my treats for your guests' pets."

She took my arm, smiling at some of those guests as she pulled me aside. I noticed a few sad-looking dogs watching and mentally promised them I'd be back.

"Are you trying to undermine Harris's pet store by showing up here?" she demanded softly. "He has enough to deal with now that Myra's gone. Or is that part of it? Maybe that's why you killed her."

My grin disappeared. I glanced around. A lot of people were watching us, not just the dogs, but Elise at least had the courtesy to keep her voice down as she accused me.

"I didn't do anything to Myra but respond to her insults about my Barkery. And now—well, if Harris wants to give out treats to encourage people to come to the Emporium, fine. And if you'd think this through, you'd know that you'd be a better manager here, even a temporary one, if you gave people special, unanticipated benefits, especially for their beloved pets. I'm helping you here, Elise. Don't you see that?"

I realized that I was laying it on a bit thick, but I was delighted to see Elise's furious stare seem to melt a little. Did she feel a little insecure here in her role as substitute person-in-charge?

"Why don't you come into my office for a minute, Carrie? I might let you pass out some of your treats afterward, but we'll need to establish some rules."

Rules I probably wouldn't like. But what I did like was the opportunity to go into her office and ask a few questions. Maybe more than a few, about her and her family and ... well, I'd just have to see how far I could go.

"Sure," I said. "But first—"

I reached into one of my bags again and handed out small pieces of biscuit to the dogs who'd been waiting so patiently while we argued.

SEVENTEEN

I SAT IN THE chair Elise designated, across the desk from her.

"Would you like something to drink?" she asked. "Coffee? Water? Soda?"

That sounded a lot nicer than I'd been anticipating. "I'd love some coffee with cream," I told her. I half expected her to tell me the price, but instead she lifted her phone receiver, pushed a few numbers in, and ordered my coffee and a latte, presumably for herself.

I'd wondered before what Elise did for a living—real estate sales? Nothing? Apparently her family trusted her enough to put her in this position, at least for now.

She was probably in her forties. I'd noticed how slender she was when she'd led the memorial service for Myra, in her black dress. Her hair was a deep blonde, probably not her natural color, and it waved softly about her face. She wasn't beautiful, but neither was she unattractive. I figured that her excellent makeup job, with arched brows and perfect lashes and pink lips that were full but not huge, were probably at least partly thanks to her family's wealth—which enabled visits to salons and purchases of the best brands of makeup.

Did that sound catty or jealous? I was neither. I didn't really care, except that I felt relieved we were getting along now. Or at least she wasn't still telling me how unwelcome I was here.

Did that mean it was time for me to ask some cagey questions about her family and how each of them had really gotten along with Myra? I'd have to use some finesse so I wouldn't be totally obvious. But how much subtlety could there be in indirectly asking a person if she, or someone she was related to, had hated her sister-in-law enough to have killed her?

Might Elise have done it herself to get this position? Some other reason? A combo?

I decided my best approach was to be candid—sort of.

"I know I could have given out treat samples someplace else, Elise," I began. "Someplace where no one had told me I wasn't welcome."

Her half-smile was wan. "I hope you understand why I said that."

"You thought I had something to do with your sister-in-law's death. Yes, I do understand. I hope you understand that my coming here then, and now, is my way of saying I didn't do anything. I realize you could assume it's just the opposite, that I'm rubbing your and your family's noses in my misdeed, so to speak, and gloating over the fact I haven't been arrested."

She laughed. "Appropriate analogy," she said, "but I gather that the best people dealing with dog training these days don't rub bad dogs' noses in their mistakes."

"True." I smiled back at her. "Anyway, I'd imagine it's pretty stressful for you to take over running the resort now that Myra's gone, especially under these circumstances."

"You could say that." She nodded, pressing her lips together.

A knock sounded on her half-open door, and Gwen came in. She held a tray with two steaming orange coffee mugs on it. "Here we are, ladies." Her glance toward me appeared quizzical. She obviously knew I'd been all but kicked out of the restaurant a week ago by the same woman who was showing me hospitality now. She also knew I was curious about a lot of things—and that I was Neal's sister.

"Thanks." I smiled at her as I had at Elise, but this wasn't a good time to start a conversation with her. I felt certain, though, that Neal would soon know where I was.

"Let me know if you'd like anything else," Gwen said.

"We will, thanks," Elise said, clearly dismissing her. That was fine with me. I needed to continue our conversation and hopefully get things right.

Or at least not put myself back in the position of being un-welcome.

"I realize that you and I got off on the wrong foot," I began, still not quite sure how to approach this. "I felt glad, though, that Walt seemed to recognize I wasn't all bad."

"My husband thinks that about a lot of people he shouldn't." Elise's mutter was directed into her latte, so I had to strain to hear it.

What did it mean?

I forced myself to laugh. "I hope you don't mean me—and I have to admit I don't always understand the intricacies of how married people interact with one another and with other people." I had a lot of married friends whose relationships I'd observed, so that wasn't exactly true, but I thought it appropriate to say. Maybe. "Anyway, Walt seems like a nice guy. I gather he's been accepted well into your family, like Myra."

Elise's attention was suddenly on me. "What do you mean?" Her tone was cold. And I wondered what that meant.

I had an odd thought suddenly. Myra had married into the Ethmans. So had Walt. Elise's comment suggested there might be more to the situation than that, although I couldn't be sure what.

But I might be able to get that information fleshed out if I approached this carefully.

"I've lived here long enough to recognize how … respected your family is," I said. "The Ethmans do wonderful things for Knobcone Heights, and not just by owning a great resort that attracts people here and keeps them coming back." Was I laying this on too thick? I didn't think so, judging by the interest now apparent on Elise's face. "I didn't know Myra well enough to understand how she came to run this place, but I'd imagine her shoes will be hard to fill, at least if you haven't done this before." I watched Elise's face, hoping she wouldn't consider that an insult.

Her nostrils flared a bit as if she was attempting to suppress some anger. "Oh, I think I'll do just fine filling her shoes. Better than the way she tried to fill mine."

I watched her eyes narrow, as if in anger, as she said this. What did she mean?

I started to ask, but Elise stood abruptly, hands poised on the edges of the dark wood desk. "Go ahead and give away your dog treats, Carrie. In fact, let's both go into the lobby. I think it's a great idea to hand people more than they expect so they'll consider coming back. I actually appreciate it, since I'm just getting started here and intend to do all I can to increase our sales. Come on." She beckoned to me as she headed for the door, her coffee cup still on her desk.

What had just happened here?

On the one hand, I was glad I was welcome to give away dog biscuits. But I hadn't achieved my real goal of finding out more about some or all of the Ethmans.

Or had I?

What had Elise meant by that comment about Myra and she filling each other's shoes?

A wonderment that could explain a lot pierced my brain. Had the two non-blood-related Ethmans—Myra and Walt—been having an affair?

If so, that would explain Elise's attitude.

It would also have given her a motive to kill Myra.

I could just be jumping to a wild conclusion. But maybe not. I recalled Walt's sadness at Myra's memorial. I wouldn't come right out and ask—not Elise, at least. Who might know? Neal? Someone else around the resort?

I needed to ponder how to approach this, and with whom.

But I also wanted to take advantage of having Elise's attention and perhaps being on her good side. Until I wound up accusing her of murder ...?

I stood too. "Yes, let's go give away some more of my treats. And if this goes well we could do it again sometime."

My mind was racing even as we started walking. Was Elise helping out at the resort solely as a favor to her parents, or did she actually have aspirations to take over running this place? I'd gotten a sense already it was the latter.

If so, yes, it would be a possible motive for her to kill Myra. And if Myra had been having an affair with Walt, and Elise thought she could get even by murdering her and stepping into her shoes here ... well, those together would definitely have provided a logical reason for her to have disposed of her sister-in-law.

It took us barely a minute to get into the busy lobby with its undercurrent of conversations. I saw Neal in the distance, behind the desk. He saw me, too, around the side of a woman in a beige dress whom he was helping.

I needed to talk to him, run the possibility of the Myra-Walt affair by him. He'd seen Myra a lot. Had Walt come by here much, maybe to do some handyman work or room remodels?

Or visit Myra . . . ?

"Here we are, folks," Elise called, crouching to beckon a cute basset hound mix toward her. She smiled up at the owner who was holding the leash. "Free samples of some wholesome, fresh-baked dog treats, courtesy of Knobcone Heights Resort." She glanced up at me with her hand out, ready to give the dog a biscuit. I raised my eyebrows and she added, "Oh, and the wonderful new shop Barkery and Biscuits."

I cooperated then by handing her some of the biscuits. The dog seemed to enjoy it, and the action spurred the others with dogs in the lobby to head our way.

I hadn't spent a lot of time at the resort before this week except for the occasional meal or visit to see Neal, but my opinion during the last few days was that it certainly catered to a lot of different kinds of guests. The lobby was, as usual, crowded. Some people were dressed up, like the woman still talking to Neal. A guy in a suit stood beside her. Here for business?

Others, like the basset's owner, were in jeans and T-shirts, wearing backpacks. Neal would have been better off talking to them, since he might have been able to sell them one of his hikes or boat outings.

But I was making assumptions that could be entirely untrue. What was clear for the moment, at least, was that Elise was acting as if she had invited me, and was using my presence and my biscuits to score points with at least some of the guests.

Which might help to secure her position here at the resort into something more permanent, if that was her goal.

If so, my idea about her possible motive was stoked all the more.

We soon had quite a crowd around us, even petless folks. Most said they'd take a treat or two home with them, maybe even to help make themselves feel better about not having brought their pooches along on this trip.

I laughed and handed out samples—and told them they could make themselves feel even better if they stopped at my Barkery and picked up more than a sample to bring home. I had a feeling that at least some of them would do just that.

Soon, all the treats were gone. "This was a good idea," Elise said. "In fact, I'd enjoy having you to do this again. But next time, get in touch and schedule it."

She was actually smiling at me.

"Of course." I smiled back.

It looked like our short, friendly get-together was about to end. That was okay with me, for now. I had some new things to think about and look into.

But I didn't want to leave without one more inquiry.

"I've got a question for you. I have a lot of good recipes I'm trying, but I want to attempt even more. I may need some help. It might be way off base, but I heard the resort's restaurant"—namely, Myra, who'd apparently been in charge there too—"recently let a chef go from the restaurant. Do you know how I could find him? Maybe I could pay him to create some recipes."

"Right. Manfred Indor. He got sloppy with his cooking here." No longer did Elise look friendly. "But hey, maybe he'd do better cooking for animals. Sure. Come back to my office. His contact information is probably on the computer. You know that he messed up here.

Myra told us how he'd used inferior ingredients in a meal prepared for an important party, so don't consider this a referral or recommendation."

"I won't." That wasn't the story I'd heard, but if it was the one that had gotten out and harmed Manfred's reputation, he might have been even more strongly peeved with Myra.

Her smile came back, at least halfway. "Maybe this would be a good thing since he messed up with his people food. Manfred at least deserves a cooking demotion. You'll have to let me know how it works out."

"Of course," I said.

And you might wind up being glad if I determine he's the one who killed Myra, I thought.

That way I'll stop suspecting you.

EIGHTEEN

I SAID GOODBYE AND left Elise in her office along with the empty bags with my Barkery and Biscuits logo on them. She'd probably just toss them, but for now they'd be a reminder of how the formerly unwelcome Carrie Kennersly had jumped in to help Elise make a good impression as the current resort manager.

Maybe Elise wouldn't have any questions about why I'd been so helpful. She knew I was promoting my shops, right? Why would I have any ulterior motive?

I gnawed gently on my lips to hide any wry smile that might otherwise have emerged. When I went into the vast lobby this time it was just as crowded as before, and when I looked over at the registration desk I didn't see Neal.

Not till I glanced toward the door that led toward the beach.

My brother caught my eye at the same time and gave a nod that told me to join him. I made my way gently but determinedly through the maze of people, some of whom had their dogs with them. A few tried to stop me, but I held up my empty hands and shrugged. "Sorry," I said to a couple of them. "No more treats here right now. But please visit my Barkery."

I finally reached the door, and as I got there Neal pushed it open. I followed him onto the patio with the stairway down to the sand. A few people stood out there, mostly in pairs, staring out at the lake, which was shimmering brightly this afternoon. I followed him to the far end of the patio, which was empty.

"So how did it go?" My good-looking brother stared down at me as if trying to read my thoughts. Not that I was trying to hide them from him.

"Surprisingly well." Then I said in a low voice, "Do you know whether Elise has any aspirations to make her new managerial slot permanent?"

Neal blinked and his brows knitted together. "Really? That's the impression you got?" Before I could respond, he continued, "Very interesting. She's always hung out here a lot, and she seemed to be happy when she was helping, but then she was mostly following Myra's instructions."

"Was she doing that recently?"

Neal's expression grew pensive. "No, lately she didn't come here very often. And when she did, it was to have dinner with her folks and Walt, not to hang out and do something to help the resort."

That didn't prove anything, but neither did it dispel my wonderment about whether Myra and Walt had had something going.

Well, why not ask someone who might have observed it, even if he didn't recognize it at the time?

"Neal," I said, "a possibility occurred to me that might be completely ridiculous. But something Elise said made me think she was … well, a bit unhappy with Myra. And the context was—okay, let me just ask." I glanced around first and fortunately didn't see anyone standing nearby. In fact, most people had their backs toward us as the groups who hovered on the patio continued to watch the water, which now contained a few noisy motor boats rushing by.

"What?" Neal looked both interested and curious.

"Did you ever see any indication that Myra and Walt were...let's say, better than friendly in-laws?"

Although Neal shook his head, it was slow and looked as if it was more in surprise than denial. "How you come up with stuff like that out of the blue, Carrie—I'm amazed. And impressed. You don't even know these people, do you? At least not very well."

"I need to get to know them better now," I said. "As long as I'm considered a possible suspect in Myra's death."

"Are you saying Walt might have done it?" His tone sounded incredulous, though his expression was more calculating.

"Maybe. But I'd be more likely to suspect Elise, if she caught them in something. Especially if she was jealous because Myra was running this place." I nodded toward the resort's lobby.

Neal laughed aloud, but softly. "I knew you were an intuitive witch," he said. "But you mostly aim that toward the animals you care for. I can't say for sure that you're correct, but I had a few suspicions of my own now and then. Not that I particularly cared. It wasn't my business who was screwing who around here, as long as it didn't affect my job."

I nodded as I pondered what he'd said. The answer was yes. My brother had suspected that Myra and Walt had something going.

Had that in some way led to Myra's demise?

Elise certainly had reason to get rid of her. Maybe Walt did too, if she threatened him with exposure. He seemed to be a successful-enough building contractor, but it surely didn't hurt him to have the financial cushion of being married to a wealthy Ethman. If his relationship with Myra became public, Elise would have felt humiliated and might have divorced him.

So it was better for Walt, too, if Myra was out of their lives, assuming he didn't really love her.

Did the cops know or suspect any of this? I had no proof of anything, so running to them and trying to point them toward these people as better suspects than me might make them hang on to me even harder.

But I'd check things out as best I could. Look for proof. Give the detectives the benefit of my inquiries if the appropriate occasion arose.

And in the meantime...

"Thanks for your insight," I told Neal. "It might not mean anything. I realize that. But it doesn't hurt—"

"To know about other people who might have had a whole lot more reason than you—or me—to kill Myra," he said.

I smiled. "Which brings me to my next idea."

"Which is?" By now, Neal's grin was huge.

I told him about my other thought, that the fired chef Manfred Indor might have resented the manager who'd canned him.

"I figured that might be one way your thoughts were headed," Neal said. "I never knew Manfred well, but I know someone who did. Let's see if Gwen can tell us more about him. Wait here a second."

As Neal hurried into the lobby, I saw him take a sharp right turn—toward the restaurant. When he returned with Gwen a few minutes later, she looked a little frazzled but stayed at his side, talking to him as they approached me.

I'd noticed last week how attractive she was, with her dark hair and friendly demeanor. She wore a chocolate-colored skirt today with a white blouse and coppery pinecone necklace, clearly helping to promote Knobcone Heights and the resort. Her glossed lips glowed in the late afternoon sunlight, and she smiled as she continued to converse with Neal.

When they reached the edge of the patio where I was leaning on the railing, both stopped. Neal appeared happy too, with a large smile on his face.

I thought once more that there must be something between him and the pretty server, but I wouldn't mention it again now since she was standing right there. Later, though...

"Gwen said she'll give us more info about what happened with Manfred, Carrie." Neal grinned down at her, then toward me.

"I'm all ears," I said.

"Our Manfred was quite a character." Gwen rolled her deep brown eyes.

"*Our* Manfred?" I had to ask.

"He was the main chef when I started working here a year ago." She turned to look dreamily out over the lake. "I heard from him, and from the other servers, that he considered this place his, and that he also considered all of us a team. We were one many-tentacled unit, in his estimation. Or that's what I gathered."

"Interesting," I said. "Then it must have been hard on him when his unit dumped him—or at least its leader did, if I understand correctly."

"I'll say. And the way, and reason, it was done..." Gwen's voice trailed off.

"Tell me." If she was looking for encouragement before continuing, I'd definitely give it. Or was it something else?

She turned to look at Neal, as if his encouragement was what was lacking. Or maybe she was worried about whether gossiping more with his sister, whom she didn't really know, was such a good idea.

Especially since she knew why I was asking: I was trying to potentially pin a murder on her former unit-member.

Neal nodded at her, possibly conveying that I was an okay person. Or at least giving Gwen support in going further.

Rather than looking at me, she leaned on the railing beside me and again looked out over the lake. It was less sunny now, and there was a kayak rowing team nearby. As Neal followed her gaze, I saw a wistfulness in his expression, as if he'd like to be out there with the rowers—maybe leading them on one of his beloved expeditions.

Maybe I was wrong about his feelings for Gwen.

Or maybe he wanted to be out there with her.

"Okay, here's what actually happened," Gwen finally said. "Cohesive unit or not, Manfred was the one in charge of food, or at least the special recipes he used for the restaurant's most gourmet dishes. One afternoon a couple of weeks ago, Myra came into the kitchen and told him and the rest of us that there would be a very special party here that night. She wanted a very special menu, too, since the guests were people with a lot of influence down the hill, mostly from L.A. and San Diego. If they liked their experience here, in the restaurant as well as at the resort, they'd not only return but would also tell their affluent friends about it."

"Sounds reasonable," I said.

"Yes, on the surface. And maybe below it." Gwen again looked toward Neal.

"You were all briefed," Neal suggested, "in a way that you recognized meant your jobs were on the line." When Gwen nodded, he looked toward me. "That was one of Myra's favorite ploys. If she wanted something done 'right'—meaning her way—she would make sure everyone knew that, if anything went 'wrong,' heads would roll down the San Bernardino Mountains. Fast and hard."

I'd suspected something like this was the case when Neal occasionally seemed irritated when he returned home after a day's work, but he'd always slough off my questions. He would just say there'd been some stuff going on that day involving the management but that it all had worked out fine.

Meaning, I now figured, that Myra had been satisfied with whatever the result had been.

"That's it," Gwen agreed. "Then Myra was nasty enough to tell Manfred that she not only wanted his proposed entrée of beef Wellington changed, but she had chosen chicken Parmesan, which was much more mundane to him. Then she told him his recipe for chicken Parmesan was okay, but she wanted him to change it to meet her specifications, which she handed him. Those of us who were near them in the kitchen could almost feel the earth shaking beneath our feet as Manfred's temper got ready to explode."

"And did it?" I figured I knew the answer but asked anyway.

"Did it ever!"

"I even thought I felt the explosion out by the registration desk," Neal said, his eyebrows raised in irony.

Gwen looked at him in what appeared to be fond amusement. "Maybe so," she said. "I'm sure you at least heard the argument."

He nodded. "It shook up everything. I even wondered whether the people I was checking in would turn around and flee. We didn't know what it was about at the time, and it was quick. Later, when Myra came back our way, she gave her usual instructions. We were not to discuss, even among ourselves, what we may have heard. It no longer existed. Not being the greatest direction-follower, I did initially attempt to get some info about it, but everyone else had been intimidated enough to follow what she said." He looked down at Gwen. "I still heard rumors. And I think I've only convinced Gwen to give you details now because Myra's not around to follow through on her threats."

Gwen's smile toward him looked fond. "I agree that there won't be consequences now that Myra can't instigate them." Then her expression morphed to something more troubled. "But—oh my, Carrie. What I've told you—you're running with it, aren't you? Are you jumping on the possibility that Chef Manfred was the killer—or trying to protect yourself by trying to make him look like the top suspect?"

I liked Gwen. She seemed like an intelligent, intuitive woman who could aspire to doing a lot more with her life if she decided to move on from being a restaurant server. If she had a relationship with Neal, that could be a very good thing for my smart but sometimes mentally lazy brother.

I shrugged one shoulder. "I'm still looking into all possibilities. And I'm not making any accusations. Not yet, at least. Even so—" Did I dare ask her opinion about whether Manfred could have been angry enough to do something drastic to Myra?

She seemed to hear my unspoken question. "You know, Carrie," she said thoughtfully, pursing her shining lips as she looked at me, "I like Manfred, despite his egotism. If I had to hazard a guess, sure, he could have wanted to get back at Myra. But in my opinion, he'd do something more subtle—like sabotage one of her parties. He wouldn't have had a chance to gloat if he'd simply murdered her." She put her hand up to her mouth, and I noticed that her short but well-shaped nails were as glossed as her lips. "Sorry. That sounds horrible."

"But helpful." I leaned toward her and gestured for Neal to come closer too. "I appreciate your information and advice, Gwen.

And if you happen to have any other ideas about people who might have disliked Myra and had no need for subtlety if they decided to deal with her, I'd appreciate your letting me know. I'm already looking into other family members, by the way."

"That would be my first thought," Gwen said. "Did you tell your sister about Myra and Walt Hainner?" She looked at Neal.

"You knew about that?" I asked.

At the same time my brother said, "Then my suspicions were true?"

I laughed softly. Gwen could be a real asset in my investigation into who could have killed Myra.

Briefly, a thought came into my mind. Could she herself have had something against the resort's big boss—something stronger than her concern about getting fired? She might have been smart enough and subtle enough to resolve it and direct attention to others—like me.

Then I erased that thought. No way. I was just so eager to plant the blame on someone else that I was jumping to absurd conclusions.

Even so ... well, I would have a talk with Chef Manfred Indor to get my own ideas about his possible guilt.

And I might just continue to run ideas by Gwen—not only to get her thoughts about them, but also to see her reaction.

NINETEEN

TIME TO HEAD BACK to my shops. I said bye to Gwen and saw her hurry into the restaurant as I walked through the lobby with Neal.

"I like her," I said. "She's nice, and she seems smart. And pretty." I didn't look at him but waited for his response.

"Yeah, all of those." My brother was moseying beside me in the crowd, either wanting to talk more or not eager to return to work. Or both. "But there's a guy in her life and I don't get it. He lives in Riverside and they don't seem to get together much." He stopped, and when I looked at him he shrugged. "Could be he's just an excuse. It might be obvious to her that I'm interested, but it's not obvious to me that she's not. Interested in me, I mean. She seems to like me, but—Hell."

He turned and started walking again, edging through the people in the lobby toward his post.

Interesting, I thought. Despite having told me before that there was nothing between them other than having fun, my fancy-free, sometimes irresponsible brother seemed to have a genuine romantic interest in this woman—one that might not be reciprocated.

Still, he could be trying to win her attention. That would explain his working here so diligently lately. Although he mostly worked at the reception desk, along with leading some of the official resort tours, Neal also ran some unofficial tours on his own. If he didn't have enough vacation time available for this, he'd call in sick. But I knew there hadn't been many outings at the resort recently, nor had Neal had any of his own. And since he was clearly not happy about it, I couldn't believe he'd arranged it just to see more of Gwen.

As I watched, Neil returned to his post behind the reception desk and started talking to another of the employees. He lifted his hand to wave at me, but he clearly was finished with our conversation. Which was fine with me—for now.

But later . . .

I hurried into the parking lot, gulped when I paid to release my car, and headed for the vet clinic to pick up Biscuit.

Even that didn't turn out as to be easy as I'd hoped. Oh, my adorable dog was fine and clearly happy to see me. But before I could leave Faye said, "Dr. Storme wanted to talk to you. He said I should have him paged once you got here."

"I'll go into the clinic and find him," I said. "Thanks." I swallowed my smile. I'd be glad to see him too.

But my pleasure turned out to be premature.

Reed exited a care room as Biscuit and I walked down the hall. His pace was quick and determined, and he stopped as soon as he saw me.

"Glad you're here, Carrie. I was going to call you if I didn't see you. We have several unanticipated surgeries scheduled for tomorrow and not enough assistants. I know you're supposed to be off, but could you come in for a few hours?"

I swallowed hard, especially since his stare looked demanding and not particularly friendly. This wasn't the Reed I thought I was getting to know. But it was apparently his stress talking.

And my stress? A few hours? A short while, yes, but so long? "I … I don't think so," I said sadly. Biscuit, who'd started to lie down at my feet, was suddenly standing at attention beside me. She was a sweet, intuitive dog, and she clearly sensed the tension here. "I'll see what I can work out, but—"

"Okay. Fine. But don't be surprised if we—"

Arvie was suddenly with us. "Now, don't make threats we've no intention of keeping, Dr. Storme." But my sudden relief and urge to hug Arvie were dispelled by his next words. "We're already looking for another tech or two to hire, but we're not going to make any changes in Carrie's situation here."

That was especially sweet of him, since he had an interest in having my shops do well and my being there instead of here might help that. Still … another tech or two? My part-time services could become even more part-time then. It had been my own choice to open my new retail venture, but the idea of less pay, and even less time working at a job I really loved …

Well, I'd asked for it. But I really wanted it all—and a treasured part of my life might be taken away from me.

It might anyway, I reminded myself. It was worse—much worse—that I was considered a murder suspect.

I looked at my beloved senior mentor and smiled. "Thanks, Arvie," I said, as one of my tech coworkers walked by and glanced quizzically toward us. I waved without really looking at him. I instead looked from Arvie to Reed and back again. "As I said, I'll see if I can work anything out for tomorrow. I do have an couple of assistants lined up to help at my stores but haven't required either of them to work alone much." And I didn't have someone else lined up who could come in and help, if necessary.

"I like your stores, Carrie," Reed said. "Don't get me wrong. But I think you're going to have to make a choice."

"We'll see," Arvie said. "But that's in the future. Right now, please just let us know as soon as you can about tomorrow, and I'll also see who else around here might be able to help out. Now, I've a kitty waiting for me down the hall so I've got to go. Give us a call if you can help, Carrie."

"Okay."

I watched Arvie stride down the hall, then looked again at Reed. Had I been mistaken about his interest in me as something other than an assistant here on the job?

Maybe not. His expression was softer now. "Sorry, Carrie. I was out of line, but a couple of those surgeries tomorrow are mine and I'm concerned that all the right details be in place before I perform them."

So he considered me a "right detail"? That didn't make me feel much better. "I understand," I said, attempting to make my assertion feel true. "Anyway, like I said, I'll see what I can do. But—"

"But yes, I know, your new venture has priority in your life."

But so do the animals here, I thought.

And, perhaps, Reed . . . ?

A man holding one of the patients walked down the hall, a welcome interruption. I pulled my gaze from Reed's deep brown eyes and said, "I'll talk to you soon." And then Biscuit and I left.

———

Now what could I do?

Well, the first thing was to go back to the shops that had helped to cause this crisis in my vet tech career.

I drove Biscuit and myself there slowly as my mind cranked around possibilities. Maybe it was already time for me to hire another assistant at the shops, but how could I afford it? Go full-time again as a vet tech to pay for extra staff and let my helpers run my new, fun, potentially exciting venture? I didn't think so.

I parked in back and took Biscuit around the side of the building to enter the door into the Barkery. There were no customers, and after hitching Biscuit to her crate I went into Icing. Also empty. But both Judy and Dinah entered from the kitchen.

"Sorry for not coming into the Barkery," Dinah said, "but we knew it was you since we saw you park out back."

I nodded. "No problem. And at the moment it's probably a good thing that it's empty. I have a problem, and I hope you can help me with it."

I got a cup of coffee from our urn at the back of Icing, then explained my dilemma to my assistants, who both regarded me with concerned expressions. "I realize that when you agreed to stagger your weekdays working here you assumed I'd be around most of the time—that I'd keep my hours at the veterinary clinic to a minimum. But they need me tomorrow." I looked at Judy. "Are you okay being in charge of both shops yourself for potentially a couple of stretches of more than an hour or so each?"

"No problem at all," Judy said. "I think we're both getting used to our dual duties here, and keeping an eye on two small shops at a time—well, I'm up for it. How about you, Dinah, if Carrie's schedule at the clinic is heavy like that?"

Dinah was fine with it too. A huge weight lifted from my shoulders. "I can't thank you both enough," I said. "And as time goes on and we're as successful as I'm sure we'll be, I'll give you raises and add some more help." Even though neither one had encouraged my hiring someone additional, I suspected they both would agree if I made that decision.

We engaged in a brief hug fest that lasted only a minute, since we heard the bell on the Barkery's door ring. I headed toward the other shop.

I enjoyed waiting on the customer who'd just come in, another local whose dog I knew from the clinic. I smiled and laughed a lot as I sold her several kinds of treats for her little schnauzer. I felt so darned good. This was all going to work, and work well. I even heard the bell on Icing's door ring while I was busy.

When the customer left, I gave Biscuit a huge hug, then walked back into Icing to thank my wonderful assistants yet again and to say good night, since it was nearly closing time.

They still had a few customers, so for the next ten minutes I stayed busy there, too.

When we again heard the bell go off on the Barkery side, I began wondering if this system would work in the long run—but was grateful when both Dinah and Judy headed for that shop.

My Icing customers finally left, so I was able to close up there, then headed into the Barkery to relieve my assistants and finish that shop's business for the day too.

But as I walked in, I stopped so abruptly I was nearly hit by the closing door.

Dinah was there, behind the display case, helping just one customer.

That customer was Detective Bridget Morana.

I suddenly felt ill. After discussing their varying work schedules with my sweet and accommodating assistants, my mood had morphed into relief. Happiness, even. I'd potentially resolved, for now at least, a major concern in my life. Was that just a fantasy on my part, a bandage over an issue that was comparatively minor while I gushed blood from a much more vital area?

Okay, maybe that was a bit too ugly and graphic a metaphor, but I was worried. Was I about to be hauled off to jail for a murder I hadn't committed? In fact, the only time I could probably be motivated to kill someone was if they majorly threatened my closest family—Neal or Biscuit—and even then I'd only do it if it would save my loved ones from harm.

But, hey, I'd had a relatively painless session with Bridget's partner Wayne that morning. Maybe they were playing tag team, trying to unnerve me by showing up individually and seeing if, in fear, I blurted out the evidence they needed to haul me in. Wayne had even indicated he'd hoped I'd spout out a confession.

Not going to happen.

I forced myself to smile and drew closer to my good buddy Bridget.

"Well hello, Detective," I gushed. "How nice to see you. Do you happen to have a dog as well as your delightful cat?"

"No, I actually just hoped to catch you before you closed and figured I was more likely to see you in your dog bakery than the people side." Her tone and demeanor were friendly, not accusatory, and I didn't trust them, or her, one bit. Today she wore a beige knit shirt over khaki slacks, and, with her light brown hair, she could easily disappear into a crowd and be able to study whatever subject she chose without being noticed. But as I'd seen before, her bushy brows were raised in an ironic arch that dimmed my idea of her easily blending in.

"Guess you were right." I was proud of myself. I still sounded amazingly friendly, though I wanted to yell at her, throw her out, ask what she really wanted…

But I didn't need to ask the latter. She answered it for me. "I'm glad you're still open. I wanted to buy some people-cookies from you. I'm having a few friends over tonight and want to give them a special treat."

Was she trying by flattery to get me to relax? Once again, that wasn't going to happen—though I might allow her to think otherwise. "Well, thanks. I'm flattered that you'd like some of my cookies. Icing on the Cake is actually closed now, but come next door anyway and pick out what you want."

Leaving Biscuit there, I ushered Bridget through the door between the shops. Judy, who'd probably gone into the kitchen before, was now in Icing, rearranging things in our display case for the night.

"What would you like?" I asked after leading the detective to the glassed-in front of our display.

Bridget looked at me for a long moment, and I could just guess what she was thinking: *Oh, how about a murder confession? Or, failing that, a slip of the tongue that'll lead me to the same result?*

Instead, she turned to study our baked goods. "How about a dozen of those great-looking sugar cookies. Better yet, make it half a dozen of them and half a dozen chocolate chip."

"Of course. Judy, could you pack them for us?" I aimed my false, overly happy grin at my assistant. I saw her startled expression, but she turned away quickly and began to do as I asked.

"Anything else I can help you with, Detective?" I asked in a tone as sweet as the cookies I was about to sell her.

"I can't think of anything, can you?" Bridget regarded me intensely, with the penetrating expression I'd seen before, though her tone too was light.

"Nope, but please come back anytime to buy some of our treats." That hurt like a knife stuck into my palm, but I figured it needed to be said to keep her, hopefully, from coming back. Ever.

But her response was, "Of course. In fact, I think I'll be back here a lot, Carrie. Thank you."

With that, she paid the bill in the amount Judy quoted and left.

"Are you okay?" my assistant asked when she was gone. "It's time for us to leave, but if you need some help now or anything, I'll be glad to stay."

"Me too," said Dinah, from the doorway.

I had to take a deep breath to be able to answer. "No, but thank you both. You've done more than enough for me by being so wonderfully flexible about your hours. I'll see you here on Tuesday morning, Dinah."

"You definitely will, Carrie." Dinah went back through the kitchen door.

"Are you sure you're okay?" Judy asked when she was gone.

"Absolutely," I replied as brightly as I could muster.

"Guess I'll go now too."

"Great. See you tomorrow morning. I'll lock up the Barkery, and Biscuit and I also will go home now."

When Judy disappeared through the kitchen door I found myself clutching the end of the display case as if I'd collapse otherwise. Then I stood, straightened my shoulders, and went in to check that Icing's front door was locked. Heading into the Barkery, I locked its door too, and gave Biscuit a huge hug.

TWENTY

"TIME TO GET OUT of here, girl," I finally said when I could breathe and didn't feel like crying. Sure, my eyes had gotten a little damp, but I was determined not to let those cops get to me.

Especially since I figured that was exactly what they'd planned with their much-too-friendly visits.

But as it turned out, we weren't leaving the shops immediately after all. Before I'd untethered Biscuit from her crate, my phone rang. As I drew it out of my pocket my breathing stopped again. Was it one of the detectives with another question? Would they suggest another purchase from one of my stores that would sound delightful but have some underlying meaning I couldn't yet decipher—only worry about?

Drat. I wasn't going to let them get to me that way.

I held onto the end of Biscuit's leash, though, as if it tied me to sanity. In a way it did. My dog was there for me, sitting and watching me with her big brown eyes, wagging her golden tail on the floor.

I couldn't help smiling at her. And when I looked at my phone, relief washed over me. I recognized the number even though I hadn't programmed it in. It was Jack Loroco.

"Hi," I said, immediately wondering about the reason for his call. At the same time, a pleasant feeling washed through me. He wasn't a cop. And even though this was undoubtedly a business call, we'd parted on good terms and had even flirted a bit.

I wouldn't mind a little more of it now, especially considering how my last visit with Reed had gone.

"Hi, Carrie. It's Jack Loroco. I just wanted to let you know I'm heading back up to Knobcone later this week, probably Friday."

Nothing certain, it seemed, but whatever the reason or timing, it might prove pleasant to me. He'd presumably been back at his job. Did he now have the authority to make me an offer to buy my recipes? If so, I wasn't ready for it, but it would still feel good.

I assumed his pending visit was for something like that, though. We hadn't flirted enough for it to make sense for him to come dashing up here again so soon, possibly in the middle of a work week, simply to get together with me.

"Great," I said, then added, "I hope I'll see you then."

"That's why I'm calling. I hope to see you too."

No explanations as to his reason, and we chatted about pleasantries like the weather and Knobcone Heights for another couple of minutes.

And now I had a good reason to look forward to … well, whenever.

———

I wound up having a reason to look forward to that evening, too. I also received a call from Reed, this one as I pulled into my garage.

"Mind if I come over for a little while?" he asked. "I want to apologize for my attitude before."

He did? And how did I feel about that?

Mostly good. "Sure," I said. This would make it two nights in a row that he'd come by my house. I hadn't eaten yet, but I didn't feel like fixing anything. "Have you had dinner yet? I haven't, so I could go get us some fast food if—"

"Don't bother. I'll be there in about half an hour, and I'll bring the food. Is it okay if I bring Hugo?" That was his Belgian Malinois, a smart, friendly dog I'd seen several times before, sometimes at the clinic's doggy daycare.

"Fine."

"Great. See you soon."

———

It turned out to be a pleasant evening.

As always, Hugo and Biscuit, although they weren't best buddies, got along fine after their initial wary sniffs.

Reed, dressed in a snug blue T-shirt over jeans, brought a roast chicken dinner, and, even better, another bottle of wine. He'd obviously thought about the stress he'd put on me earlier about my working hours at the clinic and seemed to regret his attitude. "I'm just glad Arvie made it clear that whatever time you can put in at the clinic will be most welcome."

By then, we were sitting in my kitchen, eating. Neal hadn't called and he wasn't home yet. I didn't know if he was working late or out having fun. For all I knew, he could be out on a date with Gwen.

The dogs sat at our feet. Hugo was tall enough nearly to place his chin on the table but was well trained and well behaved. When Reed told him "down," he lay on the floor, head up and eyes pleading for a treat, but he didn't move.

Biscuit wasn't quite that good, but though she sat beside me and begged, she wasn't too pushy.

"I'm glad too," I responded to Reed. As we continued talking, I wound up crying on his shoulder—figuratively, thank heavens. I didn't even get a bit teary this time. Of course, most of what I talked about involved the logistics of working with my two assistants to make sure I could keep both shops open every day during reasonable hours and still maintain my part-time hours at the clinic. Plus, I admitted I was considering hiring another part-timer soon.

I didn't mention my concern about the visits from the detectives. I didn't want to ruin my mood and possibly his.

"I realized your new businesses were challenging," Reed said, "but not as complicated as that." The expression on his nice-looking face, which at this hour had plenty of after-five-o'clock shadow highlighting it, seemed concerned. "Maybe it would be better if you devoted all your time to your new venture."

"Nope," I said. "I want to do it all."

"And I'm sure you can do anything you want." His deep brown eyes grew warm and I had to look away. I liked this guy. A lot. And since I sometimes had a short temper myself these days, I couldn't hold his stress against him.

"Pretty much." My tone was teasing, but I meant it. That was one reason I'd leaped into my new venture yet hung on to the work I so enjoyed. I never wanted to limit myself when I didn't have to.

I certainly didn't want a stint in jail to do it for me…

"What's wrong, Carrie?" Reed sounded worried.

I must have unwittingly allowed my fears to show on my face.

"Nothing, really." But as lightly as I could, and without going into details about police harassment, I mentioned my concerns about being a murder suspect.

"The police are full of crap." He stood so fast that both dogs did too, looking from Reed to me and back in confusion.

I was also confused—since Reed was suddenly right beside me, pulling me gently to my feet. He took me into his arms and held me tightly against him. My cheek pressed against his hard chest, and I felt a sudden sexual yearning being that close to him.

But was I ready? We'd known each other for a couple of months, but that wasn't very long. And tonight was certainly not the best time to get to know each other *that* way—not after his disturbing attitude this afternoon, never mind that he was here to apologize.

"I'm so sorry about all the bad stuff you're going through, Carrie," Reed whispered into my ear. "And I don't want to add to it by coming on too strong. But one of these days—well, I'd like to get to know you better." He lightened his hold and we kissed—warmly and caringly, but that was all.

Then he released me. "I really appreciate your working things out to come to the clinic tomorrow." I'd already told him that one of my assistants was on board to watch both shops. "It'll be great to see you then too, and get your amazing help."

We soon took Biscuit and Hugo for a brief walk. And then Reed and his dog left.

I couldn't help but wonder what his real motivation had been for coming by that night. He clearly liked me—or at least appreciated my services as a vet tech. I'd started believing he liked me for more than that...and now? Well, he'd said he did, and I hoped it was true. But I was a bit wary and knew I'd remain that way.

And as I watched Reed's car go down the street, I saw my brother's arriving back home.

Where had Neal been? He told me as soon as he came inside, and I shared a smile with him. He'd taken half a dozen tourists from the resort on a boat ride around the lake, complete with water skiing before sunset.

————

To my surprise—and relief—the next day proceeded without a hitch.

Biscuit and I went to the shops even earlier than usual after I fortunately got a good night's sleep. I was pleased when Judy arrived a few minutes before I expected her. As a result, we finished baking both kinds of treats and got them arranged in their respective cases early too.

I called Arvie as soon as the veterinary clinic was set to open and we decided on the hours I would be there—two shifts, one mid-morning and one in the early afternoon.

I was still at the shops for the first customers of the day, staffing the Barkery when they arrived, then heading over to Icing to check on how Judy was doing.

Everything was smooth there as well, and so I left Judy in charge. I took Biscuit with me to the vet clinic, signing her in at her doggy daycare. Then I got to work at my other job.

The first surgery of the day that I assisted with, where Reed was operating, went extremely well. The male pit bull mix had been in a fight some time ago and needed some reconstructive surgery on his ears. He got through it just fine.

And Reed? So did he. Though he was clearly in charge during the surgery, his attitude toward me there was highly professional, and a lot more friendly afterward.

I assisted Arvie with his afternoon surgery—a male cat whose neutering by a different clinic had left some gouges that needed to be fixed, poor guy. But Arvie did a fine job, of course.

Biscuit came back and forth with me both times. On the way to my first shift I'd dropped some leftover treats at Mountaintop Rescue. Billi was there and seemed thrilled. We discussed getting together soon for lunch, or at least coffee. I'd then carried the rest of my leftovers to the clinic.

When I returned to the shops after my second vet tech shift was done, I told Judy she could leave early for the day. She'd done double duty, and I appreciated it. Now it was my turn to take care of both bakeries for the rest of this busy Monday.

Judy didn't object, unsurprisingly. And I made it clear that she'd be paid for the rest of the day.

Biscuit and I were alone after that, except for customers. Delightfully, there were plenty of those too. Fortunately, between Judy and me and during the times we'd both been around, we'd prepared plenty of dog treats and people baked goods, so I wasn't concerned about running short. I even got ideas from some patrons for new things to try. I'd never baked biscotti and apparently neither had Brenda, but some customers who visited Icing, despite expressing love for our cookies and cupcakes and other treats that we had, felt a little disappointed about the lack of biscotti.

I'd have to remedy that, assuming I found a great recipe that I could handle.

Every time a customer came in or the bell rang in the other shop I found myself worrying about who it was till I assured myself it wasn't either one of the two detectives. I didn't see them at all that day and couldn't have been happier.

It quieted down around five o'clock. I didn't need to bake any more that day.

And something that I'd wanted to do, preferably that day, finally became possible now that I could catch my breath.

It was finally time to call Chef Manfred Indor.

———

As it turned out, it was nearly an hour later, just before closing time, that I finally got the opportunity I'd been hoping for. The reason for the delay was a good one, at least: customers. A couple of chatty middle-aged ladies, Sissy and Sheila, came into Icing wanting a half dozen red velvet cupcakes each. They'd been patrons of Brenda's for years, they told me, and always tried to get some of those yummy cupcakes at least once a month. Then, for the rest of the month, they'd exercise to prepare for the next batch they brought home. They'd missed coming while the shop was in transition, and hadn't been able to make the grand reopening, but were thrilled to be here now.

Fortunately, I had enough of the desired cupcakes to sell to them. I even gave them a sugar cookie each as an appetizer.

As they were leaving, I heard the bell at the Barkery's door as well as a couple of woofs from Biscuit. I hurried over to find my thin, friendly neighbor Bob there with his dobie, Dog, who immediately pulled on his leash so he could approach Biscuit. My dog, also leashed, was on her feet greeting her sort-of friend, and the two of them traded sniffs of the nose and behind.

"Hi," Bob said. He craned his long neck so it protruded even more from his gray muscle shirt. "First time here. I had to come in and see what it was like—plus, Dog's birthday is tomorrow so I want to get him some special treats."

"Great." I told him we could bake Dog a special doggy cake or some cupcakes. "Or, if you'd like, we could use some special carob icing and just put his name on a couple of those larger bone-shaped cookies." I pointed toward the cookies in question in the display case.

"Yes!" He did a fist pump with his free hand. "In fact, I've invited some friends over with their dogs to help celebrate. Could you put their names on one of those cookies, too?"

"Of course."

That took about ten minutes, slightly beyond my six o'clock closing time. I already had the icing made but had to be careful about spelling "Thelma" and "Gingerbear" and "Whitney" on the cookies. "Dog," at least, was easy.

"Thanks," Bob said as he paid and yanked gently on Dog's leash to tear him away from where he lay on the floor near Biscuit. Biscuit, too, seemed reluctant to let her friend get away, but it was time. "See you around. And if these are as good as they look—assuming Dog tells me his opinion—I'm sure we'll be back for more."

I thanked him and watched them leave, then made a quick round through Icing and the kitchen, locking doors.

Then, finally, it was time to make the call I'd wanted to all day. I took the number Elise had given me for Chef Manfred and pressed it into my phone.

I'd sat down on the floor beside Biscuit before I did so. That way, she wouldn't feel so lonely after her friend Dog left. And I had her company and support of sorts while I made the call.

"Hello?" The voice was male and gruff and quizzical, with perhaps a hint of a Slavic or German accent. He clearly didn't recognize my number, assuming he'd answered on a phone with caller ID. Of course there was no reason he should know it.

"Hello, Chef Indor. My name is Carrie Kennersly. I think you know my—"

"Brother. Neal. Right?"

"Right," I said, wondering if he always spoke in one-word sentences. "I know you used to work at the resort too. I've heard really good things about your baking skills, and I have a rather odd request. Have you heard of Icing on the Cake?"

"Yes."

"Did you know that its former owner, Brenda, sold it to me, and that I've changed it so that half's still Icing and the other half is a dog bakery?"

"No."

So what do you think of that? I wanted to demand. But that would require more than a one-word answer.

"Well, that's where I am," I said instead. "And although I've got some good recipes, I'm interested in more, for both shops. I can't hire anyone full-time now, but I'd love for you to come in and advise me and maybe even sell me some additional recipes. Are you interested?"

"Yes, but I have a new job now."

Hey. A whole sentence.

"That's even better, since I can't take you on as an employee. Are you willing to advise me?"

"Yes."

We were back to that. Or maybe we'd never left his tendency to be brief.

"So when can you come and talk to me about it?"

"Tomorrow morning. Eleven o'clock. Okay?"

My turn to be brief. "Great!"

TWENTY-ONE

DINAH WAS THERE WITH me at the shops the next morning, and since I didn't want her participating in my conversation with the chef, I sent her on a mission to take yesterday's leftover dog treats to the veterinary clinic. I'd bring some for Mountaintop Rescue later, since Billi and I had arranged to meet for a short stint at Cuppa-Joe's.

In fact, both Dinah and Judy seemed to enjoy taking our extra doggy baked goods places where they could be used to full advantage. They'd previously told me they'd be doing that as much as possible, now that they worked for the Barkery as well as Icing.

I'd smiled at that, although in the interest of the Barkery turning a profit I'd cautioned them to only take treats that I'd packed up and authorized. That way, I could make sure that what they were taking was close to—but not quite—going stale, and the Barkery's reputation would be enhanced, not spoiled. Since my assistants had begun staggering their schedules, those ventures would worked out well as part of their breaks.

So far, I'd had no trouble running both shops alone. Of my assistants, only Judy so far had done so, yesterday. Dinah was going to get her first crack at it this afternoon when I headed to the vet clinic for my shift—only one shift scheduled today, for an hour. No surgeries, fortunately, so I'd be back to doing the normal stuff like shots and flea treatments or whatever.

It was now nearly eleven a.m. The morning's baking had been completed hours ago for both shops, unless we got low on something or needed to work on a special order. I hung out in the Barkery to be close to Biscuit. Besides, that was where I'd told Chef Manfred Indor I'd meet him.

I chatted with Biscuit while reorganizing the cookies and biscuits in the display case. We'd had a couple hordes of visitors earlier and had sold a lot, especially one of our favorite kinds of dog cookies, the small round ones with a slight carob flavoring. Since it resembled chocolate but was safe for dogs, I certainly could understand its popularity.

"I know you like these too, girl." My little golden furry friend was sitting up watching me, her head cocked. If she hadn't been restrained with the leash I figured she'd be right beside me trying to rearrange the items in the case. Better yet—in her estimation, at least—she'd be sampling, or guzzling, them all. "But moderation is much healthier than giving in to our impulses."

It was fine for me to spout such platitudes, but I didn't always follow them myself—another good reason for me to spend more time in the Barkery than in Icing. Although I did sample the healthy dog treats, I didn't overdo it here as much as I might on the other side of the door.

Biscuit continued to wag her tail in a cheerful but pleading way. I couldn't resist. I took a cookie and broke it in half, putting one part on the counter near the display case for the future and handing the other to my clearly delighted dog.

That was when the bell over the door rang. When I looked up, a large man stood there. By large, I mean not only tall but rotund; his belt outlined a protruding gut covered by a white knit shirt tucked into beige jeans.

"Carrie?"

Since he asked with one accented word, he confirmed my initial assumption. This was Chef Manfred Indor.

"Yes. You're Manfred, right?" I didn't need to confine my own speech.

"Right." He moved farther into the store, not looking at me but everywhere else. As he got close to Biscuit, he bent and patted her head. Only then did he deign to stand straight and regard me with cool, dark eyes. "Nice store. I like dogs."

Ah, good. We might actually have a conversation, especially since he'd again graduated to multiple words.

"Great," I said. "I do want to talk mostly about this part—the Barkery—since the former owner of Icing on the Cake left me a lot of great recipes for people baked goods. I take it that you'd be okay coming up with ideas for more dog treats."

"Yes."

"Do you mind going outside to talk?" A few tables and chairs were already set up on the patio there, as they'd been on the night of the grand opening.

"Fine."

I made myself forbear from groaning. After all, even when he used single syllables he was being responsive to what I asked.

I unhooked the end of Biscuit's leash from her crate. She might as well enjoy being outside with us.

When we were on the patio, I motioned for Manfred to take a seat on a chair at one of the round wrought-iron tables. I hoped the frilly, decorative chairs were strong enough to hold him. They should be, since they too were iron. When Manfred lowered himself onto one, he seemed to hold his breath as if he also had some concerns about the chair's endurance, but in a minute he was planted there, nodding a little.

The temperature was warm. It was late spring here in the San Bernardino Mountains, which meant that the weather could be anything from winter-icy to summer-hot. Today was a fair compromise in between. At least I felt good in my green Barkery and Biscuits T-shirt and slim jeans. I wondered, though, whether my large companion would be comfortable here. He wasn't complaining, and until he did, in a single word or more, I wouldn't suggest that we move.

"So," I said, "I'd really love to enlist your help with new and exciting recipes, more on an occasional basis—for a negotiated pay rate per creation—rather than anything regular right now. As I mentioned, I'm just starting out and don't have funds available to hire anyone besides my two current assistants."

I watched his dark, bushy brows lower into a straight line over those watchful eyes. His hair was of the same blackness, short but kinked into waves.

"Okay. I am working now. But I always like to create new foods."

"I was glad to hear that you already have a new job." And now I had to be careful with what I said. I truly was looking for new and exciting treats to serve here. But of course my main reason for talking to Manfred was to learn if he'd been angry enough about Myra's firing him to do anything about it.

Like kill her.

"Yes. Two jobs."

"Really?"

"Yes. Two restaurants at Lake Arrowhead."

That was a San Bernardino Mountains town not far from here, with a lake, of course, and some nice residential areas. A fun town to visit.

"Congratulations," I said. "But I'll bet you have to do some juggling to prepare food for two different places." I tried to sound a little dejected, which I was. Would he have time to do anything for the Barkery? Even though that wasn't the primary reason I'd asked him here, my interest in it was genuine.

"Yes. But I am good at planning my time. I can help you too. And my partner also cooks, so he will assist me."

"That's great!" I smiled at him. Now it was time for what I really wanted to talk about. "I know you used to work at the Knobcone Heights Resort, in the restaurant there. My brother Neal told me, though, that—"

"Yes, the bitch fired me." Those dark eyes turned stormy, and his thick hands clenched into fists on the table. "For no reason except that I didn't follow her stupid, uncreative instructions." But then he stared straight at me and grinned, revealing perfect teeth whose whiteness seemed emphasized by the swarthiness of his skin. "I hated her. Yes. Did I kill her? No." He leaned toward me over the round glass surface of the small table. "Did you?"

His outright brazenness startled me. But then I laughed. "No." My turn to use a single word.

"That's why I'm here, right? So you can figure it out? I know the cops are after you. They're after me too, but I think I got them to see the truth. Not me."

"Not me either. Now that we've gotten that out of the way, let's talk a bit about the time you might have to develop new recipes for me."

Because the other part of the conversation was over. Could Manfred be lying? Yes. On the other hand, he seemed intuitive and intelligent as well as somewhat bearlike. I'd keep him in mind as a possible suspect in case I needed to point to others.

But did I think he was guilty?

No.

———

Several hours later I was sitting across from someone else, at a very different table, with Biscuit again at my feet.

Billi had called to confirm our short get-together soon after I'd returned from my shift at the clinic. Dinah was enjoying some additional baking this afternoon; she'd been fine holding down the fort at both shops during my shift. I was happy to be at Cuppa-Joe's now, sitting on my favorite patio with Biscuit at my feet.

Billi was dressed casually in a silvery workout top and pants—not surprisingly, since she'd come from the Robust Retreat not Mountaintop Rescue. Her fitness club and spa were not far from Cuppa-Joe's or my shops, just down California Street on one edge of the town square and onto Peak Road. Although she said she always brought her dogs Fanny and Flip to the shelter with her, she'd left them at her spa today.

We both nursed our caffeine-laced drinks and smiled at each other. "So your shops are doing okay?" she asked. Her dark hair with its golden highlights was pulled tightly into a ponytail at the back of her head, accentuating the perfect oval shape of her lovely face. If looks were the main criterion, Billi definitely deserved to be a member of one of the town's most elite families.

"They're doing great," I said. "And before you ask, yes, I've brought along some treats for you to take to your shelter."

Kit had waited on us a few minutes ago, but now my dear friend Irma came over to say hi. "Everything okay here?" she asked.

"Everything's fine," Billi assured her, and I nodded in agreement.

Irma smiled and told us to let someone know if we needed anything else, then walked off.

Then Billi turned back to me. "And on the other front—I mean, about Myra. City Council hasn't met since her death, but we do stay in touch. I keep hearing rumbles from my fellow members about irritation that the cops haven't yet solved the murder. Some of it, I think, is to appease Les Ethman since he's one of us, but he seems cool about it—cooler than some of the others, at least. Are you still...?" Her voice trailed off.

"Am I still the number one suspect?" I sighed and took a sip of my latte. "I'm not aware of anyone that the cops are looking at more strongly. I don't even know much about evidence, what they've got or what they're looking for, except for a suspicious dog leash and, apparently, a dog biscuit from my Barkery. Wish I did know more—including that they were zeroing in on someone else."

"Me too." Billi's turn to take a sip. "Having a position of some authority in this town should come with a magic wand that we can wave and have everything that needs to be resolved get that way fast. And without hurting people who don't deserve it."

I smiled at her. "It means a lot that you believe in me, Billi."

"It means a lot that you're such a great animal person, Carrie. Such a great person in general. I'm sorry you're going through this, and if I see any way to help, believe me, I'll do so."

"Finding the actual killer would help a lot." I kept irony in my tone. I knew Billi couldn't do it any more than I could, even with her seat on City Council.

"Yeah," she said, "it would." She paused. "We don't know each other extremely well, but—well, I get the impression, especially from your efficiency in running both new businesses while having a job, that you get things done when you need to. So...who do you think killed Myra? I assume you've been thinking about it, maybe looking into it."

"Yes, I have," I told her. "But so far, I've got suspicions but nothing to prove who it was."

"I have a feeling," she said, looking straight at me with her gorgeous brown eyes and even lovelier smile, "that you will."

I could only hope she was right.

TWENTY-TWO

BUT OVER THE COURSE of the next week, although I thought a lot about finding Myra's killer, I didn't do it, or even try. I didn't accuse anyone of murder, or talk to people—much—about what had happened, or even consider where else to look for evidence.

That was partly because the cops left me alone. Not even any visits to the Barkery by either of my dear detective buddies. And as long as I wasn't being harassed into a state of fear and anxiety, I allowed myself to ignore the situation. Almost.

I couldn't keep my thoughts completely away from it. I was waiting for the next proverbial shoe to drop. If someone else had been arrested the news around here would be full of it. Knobcone Heights had its own small newspaper and radio and TV stations, and none of them said anything new about the murder during that week.

In the meantime, my life got into a routine.

Very early each morning, I'd rise and put Biscuit briefly into the yard or take her for a short walk. Then we'd go to the shops. There, I'd start baking, usually for Icing first and then the Barkery.

Once things were in the oven, I'd gather dog treats that were threatening to go stale and put them in two boxes. The smaller one was for the vet clinic, and the larger for Mountaintop Rescue.

Of course, I made sure we'd prepared extra treats so we always had some to give away.

While I was doing this, my scheduled helper for the day would arrive—or the one primed to be earliest on days they both came. She'd help me finish the baking, and as she finished I'd complete packing up treats from the prior day that could be given away, both from the Barkery and also from Icing, since the people from the homeless shelter down the mountains sent couriers every few days.

And then we were ready for customers to start arriving. Some days a lot came early. Some days only a few showed up. I didn't yet know what made the difference but was aware that my promotion needed to be increased. I pondered that along with ... well, whether I'd remain out of jail long enough to put any ideas into effect.

Because my time at the clinic was nearly always in the afternoon, I'd sometimes send Dinah or Judy there with the appropriate treats during their mid-morning breaks. Sometimes I'd bring treats in the afternoons. And on my way to the clinic those days, I'd time it whenever possible so I could pop over to Mountaintop Rescue, to fit with Billi's schedule. She was usually there around one p.m., on her own break from her spa, and it was always fun to see her and to get her insight on her day—and mine.

And to see the animals her shelter had rescued.

Mountaintop Rescue wasn't a large facility, but it was well designed and well maintained. The dog kennels were separated by metal fencing that was actually attractive, with rows of decorative circles adorning the top. The surfaces were all a smooth cement that could

219

be cleaned easily, with slightly raised platforms at the rear where soft bedding and toys were placed. The kennels were cleaned often.

Inside the kennels were a lot of really wonderful-looking dogs of all sizes and breed backgrounds. Cats, too, kept in a different area. Their histories, to the extent known, as well as their health records since arriving at the shelter were recorded on cards that visitors could read at the front of their enclosures.

I'd dropped in before, of course. None of the dogs there now looked familiar from my earlier visits, which was a good thing. That meant the ones who'd been there before had been adopted.

When she could, Billi accompanied me on my walk through the facility. The lovely, trim spa owner was always dressed for her other profession, and she inevitably had a smile on her face. And she always asked me, "See anyone you'd like to adopt to be Biscuit's best friend?"

Since I always brought Biscuit to daycare while I worked at the clinic I inevitably had her with me, but she waited for me in the shelter's office. And as much as I loved dogs and hated to see these guys staring hopefully at me, with my new routine I had to say no. At least for the foreseeable future.

But I didn't mind Billi's asking. I was here as much to enjoy her company as I was to see the animals—and yes, I visited the equally posh cat house too, each time.

I'd realized that Brenda's leaving town, despite its wonderful effect of making me the owner of the two bakeries, had left a gap in my life since we'd been such close friends. Now it appeared that, thanks to my shops and even the adversity of being considered a suspect in Myra's murder, I was developing a new friendship that I was finding highly enjoyable. I'd nurture it by getting together with Billi as often as possible, even for short amounts of time.

When I finished my visit at the shelter, I'd go on to my shift at the vet clinic on the appropriate days.

Even after his vague comment about returning to Knobcone Heights that week, Jack Loroco had called to postponed his visit further, so I figured that he and his company had no interest in my recipes after all. That was a good thing, at least for now. I still wanted to perfect them. And I might decide to keep them all my own, despite giving up the possibility of profit earned by selling them.

And as far as seeing Jack again?

Well, one of the good things going on now was that Reed and I were getting along just fine whenever I saw him at the veterinary hospital. Sometimes I helped him out with a patient or two and sometimes I worked only with Arvie or another of the vets, but I'd always get to see Reed long enough to say hi. Usually a very warm hi.

And he asked me out for dinner again next weekend.

Then there was Neal. He'd been pleased with his brief, almost spontaneous outing the other night, but additional scheduled boating or hiking expeditions were sparse. When I asked him about it, he expressed both frustration and hope. But at least I got to see my brother most evenings when he got off work, and he filled me in on how things had gone that day—and what he'd overheard about the investigation into Myra's death, since her relatives weren't shy about discussing the enigma.

He knew that my suspicions mostly rested on Harris or Elise. He didn't disagree—but neither did he come home with any clue or conversation that I could take to the detectives to get them on the right track, and away from me.

At least for now, they weren't hounding me.

But I wasn't surprised when that changed.

———

It started with a report on the local evening news.

Maybe it was because the media themselves were pressing for answers. Maybe the Ethmans were pushing for an arrest—possibly because it looked good to be a squeaky wheel, even if one of them was the guilty party. Or more than one of them.

Whatever it was, I sat up straight on my living room couch when I saw Myra's picture pop up at the top of the eleven o'clock news that Monday night.

Had they solved her murder? Arrested a suspect?

Was it all over, at least from my perspective?

Unfortunately, no.

And whoever had instigated it, the message was clear.

The anchor for the late-night news stared solemnly into the camera and intoned, "More than two weeks have passed since the murder of Knobcone Heights resident Myra Ethman, and the authorities have not yet come forth with an arrest in the case."

This obvious statement was followed by an interview with the town's police chief, Loretta Jonas—whom I hadn't yet met. I suspected that was a good thing, although perhaps she was more reasonable than the detectives reporting to her.

It must have been a slow news night for the station to focus on a case that was growing cold—or maybe, as I'd been suspecting, an Ethman had pushed for more answers. The Knobcone Heights Resort was advertised often on the station, so maybe the powers-that-be there felt they owed it to whoever held those purse strings to keep the story in front of the public until it was resolved.

But I was just guessing—as much as I was guessing about who was guilty.

And was this going to be enough of a thorn in the police chief's side that she'd push her detectives to start getting even more in-your-face with their suspects again? Or maybe just their top suspects—and as far as I knew, I was still among them.

Maybe the topmost one.

———

I was, unfortunately, right about that.

The next day, Tuesday, started off like all the others: an early morning Biscuit walk, then baking for both shops, an assistant's arrival—Dinah today—followed by her break late morning and waiting on customers who seemed to arrive in both shops at the same time. My own "break" that afternoon consisted of a shift at the vet clinic. All the same as ever. All just fine. Although I kept watch for a detective to pop in at the shops, neither of them did.

Until they both did, after Dinah had gone home for the day.

I was just about to close up. I'd finished waiting on my last customers in Icing, so I started there. But I moved too slowly. Just as I started toward the door, key in hand to lock it, it opened.

Detective Bridget Morana strode in, followed by Detective Wayne Crunoll.

Both wore dark suits with white shirts. Both had serious expressions on their faces—there was no indication that they'd come here to buy treats for Wayne's dogs, or anything else that would give me reason for hope this was just another simple harassment call.

"Hello, Ms. Kennersly." Bridget … er, Detective Morana, clearly did not intend for us to be on a first-name basis that day. That also boded badly for what was to come.

"Hello, Detectives." I tried to keep my tone light. "I'm just closing up for the day. But I do have some leftovers here in Icing. Would either of you like a sugar cookie?"

"No, thank you," said the lady detective in charge. I glanced toward her male counterpart and he just watched me, not even deigning to respond.

"I assume you'd like to talk," I said. "Is it okay if we go next door so I can be with Biscuit?"

"Fine," Detective Morana said, and as if he had been given a direct order, Detective Crunoll joined me as I locked Icing's front door, then proceeded into the Barkery. Although Biscuit stood up in her crate, I just smiled at her—somewhat grimly, I knew—and went to lock that shop's door too.

While I did that, Detective Crunoll, who was trying to remain near me, gathered three chairs.

They waited for me to let Biscuit loose so she could stay close to me. I sat down as they joined me. My knees were suddenly so weak that I might as well have melted into my seat. Instead, I let myself bend over just far enough to give Biscuit's furry head a gentle rub, wishing I could throw myself onto the floor and hug her. Instead, I just straightened up.

I considered asking breezily what had brought them here—the TV news or something more significant—but decided to let them start the conversation however they chose to.

I didn't have long to wait.

"We have some additional questions for you, Ms. Kennersly." Bridget Morana had an expression on her face that, like others I'd seen on her, I couldn't read. If I'd hazarded a guess, I would have said it looked smug. Why? Did she think she had some evidence that would allow her to arrest and possibly convict me? Her bushy eyebrows were raised a little. Her mouth curved up just a bit in a not-quite smile.

I wondered if it was now time to find myself a lawyer.

"All right," I said slowly, not really meaning that it was at all okay with me.

"How often have you shopped at the Knob Hill Pet Emporium?"

That seemed an innocuous enough question. I hoped. "I used to go there every couple of weeks, but once I purchased Icing on the Cake and started turning half of the building into my Barkery, I stopped going there. The Ethmans weren't especially welcoming to me once they believed they would have competition—even though I explained to them that what I was doing wouldn't really compete with them."

"Right. Well, what kinds of things did you buy there?" That was still the lady detective. Her expression hadn't changed, so I assumed I hadn't said anything she hadn't expected.

Detective Crunoll appeared to be paying less attention. His gaze wandered around the shop.

What was he looking for?

"Sometimes food for Biscuit," I said, responding to the pending question. At her name, my little golden dog looked up from where she lay by my feet and started wagging her tail. "Occasionally a toy for her. That kind of thing."

"And how long ago did you last buy a leash there?" Bridget's expression had finally changed. It now appeared like a *gotcha* look. And now I understood where she was going with this.

She wanted me to admit that I'd bought the kind of leash—the very leash—that had been used to strangle Myra as she was being killed.

Which I hadn't, of course. But if I denied buying even a similar one, I felt sure she would believe that was a lie. Maybe she even thought she'd be able to prove it—which she couldn't. Not actually.

I decided to try to respond, but again wondered if it was lawyer time. I'd be careful. I figured these two must be recording this conversation. If so, were they supposed to warn me? It didn't really matter since I'd assume it anyway.

"I'm not sure whether I ever bought a leash there," I began. "If so, I don't recall it. And if what you're asking is if I bought the one used to choke Myra Ethman, the answer to that is a definite no. I use this kind." I pointed to the black one I used to anchor Biscuit to the wall in the Barkery. "I also have a shorter one at home that I sometimes use to take her on walks, a flat, woven nylon thing. A blue one. From what you showed me, it was a beige, ropelike mesh leash that was used on Myra. I don't have one of those. And this one and the one at home I bought from a major retail chain some time ago, the store on the road to Lake Arrowhead."

"Do you have the receipts?"

I shook my head. "I doubt it. As I said, it was quite a while ago."

"Then what would you say if I told you that Harris Ethman has a duplicate receipt from when you bought the identical kind and color of leash that was used for ligature strangulation of his wife, rendering her unconscious?"

TWENTY-THREE

I SWALLOWED. HARD. LAWYER time had finally arrived. Probably. But first I looked into Wayne's eyes, which had turned hard and accusatory. Then I returned my gaze to Bridget. Her expression hadn't changed, except perhaps to grow even more smug.

Why? Had Harris manufactured some kind of old receipt? If he had anything, it wasn't real.

But maybe these detectives didn't care about the truth, as long as they had a potential suspect in their sights.

"What I would say is that he's lying," I told them as coolly as I could muster. "And that his accusation should make you want to arrest him, since he's trying hard to point fingers at someone else. He clearly had access to that kind of leash if it's sold at his store. He had more motive and opportunity to kill his wife than I did, and since she was hit on the head while unconscious—right?—it had to be someone strong as well as angry. And of course he'd want to turn your attention elsewhere—like to me."

"We considered all of that, Ms. Kennersly. It's why we're not placing you under arrest just yet. There are a few other things we're looking into first. But we wanted your answer, and your reaction. Now we have both." She rose, and so did Wayne, at the same time, as if her words had been his cue. "We'll see you again soon." Within seconds, they were waiting at the door for me to let them out.

I did so gladly. As I shut it behind them, I rested my forehead against it while slowing my breathing to something resembling normalcy.

What was I going to do now?

The first item on my agenda now was clear—but how would I find a lawyer? Neal knew of some, but would any be the right one? My mind searched frantically for any attorneys who'd brought their pets to the clinic. I knew of a couple, but one was a big shot with his own firm who I believed worked for the Ethmans. Definitely not him. And the other worked for the area's largest real estate company, if I recalled correctly.

I needed someone who dealt with criminal stuff, even though I wasn't a criminal. At least not yet.

I could do a search online, but I didn't want to pick out just anyone.

Then it dawned on me. Billi Matlock might be able to help. Not that she'd ever needed a criminal lawyer. Or at least I didn't think so. But since she was on City Council, and because she was a Matlock, she probably had some contacts she trusted who might be able to make a good suggestion or two.

I went through the kitchen and into the office, where I kept my purse. I pulled out my phone and called Billi.

Maybe Cuppa-Joe's hadn't been the wisest choice for where to meet this time, since I didn't want anyone eavesdropping or knowing what I was asking. But it was convenient, I was able to bring Biscuit, and I felt comfortable there.

I had already told Billi a bit of what I needed to pick her brain about. I'd also requested that she be discreet, both now and later.

We sat on the central patio again today, a table away from where we'd been a week ago when we'd also briefly discussed my being a murder suspect and how I was bound to turn that around soon.

Now, I absolutely had to.

We'd already ordered our drinks—same as last time, both filled with caffeine. And now we waited.

I leaned over the table toward Billi. Since her work day was over, instead of workout clothes she wore a lovely knit shirt in a floral print over deep green slacks. She had again left her dogs at her spa.

"I had some visitors a little while ago," I said to her.

"I figured that from what you said. Those detectives again?"

I nodded and briefly told her their claims about the leash. "I buy things for Biscuit a lot, and from different places, but I really don't believe I bought a leash for her from the Ethmans' shop. And even if I had bought one of the exact same type a few weeks ago—which I didn't, particularly since I knew I was persona non grata there—I absolutely didn't use it to strangle Myra. Shouldn't they be looking for a man, anyway? I'm reasonably strong, but I don't think I could strangle someone to unconsciousness with a leash. And killing them by striking them with a rock? Ugh."

"If you took the person by surprise you probably could knock them out, and anger, or determination, can give people a lot of extra strength." Billi regarded me assessingly. "But I believe you, Carrie. And I figured from what you said when you called—"

Kit arrived then with our drinks. It was a welcome break from our intense conversation, yet I needed to continue talking to Billi, so I thanked our server and smiled—waiting for her to leave. I think she sensed it, since she gave me a slightly hurt look instead of her usual toothy smile and moved away quickly.

I'd have to be particularly generous with my tip when we got ready to go. But that wouldn't be for a while.

"Anyway," Billi said, leaning over the table toward me, "I gather you're looking for a lawyer."

I nodded, then glanced around to see if anyone appeared to be eavesdropping. Fortunately not.

"I have contact info for a guy some members of my family have used. He does all kinds of courtroom work, including criminal." She pulled a business card out of her large brown leather purse and handed it to me.

I looked at it. His name was Ted Culbert, and the firm name contained his name and several others.

I'd call him tomorrow.

Right now, I would enjoy the company of my friend Billi.

And hope I'd be able to do so again.

———

I wish I could say that the next couple of days faded into the same routine as the past week.

They didn't.

Oh, sure, they still contained most of the same activities, from walking Biscuit to baking to running the shops—and even a shift at the veterinary clinic.

But I also worked in first a phone call, and then a visit, to that attorney. I didn't tell Judy where I was going, only that I had an important meeting to attend. Was it wise to be secretive with my staff? I wasn't sure. But I also didn't want to broadcast what was going on—and how concerned I was about it.

Ted Culbert's office was in a part of town near the elite area—on one of the curving downtown streets off Summit Avenue toward the lake. Driving, to save time, I dropped Biscuit off at daycare. I'd do my shift at the clinic after my meeting and pick her up then.

The law office was on the third floor of a four-story building. I reached it by elevator, and when I went inside the waiting room I found it was as posh as I'd figured it would be.

This wasn't going to be cheap. I'd already asked about Mr. Culbert's hourly rate and it made me gasp.

But hopefully expense would buy me excellence. And I only required half an hour at the moment, to get him on a retainer. Then I'd have to see how much I'd really need him.

I prayed this would be our only meeting.

It went as quickly as I'd hoped. The nice-looking man in a suit behind his regal-looking wooden desk asked me to call him Ted. I told him why I was there—and of course he'd heard of Myra Ethman's murder and the fact that someone who'd argued with her the evening before was one of the suspects.

I liked his attitude, and his confidence that he could help fix things for me if and when I needed him. His smile was a killer one—which gave me hope that he'd do all he promised and keep me from being arrested as a killer.

Then I left.

———

Maybe it wasn't the smartest thing for me to do, but before heading back to the shops after my shift at the vet clinic, I stopped at the Knob Hill Pet Emporium.

Harris was there. He was waiting on some customers as I entered with Biscuit. Purposefully, I headed with her toward the area where collars and leashes were displayed. The detectives had shown me that picture of the ropelike, beige leash used to strangle Myra, which supposedly rendered her unconscious before a rock was smashed into her head.

The Emporium carried a number of different leashes, and when Harris finished with his customers he approached me and said, "You looking to buy another one so you can use it on me?"

I glared at him. "Why would you tell the police that I bought the kind used to hurt Myra here? I didn't."

"Then where did you buy it?" His grin looked so smug I wanted to slap it off his narrow face. The way his eyes turned down at the edges didn't look sad to me now. It looked evil.

I didn't respond directly to his absurd question but smiled slightly and said, "Just so you know, when they came to visit me I felt fairly confident that they believed me about the leash. Which then sets them onto you, since you clearly have access to what's in your shop."

His smile disappeared. "Don't you accuse me, bitch."

"Why not? You've clearly accused me. And you had a lot more motive than I did. Were you angry about Myra's affair with Walt Hainner, or did you just want to make sure she didn't divorce you and take away all her nice backing for this store—and your life?"

"You—" His tone and demeanor were furious, but fortunately I didn't have to defend myself since some customers walked in and Harris was suddenly all nice-guy again.

"Time for me to leave," I said pleasantly, and did.

———

"What's going on, Carrie?" Judy asked when I returned to the shops, entering the Barkery because I had Biscuit with me. "You just got a call from Harris Ethman. He said you'd better call him back when you got here. He sounded so mad … and when I tried to get him to say what he wanted, he said that you'd better not try to pin his wife's murder on him when you're the one who did it." She looked extremely troubled as she stared at me and asked in a hoarse whisper, "Did you?"

"Of course not," I asserted. Then my shoulders fell. "I didn't do it, but the cops appear to think I did—and they're getting nastier now, maybe because the local news is pushing them to solve the case. I don't know what I'm doing, but I'm going to try hard to figure out who did kill her so I can get the authorities heading in the right direction. And that means far away from me."

"How awful." That was Dinah, who'd come in for a few hours that day. She must have heard us talking, and she entered the Barkery from the Icing door. "I'm so sorry, Carrie." She approached me and gave me a hug. "We believe in you. You couldn't have killed her."

"That's right," Judy said, hugging me, too. "Let's just hope they get their suspicions pointed in a different direction soon."

I was never more grateful for having inherited these hardworking, sweet assistants, and I hugged them both back.

———

I decided not to return Harris's call. I couldn't imagine anything he'd have to say to me right now that I'd want to hear. Instead, I told my assistants that if he called me again, they should be polite and say they'd give me the message, but nothing more.

But that unanswered call gave me even more impetus to do something as fast as possible.

I'd called Neal earlier and cleared it with him to go to the resort just before his shift ended for the day. I'd told him why, but promised that instead of my going there to accuse Elise or anyone else in the extended Ethman family directly, I would be more discreet. Sort of.

But I didn't want to do it at my brother's expense. He needed to be onboard with what I intended to do.

Of course, he could ignore his rash sister.

Since we weren't busy, I even closed the shops a little early. To reassure my assistants that I wasn't just going home to cry, I even told them what I was going to do.

One way or another, I was going to find out who really killed Myra. I had to, if I hoped to get on with my life.

I wasn't sure whether the authorities just didn't want to dig too deeply into where the members of the town's leading families were the night Myra died, or if they had other suspects they were giving as hard a time as me, or whether they were simply focusing in on me because I was convenient after my argument with Myra, or if they thought the biscuit from the Barkery was a key piece of evidence. It didn't matter why.

What mattered was finding the truth so they would leave me alone.

Since it was late enough, I took Biscuit home, fed her dinner, and walked her, then left her there. I drove to the resort and parked in its lot, then walked inside the main lobby.

As I'd anticipated, Neal was at his usual location behind the desk. The place wasn't very crowded that night, and I wondered whether that was because the resort wasn't filled, or because people were dining here and elsewhere or otherwise enjoying their evening at Knobcone Heights.

It didn't matter, at least not to me. In fact, it was probably better this way, since tourists wouldn't have the answers I needed.

Too bad I hadn't invited Reed to join me here for dinner again. But that wasn't necessarily the best way to ferret out the information I hoped for.

Instead of heading for the dining room, I walked the perimeter of the lobby, checking out the areas where the Ethmans' offices were.

The office doors were closed, and I couldn't tell if the rooms were occupied. Neal would know, but he was talking to a few visitors so I couldn't just go ask him. Instead, I headed toward the rear of the lobby, to the door to the spa that overlooked the hill down to the beach. It wasn't locked, but neither was anyone in there. It wasn't somewhere I'd be able to ask questions. At this hour, I'd also not be able to quiz lifeguards at the beach or employees who helped rent boats out to visitors.

Maybe I needed to grab a bite to eat after all.

First, I'd scan the crowd at the restaurant to see if I could get a table ... and also to see if anyone useful was there.

There was! To my surprise, not only was City Council member Les Ethman there, but he was eating by himself in the crowded dining room; I didn't see any vacant table, not even along the inside walls where there was no view of the lake. Les definitely looked lonesome. Or so I told him as I joined him.

"I'm fine, but of course you can sit here, Carrie." Les rose and pulled out the chair at his right side. His smile was wide, its edges pointing cheerily at the sides of his down-turned eyes. I was used to seeing Les dressed up, but tonight he wore a casual, brown knit shirt with a collar.

"What are you eating?" I asked. Only a salad was in front of him.

"I've got a burger on the way. What would you like?"

"Probably the same." I'd already looked around and still didn't see any of his relations, either by blood or marriage. My goal tonight had been to latch onto one or more Ethman besides Elise or Harris, whom I'd already quizzed in my way, finding a way to chat with them without, hopefully, creating any more animosity—even as I charmed them into giving me their opinion on who killed Myra. And as I spoke with them, I'd see whether I got any vibes of guilt.

I'd never imagined that the Ethman I'd be dining with would be Les, the nicest member of the family.

That didn't mean he wasn't Myra's killer, but he was the one I considered least likely. And he and I already had a friendly relationship, partly thanks to his dog Sam.

A male server came over and brought us water. I didn't see Gwen and wondered if she was there that night. I'd keep an eye out for her. It would be good to see another friendly face in here. But the one across from me was friendly enough.

"Just so you know," Les said, "I didn't start out eating alone. Elise was with me. But you know she's running the resort now?" I nodded. "Well, she got a call and had to take it in her office. So here I am on my own. I'm delighted that you joined me, though."

"I'm delighted too," I said as my mind raced through scenarios to quiz him about.

The male server returned and I ordered. When he'd left, I opened my mouth to ask an innocuous question that I thought I'd be able to use to segue into a discussion about Myra's murder and who might have done it. Les himself? I hoped not, but couldn't cross him off the list yet.

"So," I began.

At the same time, Les asked, his voice low as he leaned sideways toward me, "Tell me, Carrie. Is it true that you killed my niece-in-law Myra?"

I'd been reaching for my water glass and stopped, staring at him. "I was going to ask you the same thing—only a lot more subtly."

He smiled, though it wasn't the warmest smile I'd ever seen on his gracefully aging face. "Touché." His expression grew darker than I'd ever seen before. "The thing is, Carrie, the City Council's members have been talking behind the scenes, worried about what having an unsolved murder is going to do to Knobcone Heights's reputation. I know it's our police department that is supposed to solve the case, but right now the entire town looks bad, a small municipality where evil things happen and don't get resolved right away. We're therefore putting pressure on law enforcement to solve this, and fast."

Billi Matlock had said something similar, although she'd implied that one reason the Council was majorly concerned was for Les's sake.

He stopped talking as the server brought his burger and mine, too, along with my salad, the kind Les had been eating on my arrival.

I no longer had an appetite, not that it had been especially intense before.

"Thanks," I said brightly as Les also said thanks quickly, as if he too wanted the server to leave fast so we could continue this conversation.

But did I want to continue it? The one Ethman I'd really liked and pretty much trusted, whom I wanted to trust me … didn't.

Yet did I really have any choice? And maybe, if my initial instincts were right about Les and he decided that I was telling the truth, that I was innocent, he would actually help me to clear myself—even if it was at the expense of one of his relatives who did happen to be guilty.

"Okay, Les. I'd like to be honest with you, and to trust you. Now I'm not sure I should, any more than you think you can trust me. But here's what's going on."

The first thing I told him was that, despite our minor argument the evening before Myra was murdered, I hadn't hated her. I hadn't liked her either, but my feelings wouldn't have led to my killing her, and I hadn't.

I then told him about my unwelcome visits from those detectives, including the most recent one.

"I came here tonight hoping to figure out how to question some of Myra's relatives, since they knew her a lot better than I did and maybe had more of a motive to kill her." I looked at him. "I don't think you did it, but tell me if I'm wrong—and if you had a reason to do away with your niece-in-law."

TWENTY-FOUR

SURPRISE, SURPRISE. LES TOLD me there were times he hadn't been especially fond of Myra, especially when he heard she'd been nasty to some of the employees at the resort—or to Harris.

But he didn't consider that a motive to kill her, any more than I thought my argument with her was.

"And no, before you ask again, I didn't kill her," he said forcefully, although he kept his voice low. The tables around us were filled and the people I glanced at appeared to be involved in their own conversations, but ours might be a lot more interesting, so I was glad to keep it quiet.

"Same here. So now we've gotten that over with, let's both assume we're each telling the truth and move on."

Would I remove him from my mental list of suspects? No, but he'd been near the bottom before and would remain there. I hoped he felt the same about me—assuming he chose not to exonerate me altogether.

The table to my right emptied of diners. The man and woman who'd been sitting there looked at us before they left. Because they recognized our illustrious City Council member ... or because they'd been eavesdropping?

"Maybe," I said, "we'd be better off putting this conversation on hold till we're done eating. Assuming you want to continue it?" I hoped he did. Of all the people I could discuss this situation with, Les knew more of the players more intimately than anyone else— or at least anyone I might be able to get to talk to me.

So that's what we did. We talked about pleasantries during the rest of our dinner, including how my shops were doing, how our dogs were doing, and generalities about Knobcone Heights and matters the City Council might be considering soon—not including chastising the police department for their slowness in solving a murder.

From there, after I convinced him I'd pay for my own meal, we adjourned to the resort's bar. On the way through the well-lighted but nearly empty lobby I glanced toward the desk and no longer saw Neal there.

He knew where I was, and I assumed he'd peeked in to see who I was with. Wisely, he hadn't interrupted. But I figured he'd be full of questions later.

Maybe I'd have a few answers for him then.

The resort's bar was substantial in size, and there was a television in the main area that was broadcasting a game—British soccer, as far as I could tell. There was a small crowd watching, and other patrons were seated at even more intimate tables than in the restaurant.

There was also a patio area overlooking the lake that wasn't open for customers, but when Les made it clear to the chief bartender who he was, he had no trouble getting them to open it up for us.

It was noisy enough out here, with the water and occasional sound of boat motors, that I doubted there'd be any equipment turned on to record patrons' conversations. It was a good place to talk, even though it was a little chilly.

"Okay," I said after our drinks were served—mine a hearty glass of a delightful Cabernet from the Napa Valley, and Les's a locally brewed beer. "For purposes of our conversation and, hopefully, the truth, we're both innocent. But let's try some hypotheticals now." The first one I threw out was the one that seemed to contain the most logical motive. "What if Myra was having an affair and Harris found out? He might have wanted to dispose of her out of anger or embarrassment, or to keep her from getting a fortune from him if he divorced her. Or maybe her lover's wife wanted to get rid of Myra to end the affair."

Les's smile under the bar patio's dim light was full of wryness. "Or perhaps her lover's wife had the motive of wanting to get rid of Myra so she could take her place in running this resort."

I nodded as I smiled back at him. "I think we're on the same wavelength."

"Maybe, and I've considered Elise a possible suspect all along, although I hate the idea that my niece might not only be a killer but that she could have killed a relative, even one by marriage. I've dropped enough hints that I believe the police have looked at her too, but so far she's free. I still consider her a possible suspect, and maybe more probable than you. But I'm not a cop and I have no evidence, just suspicions." He took a long swig of his beer, not taking his eyes off me. "Who else?"

I went through my sparse list, including Manfred the chef and even Jack Loroco, who'd argued with Myra some time ago.

I didn't hint that Neal could be on the cops' list, although he certainly wasn't on mine.

"Then there's your brother Trask and his wife Susan," I said. "If they found out about the affair, maybe they'd have wanted to dispose of their daughter-in-law." I shrugged one shoulder. "I don't really suspect them, but neither can I completely discount them."

"I think you can forget about them," Les said, "although that could just be my Ethman blood talking."

Soon we left my suspects and got into his, but he'd pretty much considered the same list I had—or at least that was all he was admitting.

We'd ordered second drinks by then, and as we spoke I sometimes glanced back inside the darkened bar through the window, and sometimes toward the even darker lake.

When we were finished with our drinks, our discussion was over, too.

"'Fraid we didn't solve it." Les shook his head. He looked even older in the dimness, since the shadows emphasized the lines in his aging face.

"No," I agreed. "But I hope you trust me a little more now, and that our presumption of each other's innocence is the reality we'll both go with."

I watched his face to see if there was any indication he was hiding mistrust, but he just looked at me, and then, as we prepared to leave, he gave me a hug.

"I hope for both our sakes that this gets resolved soon, Carrie. I know I'll have to deal with the situation some more at City Council, and until someone's arrested I can't express my opinions there about who's innocent or guilty—not without getting myself and my family into even more trouble. But I'm glad we talked. And, yes, I still believe you're innocent."

"Thank you, Les. I can't tell you how much I appreciate it. I'd hate to think you really believed I could have done this—and brainstorming with you was … well, it was enlightening, but even more, it made me feel like a person again, not just a suspect."

He insisted on paying the bill this time, and as we walked together through the bar and then into the lobby, he stopped and looked down at me.

"I hope you're not lying, Carrie. Oh, and I'll bring Sam in one of these days for some more of your Barkery treats."

"Thanks." I gave him another brief hug before heading to the parking lot.

———

Neal was watching the end of an L.A. Dodgers baseball game on TV when I got home. He must have been listening for me, since he, along with Biscuit, sprang into the garage as I drove in. They both stayed in the doorway, Neal holding onto my girl's collar.

We talked for a while. I told him about my conversation with Les Ethman. He'd already heard, of course, about my confrontation with the cops the other day as well as my visit to the attorney. My bro was clearly concerned about me but had no suggestions or further insights, and so we soon both went to bed.

A couple more days passed. Thursday and Friday were ordinary—as ordinary as anything was these days.

Then came Saturday. It should be no different from any other weekend day as far as I was concerned. I got to my shops early with Biscuit and dug in.

One good thing about it being the weekend was that both Judy and Dinah were on board to help out. The routine we'd gotten into during the week was working out fine, and they both remained flexible if I needed them, but it was better now that we were all around when the crowds came in to shop at both stores.

Crowds! I couldn't have been happier...about that. We sold lots of both kinds of baked goods that day, and also on Sunday. Then the next week arrived and all worked out well again, even though Dinah and Judy still alternated which days they came in to help out. They quarreled a little when they were both around, but not a lot. Fortunately, they both seemed to enjoy what they were doing here. Neither made noises these days about wanting more—or less—responsibility.

And during all of that, I still managed to put in an hour or two most days at the vet clinic.

We baked. We sold dog treats and people treats. I packed up left-over dog treats to be taken to the vet clinic and, mostly, to Mountaintop Rescue. I also selected leftover people treats to periodically be picked up and taken to homeless centers down the mountain.

I talked to Brenda now and then. Her mother remained about the same. She missed Icing, and me, and hoped to visit someday soon. And I would be delighted to see her.

But oh, how I loved the routine—even as my mind still grappled with the problem looming over me now like an alien spaceship in a classic movie, ready to swoop down and change my life forever.

My potential arrest for murder.

I didn't see the detectives, nor did I hear that they'd arrested someone else. The media kept prodding, and the next City Council meeting would be on Friday. I knew what Les had said, and that local citizens wanted answers.

So did I.

I got a call from Jack Loroco. He was finally able to get away and venture up here again—soon. He still wasn't sure when, though. Hopefully on the weekend.

I saw Reed often at the vet clinic, and although he asked me to join him for coffee a couple of times, I declined and took a rain check—and, yes, there was a rainstorm predicted for this mountain community. Soon. So maybe I'd use that as an excuse to join Reed.

But the reason I saw him next wasn't at all what I'd anticipated. He called me late on Thursday. "Carrie, could you please come to the clinic when you close up your shops today." It was phrased as a question, but the tone made it a command.

"Sure," I said, then added hesitantly, "Is something wrong?"

"See you later," he said without answering. "Arvie will be here too." And then he hung up.

I felt a bit stunned. We hadn't gone on another date recently, but we talked often. I'd gotten the sense that we were at the beginning of what could become a good relationship.

But Reed had surprised me before with his bad mood. And I had no idea what was going on now.

I considered ignoring his command. But I was curious.

And if Arvie was involved...

I locked the doors, loaded Biscuit into my car, and drove toward the clinic. I realized while driving that I had some leftover treats I could have brought along, but I'd be there tomorrow and could take them then. Or, as I'd been doing, I could send one of my assistants.

No doggy patient would be deprived as a result of my mood-initiated forgetfulness that night.

The clinic was quiet. It was late, too late for doggy daycare, so I just brought Biscuit in the back door with me as I headed down the hall past the examination rooms and toward the end where the veterinarians' offices were located.

A door opened about halfway down the hall and Yolanda, my fellow vet tech, hurried out with a plastic bag in her hands.

"Hi," I said, smiling at her.

She just glared as she passed, not even bending to greet Biscuit, who was wagging her tail. She headed toward the lab area and disappeared into another door. Odd. We were usually good friends.

One of the senior vets, Dr. Paul Jensin, also passed by, just nodding and mumbling hello as if I were the owner of a patient he'd never seen before.

Very odd.

I'd already felt a lot of apprehension about coming here and what Reed had hinted at. Now I felt even more concerned. Were they all somehow convinced that I had killed Myra? But why would they be worrying about it now? And even though none of them would condone murder, it was an unlikely reason for a veterinary staff to get so upset.

I tried to keep my breathing even as I guided Biscuit toward Reed's office. I didn't have to knock on his door; it opened as I reached it. He must have been watching for me.

"Come in." He stood back so I could enter.

Arvie was there too, sitting in a chair facing Reed's desk. My kind friend and mentor, dressed in his white medical jacket, turned to look at me, and I smiled tentatively.

He didn't smile back.

My already fearful mood turned almost to panic. What was this?

I knew I'd find out soon. They wouldn't have demanded my presence merely to say they were angry about some unidentified peeve. They'd tell me what it was, and then I'd deal with it.

I hoped.

Reed motioned for me to sit down beside Arvie, then reached into a drawer and pulled out one of the boxes I used at the Barkery. I knew it was one from there, even though I used some of that size and larger at Icing, since this one had a Barkery sticker on the end. Sometimes I used these boxes for transporting treats here, and sometimes I used bags—whatever worked for the batch of biscuits I was sending along on any particular day.

Reed reached across his nearly bare desk and planted the box firmly in front of me. "This was in the kitchen where we keep dog treats, including the ones from you that we give away here."

As I nodded, an even greater feeling of dread passed through me. I was afraid I knew what was inside.

I reached for the box, opened it—and saw I'd been right.

Yes, I did make dog treats resembling cookies at the Barkery, but I purposely made them look different from the human cookies sold at Icing. That way, there wouldn't be any confusion about which was which.

And yet, the cookies in the box that had been in the kitchen here—which techs or volunteers or other helpers or even vets could have fed to patients—were human cookies.

A kind with large chocolate chips baked inside, only a hint of how much showing at the top.

And although it was not always fatal, chocolate was poison to dogs.

TWENTY-FIVE

"Oh, no!" I cried. "This is terrible! Did anyone—"

"No, fortunately none of these were fed to any dogs." Arvie's uncharacteristically cool gaze seared right through me.

I couldn't blame him. I wanted to thrash myself for this carelessness. "Thank heavens," I said.

"As you know," he continued, "we usually let the techs parcel out your treats. Yolanda's the one who discovered the problem—which was fortunate, since we had a bunch of volunteers here today from the high school and would have let them be the ones to give them out to our patients." His glare softened, but only a little. "I'm sure you didn't mean it, Carrie, but if the stress you're under leads to this kind of negligence, we really don't want you to bring any leftovers here until the problems in your life are resolved."

It was Reed's turn to add his two cents. "I've heard you developed a lot of the dog treats you sell now at the Barkery while you were working here, before you started your shops." His tone was even, but accusation was woven into it. "The effects of chocolate on dogs—it's elementary, Carrie. Even if you weren't an expert, you should have known that."

"I do know it. It…it was horrible negligence on my part. I'm just so glad Yolanda noticed it. It'll never happen again, I promise." It was definitely my fault. I was the one who always packed up the treats that were to come here or to Mountaintop Rescue, whether I was bringing them myself or sending some over with one of my assistants.

At least no dog had been harmed by my negligence.

But—

"Mountaintop Rescue!" I exclaimed. "I usually give them the same kind of treats. Just a second." I reached into my purse and pulled out my phone.

Billi wasn't there. I wasn't sure whether that was good or bad. I didn't really want to let our new, growing friendship disappear because of an inadvertent act of stupidity on my part. And I didn't especially want the other workers or volunteers at the shelter to know, either.

But the really important thing was to make sure no dogs were given harmful treats, no matter who learned about my mistake.

The shelter manager on duty answered the phone. I didn't go into detail, but I let her know that some of the items sent over from Barkery and Biscuits may have been tainted. "Are all your dogs okay?" I asked.

They were, fortunately. And she wasn't aware of any of the Barkery treats being given out that day. She promised to pull all treats from the Barkery and hold them for me to pick up in the next day or so.

I wanted to get a look at them, see just how far my carelessness had gone.

"Everything okay there?" Arvie asked when I'd hung up.

I nodded shakily. "Fortunately, yes. And … and I'm so very sorry. I'm really glad my mistake was caught before there were any bad consequences. And I can promise you it won't happen again."

"True." Reed's expression looked more wry now. And did I see a touch of sympathy? Maybe. Anyone could make a mistake, right?

But I never, ever, thought I could be this careless. Being concerned and even scared about what was going on in the investigation into Myra's death was an explanation for it, maybe, since it was occupying my mind, even obsessing me. But it wasn't an excuse. Nothing could excuse this.

And I learned in the next moment how true that was.

"We appreciate your generous donation of treats here, Carrie," Reed said. "But right now … well, like Arvie said, please don't bring anything from your shop here again, at least not for now. And why don't you take a few days off? Come back on Monday?"

I glanced at Arvie. He nodded. I didn't argue. Couldn't argue. Maybe I'd be able to figure out a way to rectify this and eventually bring treats that Arvie or Reed or another vet inspected before I put them on the shelf.

Assuming they wanted to take the time to assure themselves.

Biscuit and I left a few minutes later. I understood why Reed had taken that position, and why Arvie had agreed with him.

Would they let the world know what had happened?

It could affect my business at both shops.

If so, I would have to accept it. I'd made such an awful mistake and could only be thankful it hadn't led to horrible consequences.

And if the result was a loss of customers at my stores, I still could be glad that it hadn't ended in the loss of any dog's life.

Maybe Arvie would keep the situation low-key. He knew that both my shops needed to be successful for me to pay him back on time.

But his worry about endangering dogs would trump his concern about repayment, and, if he said anything, I couldn't blame him ... only myself.

———

No harm done, really, thank heavens.

Except possibly to the ongoing success of my shops.

And definitely to my state of mind over the next day, and maybe forever. Despite the fact that the outcome could have been so much worse, I was furious with myself. *Maybe I should get out of this business*, I thought. Leave town altogether.

Yeah? And do what?

It was Friday. Both my assistants were around. They knew something was wrong.

In fact, Judy even asked me, late that morning, what it was. All three of us were in the kitchen baking. Yes, we were even baking chocolate chip cookies for people.

I'd considered using only carob from now on, for both shops. Then, if I made another mistake, no dogs could be hurt by it. Carob was okay for them to eat, even though chocolate wasn't. And carob tasted somewhat like chocolate to the human palate.

The dog biscuit found near Myra's body had even had carob icing on its ends, as did some of the biscuits we still baked here.

But no, for now we were still using real chocolate in our Icing products. After all, none of what we made here was going to end up at the vet clinic anymore, or even at the animal shelter, since I wasn't going to bring or send anything to either for a long time, if ever.

At least none of the chocolate chip cookies had wound up at Mountaintop Rescue. I'd picked up the box from the Barkery that had been left there, and all were regular doggy treats.

I'd pondered whether to tell my helpers what had happened and figured it was okay to let them know. They'd have been more horrified if what I'd done had resulted in a dog's injury or death, but I could use it as a lesson for now.

A lesson that could, in the future, require them to confirm that their boss hadn't made another horrific mistake if they were ever given another opportunity to take Barkery treats anywhere.

I could use their help.

And so, while Dinah and I worked on the Barkery side of the kitchen and Judy on the Icing side, I tried to keep my voice light as I told them of my visit late yesterday to the veterinary clinic and why—after making them promise that what I was going to say would go no farther.

"It all worked out okay," I finished. "But I was more than embarrassed. I was appalled with myself. Fortunately, no dogs were given any of the cookies, or even a taste of them. And for now we won't be donating any leftover dog treats anyplace else, not there or Mountaintop Rescue. But I'm telling you this so that if this ever changes, you double check when I pack up our leftover treats so I don't make that kind of mistake again."

"Of course." Judy looked as horrified as I felt, and so did Dinah. "But ... I did kind of wonder if combining the shops, or even just combining the kitchen and keeping them so close together ... Never mind."

She'd expressed her concerns before, weeks ago when we were getting the two shops ready to open. I just figured she wasn't happy with change, losing Brenda as her boss and expanding what her responsibilities were without being put in charge, as she'd apparently wanted. And I'd given detailed instructions on how to keep the baked goods separate.

I just hadn't followed them myself.

But both assistants had done a great job since then, and I hadn't thought since about what Judy had said. Till now.

"I understand," I said. "And I still think that having a bakery and a barkery as partially separate shops is a good idea. But let's all be extra cautious from now on about making sure that here, too, we keep the products all separate."

"Okay," Dinah said. She once again looked a little older than when I'd first met her.

Was it because of the nature of her job here?

And how about Judy?

She still looked about the same to me, although I thought she'd lost some of her seriousness. She even smiled now and then—but this situation might lead to more frowns on her part. I'd just have to wait and see.

It certainly was causing frowns from me. I was worried—about everything. I'd harmed no dogs, but I might have ruined my shops, or at least my reputation, if word got out.

I didn't think either Arvie or Reed would do more than scold me and keep me from bringing treats, but I decided to find out.

So, later that afternoon, I met with my lawyer, Ted Culbert. It was a casual meeting, coffee at Cuppa-Joe's. I went to Cuppa-Joe's with a lot of different people for a lot of different reasons, and this was yet another situation where I didn't want to be overheard.

I'd brought Biscuit, and was glad to see that Ted got along great with my little golden dog. He was fine with sitting on one of the patios, and in fact did look more casual than when I'd visited him at his office. No suit coat today, and his blue button-down shirt and slacks enhanced the blueness of his intense eyes as he looked at me often and quizzically. His hair was short and light brown and added to both his professional appearance and his nice looks.

His friendliness appealed to me too. And given my latest go-around with Reed, no matter how much I'd deserved it, I even considered flirting with Ted—although not now, not under these circumstances.

This afternoon, it was Joe Nash himself who waited on us. He shot a grin from Ted to me, as if he assumed this was a date. And since I didn't want anyone to know what was really going on, I let the sweet cafe owner—my dear, fatherlike friend—go with that assumption.

"So what's going on, Carrie?" Ted's voice was deep, his attitude concerned.

"Are we subject to attorney-client privilege?" I asked, and upon his assurance, I told him the whole story.

And then he gave me even more assurance. "No harm, no foul," he said. "Yes, it was not the best situation, but since none of the dogs ate any of the cookies, no one can claim damages for negligence. But next time—"

"There will be no next time," I told him firmly.

For the next fifteen minutes—before he had to get back to his office and I had to return to my shops—we had a pleasant conversation that must have reminded him of a date too, since as he paid he said he wasn't going to charge me for the consultation, then walked out with Biscuit and me. He said that next time, he'd be the one to call me and invite me out.

Unless, of course, I needed his legal services. And I, at least, hoped that wasn't going to happen.

He was nice enough to ditto that comment as we said our good-byes.

TWENTY-SIX

THAT NIGHT, LIKE THE night before, Neal was full of sympathy about my screwing up which baked goods I'd taken to the veterinary clinic. He brought me a glass of wine as I sat staring at a sitcom on TV without seeing it. He remained full of platitudes about how it's human to make mistakes.

I loved him for trying, but he didn't make me feel any better. This mistake could have had consequences I hated to even consider.

Was I overthinking it? Maybe, but my love for dogs kept my guilt trip going.

Neal also had no further insight, after his latest day at work, into which of his employers might be the best candidate to have murdered his former boss.

I didn't mention to him that I'd had coffee with my lawyer to find out if there could be liability issues for what I'd done even without any dogs becoming ill—or worse. Since I felt reasonably comfortable now about that not being an issue, why even bring it up?

And I certainly didn't want Neal to imagine I had any kind of social relationship with Ted. I didn't. Not yet, at least, and probably not ever—no matter what he had suggested as we'd wound up our coffee break.

Neal was aware of my sort-of interest in Reed, but not of Jack Loroco's possible interest in me, even if it was solely for business reasons.

It was better that way. For the moment, I had a lot more on my mind than even considering any kind of relationship with anyone, or allowing my brother to speculate about me.

After taking Biscuit for her last outing of the night, I went to bed. When I woke at my usual early time the next morning, I realized I actually had gotten some sleep.

It was a new day. One in which I'd think hard about what safeguards I could put into place at the shops, besides having my assistants check up on me to ensure the product mix-up didn't happen again.

Several hours later I was in the shops' kitchen finishing up a batch of bone-shaped biscuits with carob icing. *Carob* icing. I'd made sure, first thing, that all the chocolate was inside a cabinet or the refrigerator on the opposite side of the kitchen, carefully labeled. And that the still-fresh leftover items from yesterday were in the correct display cases in each of the shops.

Both Judy and Dinah had remarked on my new signage when they'd arrived, but they seemed just to accept it, both smiling their understanding. I wondered what they really thought about their careless boss, but I wasn't going to ask.

At the moment, they were both out in the shops since it was a Saturday and we had a lot of customers already.

As I took the latest batch of biscuits out of the oven, Judy entered through the door from the Barkery. "There's a guy in the shop who wants to talk to you," she said. "He looks familiar. I think he was at our grand opening. He says his name is Jack something."

"Loroco?" I asked.

"Yes, I think that's it."

I put the large, filled cookie sheet on the counter to cool, took off my apron and oven mitts, and glanced down at myself. No flour on my jeans or Barkery and Biscuits T-shirt. That had to be good enough. I hurried into the shop, Judy following me.

Sure enough, Jack was there, along with two other men he was talking with near the glass display case. When I'd seen him before he'd been dressed casually. Not now. He wore a white, short-sleeved button shirt with muted blue stripes and navy slacks. The guys with him were similarly dressed. Business associates?

My guess turned out right.

"Hi, Carrie." Jack's smile was huge as he spotted me, and he approached with his arms extended as if he wanted to hug me. I stiffened. Glimmers of attraction or not, I didn't want to appear as if we had anything going, not in front of my assistant or customers or even his friends.

But he merely shook my right hand as his left hand touched my arm—a gesture that was friendly but not overly so.

"Great to see you." Releasing me, he motioned toward the men he'd been speaking with. "I didn't get a chance to call to tell you I was coming this morning. It was a last-minute thing, but both these guys were available and I'd promised to give them a sales demo, so we left L.A. really early this morning, too early to phone you."

"If it was after five in the morning it would have worked fine for me," I said with a smile. "A baker's day starts before dawn."

"Of course." He looked a little abashed, as if I'd scolded him.

"It's fine," I assured him.

"Anyway, Rico and Dwain, here, are new with VimPets and I'm in town to demonstrate how to conduct sales calls." Jack leaned closer to me. "And maybe discuss what VimPets could do with you in the future," he said more softly.

Thanks to the way his hazel eyes caught mine, I had a sense that he wouldn't mind discussing what *he* could do with me in the future, but I wasn't ready to consider that—especially not with all that was going on around me. Plus, the thought crossed my mind that he might believe that a little seduction of my body might lead to the seduction of my recipes, too.

We'd see about that, but at the moment I wasn't interested.

"Okay," I said noncommittally. Then a thought struck me. Just as Jack wanted to find a way to use me—or at least, my recipes—maybe I could use him too. "Since you know I'm not a good potential source for selling VimPets products to, where will you demonstrate your sales calls?"

As I'd anticipated, one place was the chain retail pet store on the way to Lake Arrowhead.

The other was the Knob Hill Pet Emporium.

What if I joined them at the latter? Now that Myra was gone, Harris Ethman might be happy to have representatives of a well-respected pet supply company visit him and make suggestions for increasing his product line.

Was he relieved not to be dependent anymore on Myra ordering him around?

Would that have given him reason to kill her? In addition to it ending her affair with Walt Hainner?

Who knew? Of course, Harris was unlikely to blurt this out if Jack or I happened to pop in today. The best I could hope for was that he would be less likely to throw me out if he wanted something from the man I was with.

And just maybe I'd spot something in the shop while he was distracted with VimPets, something I could follow up on.

"You know," I said to Jack, "I need to check on some items that the Pet Emporium may carry. Mind if I accompany you?"

"Of course not." Jack's smile suggested he wouldn't mind stopping in a room at the resort with me on the way back.

————

My intent was to stay in the background, eavesdropping, while Jack performed his magic in front of his new company underlings. I wanted to see and hear Harris's reactions to the sales call now that he was truly in charge.

I'd been to the Emporium before, of course, even just last week. Now I would simply let myself relax and observe. The neon sign in front, not lighted since it was daytime, was in a scripted font, and the items in the store window all appeared as elite and expensive as one would expect, from some stylish clothing for dogs that, despite it being spring, would be ideal for the icy San Bernardino Mountains winters, to bowls and leashes and toys that even human kids of wealthy parents would undoubtedly enjoy.

I hadn't paid any attention to appearances the last time I was here, since I'd wanted to confront Harris. This time, appearances, especially Harris's, were the entire reason I was here.

The walk to the Emporium hadn't taken long. I'd considered bringing Biscuit but decided against it, leaving her in her Barkery crate for now. I'd remained at Jack's side as we walked—the opposite one from where he held his briefcase. I'd felt a bit out of place in my casual clothes and athletic shoes, but so what? In a way I wished I wasn't wearing a shirt that would identify my stores, but it didn't really matter. Harris knew who I was.

Rico and Dwain had walked on either side of us, whenever there weren't people attempting to pass us on the sidewalk. I wondered what they must think about me imposing on their sales call demo. Maybe they believed that Jack and I did have a relationship other than a potential business one. Did I care?

Not really; not with strangers. But just in case, I'd talked a bit about my recipes, not giving details but discussing the kinds of dog treats that seemed to be selling best at my Barkery.

Jack had seemed quite interested, asking me all sorts of questions about ingredients such as carob and carrots and peanut butter, plus the types of flour I preferred. I kept to generalities as I answered him, and he seemed to become even more enthused the more we talked.

I didn't mention my slip-up of delivering of the wrong kind of treats to the veterinary clinic. No one else needed to know about that.

It hadn't taken us long to reach the store and go inside. There were a couple of customers at the front counter, apparently paying for a container of pet food that peeked out of a plastic bag marked with the Knob Hill Pet Emporium logo: a rich, crownlike image in a sparkling gold that must have cost a lot to stamp on the bags.

I stood back near the door as Jack and his trainees approached Harris, who remained behind the counter. I pretended to study some of the toy balls of different sizes and materials in a display off to one side while watching what was really going on.

Harris's gaze was on Jack, fortunately, and he apparently didn't notice me—or if he did, he pretended not to, at least for now. Jack introduced himself, and Harris indicated that he did recall meeting him not long ago.

No, he still didn't carry any VimPets products. He intimated that they weren't high-enough quality, and Jack pounced on that immediately, pulling brochures from his briefcase that described how wonderful VimPets products were.

"And we're always increasing what we carry; if we find the right kind of items, the higher the quality, the better. Like mass-producing formerly homemade treats with special ingredients in their recipes." Jack glanced toward me and smiled, as if he was patting me on the back for the great stuff I baked at the Barkery and reminding me of the recipes I might—or might not—sell to VimPets someday.

I cringed a bit as Harris, too, looked in my direction. His smile wasn't at all like Jack's. Instead, it was nasty. "If you're talking about manufacturing some of the homemade crap made in Ms. Kennersly's dog bakery," he said, "then you know I'm not going to buy it."

So he had noticed me. And he clearly still didn't like me any more than I liked him.

This discussion hadn't been of any use to me so far. Nothing in it suggested that he had, or hadn't, gotten along with his wife or agreed with her product choices.

Maybe I could change that. I put down the rubber squeak-ball I'd been pretending to study and approached them, aware that Jack's minions were watching us with eyes wide and interested.

"That's fine, Harris," I told him. "Some of the foods you carry here are quite good, and adding VimPets products would make them even better, whether or not they ever include my recipes." I hazarded a glance toward Jack, and enjoyed the broad grin on his angular face, as though he was cheering me on. I looked back at Harris. "Or do you miss Myra's direction as to what you should or shouldn't sell here?"

He didn't respond for a few seconds, but the look on his narrow face grew furious and his turned-down eyes were almost frightening in the way they glared. "Don't you talk about my wife, bitch. Are you just rubbing it in that you killed her?"

Interesting reaction. Was it real, or was it an attempt to remind me, and everyone else, that I was still a major suspect?

I resisted the urge to step back. "You, of all people, know I didn't kill her." I realized I was goading him even further, but I wanted to see his response to my obvious accusation.

"I know nothing of the kind," he spat. "And maybe I should have bought those damned recipes of yours when they were offered to me so I could have people who know what they're doing work with them and turn them into something good for dogs."

I froze. "What are you talking about? What do you mean, my recipes were offered to you?"

His fury appeared to recede just a little, perhaps replaced by caginess. "Never mind." He turned toward Jack. "I might have been interested in trying out some VimPets products if you hadn't brought the bitch here with you. Maybe someday, but forget about it for now."

As if called in by Harris as the cavalry, a family entered the shop with their pit bull.

"I've got customers to wait on," Harris said. "You all can leave." He walked toward the newcomers.

"That went well," Jack muttered to Rico and Dwain, who both smiled dutifully. "But yeah, we'd better go."

As we all walked back toward my shops, I half listened to Jack's explanation to his employees about what had gone on there, interested somewhat in how he glossed over who Myra was and that her murder remained unsolved, and how well-regarded the Pet Emporium was here in Knobcone Heights.

But my mind remained on our angry conversation and Harris's comments. Had he just been trying to stoke my anger—or had his anger gotten him out of control enough to mention something that was true?

Had someone offered to sell him my excellent and proprietary dog treat recipes?

And if so, who?

TWENTY-SEVEN

As we walked, I caught Jack's glance down at me now and then. He might have been wondering the same thing I was.

Or maybe he thought I'd already tainted any possibility of a future sale of my recipes to VimPets by attempting to sell them to someone else.

There weren't many people around on the narrow sidewalks, yet we couldn't talk much with Rico and Dwain along.

When we reached my stores, he sent them inside and we stood in front of one of the two picture windows. Glancing in, I saw Dinah waiting on customers in the Barkery, but Icing seemed empty. Hopefully that was just a momentary situation. I'd ask Judy how things had been there in my absence—soon.

I also had other things to ask Judy. And Dinah.

"What was that all about, at the Pet Emporium?" Jack asked, interrupting my thoughts. I supposed he was keeping the question general to see my reaction.

"Long story," I said. "But—well, you're aware that Harris is Myra Ethman's widower."

"Yes, and as we've discussed, the police consider you a suspect in her murder. I assume they're also looking into her husband as a possibility. And I gather you're still each thinking the other could have done it—or at least that's what you each want the other to believe. Of course, one of you could know the truth if you happen to be the killer." His words were harsh and so was his tone.

I'd thought this man had some romantic interest in me. If so, he wasn't acting like it now. Was that because my presence might have negated his ability to sell his products to Harris? Because he'd been embarrassed in front of Rico and Dwain? He surely didn't believe any more than he had before that I was the killer. He'd even said previously that he had as much of a motive as I did.

In any event, his current attitude reminded me of Reed's about-face.

No matter what their underlying rationales, I supposed that my being a murder suspect didn't give me great potential to become a valued girlfriend. But all of this also made me question whether I wanted either of these men in my life, for any reason.

Jack shook his head then and reached out to hold me by my elbows. "Sorry, Carrie. That all came out wrong, but I felt a bit ... let's say, gob-smacked by the way things worked out there. I know you're not a killer, although I can't be sure about Harris. But what was that about someone already marketing your recipes?"

Ah. That was what he really cared about.

Well, me too—among other things.

"I don't know," I admitted slowly. "It could just have been Harris trying another avenue to upset me." I didn't believe much of what Harris said, but the way the statement had come up in our

266

conversation convinced me that it could have been real. Someone might have offered my recipes to him, but he hadn't bought them. Not then, at least. "But just in case he wasn't lying..."

"I'm sure you'll be looking into it." I was glad to see that Jack's face now looked sympathetic, with a glimmer of something else in his hazel eyes that suggested the romantic interest I'd been wondering about still hovered there. It wasn't all about the recipes...probably. "Anyway, we're staying at the resort tonight. I'll take the guys to the nearest chain pet stores tomorrow and hopefully give them a better demonstration of how to approach store managers and encourage them to carry and recommend our products."

"And you brought them all the way up here to do that? Why?" I couldn't help smiling as I asked. I anticipated his answer—and got what I'd been looking for.

"Of course." His own smile danced in his eyes as he regarded me sexily. "I like this place, so why not take advantage? And a certain person here is a major draw, especially since she's got something I want."

"Recipes?" I teased.

"Among other things." He winked at me, then headed into the Barkery.

———

While Jack and his trainees remained in the Barkery, and then more people came into both shops, I hugged Biscuit in the Barkery since we both needed it. Then I waited on some customers and had time to ponder the best way to approach my two assistants— who both had access to my recipes.

When I'd taken over the store from Brenda, I'd asked her what she did to make sure that anything she considered her very own recipe wasn't going to be broadcast to the world by her assistants. She said they'd both signed an employment agreement when they started working there.

In fact, she gave me copies of those agreements, and I modeled a similar one for Judy and Dinah to sign. It included the recipes I'd bought from Brenda along with my own pet recipes that I'd developed while working as a vet tech. I'd always baked mine at home, all by myself, so there was never any prior question about their ownership.

But now maybe I needed to run the agreement by Ted, to make sure they would hold up as legal documents. If they wouldn't, maybe I didn't really want to know it, since I'd already have blown my proprietary interest.

Of course, it would also give me another excuse to see Ted...even though I knew I'd be better off right now dealing only with men I didn't find attractive. I needed no further distractions.

I needed solutions.

Interesting, though, I mused as I did some cleanup work in the kitchen while my assistants remained in the shops. My concerns seemed to leap from one item of importance in my life to another—each would have been difficult in itself, and now I was confronted with multiple issues. I remained a murder suspect, and the stress of that may have caused me to make a potentially horrendous mistake: providing real chocolate treats that could be lethal if a dog had eaten them. And now someone might be trying to steal my recipes.

Was that easier to deal with than the other two? Maybe—especially if I could figure out who, if anyone, was guilty and make sure it never happened again. And assuming it had been one of my employees—who else could it be?—I wanted to confront both of them for answers. But I needed to handle the situation with some finesse or I'd have no assistants left.

Which, if it turned out I was right, might actually be a good thing...

Damn it! I needed those answers. But I also needed to ask the questions in a way that wouldn't seem overly accusatory. Maybe.

Should I talk to Judy and Dinah together? Probably not. Although if I confronted them individually, they would most likely each say that if there was a problem the other had been the one to instigate it.

They'd probably do the same thing if I met with them together—and we'd be back at square one, as we'd been when Brenda left, when the two of them didn't appear to like one another. They seemed to be getting along better now—most of the time.

Of course, their apparent camaraderie wouldn't matter if I had to fire one for insubordination or worse.

It was getting late. Maybe I should consider this overnight, I thought—and talk to them tomorrow, either alone or together.

Only one thing was certain. I needed to think this through, to decide on an approach designed to get me answers.

I wasn't surprised when Jack invited me to join him and his employees for dinner when my shops finally closed. Since they were eating at the resort's restaurant, I had to accept.

I said goodbye to my assistants for that night, wondering which, if either, was a traitor. My mind whirled about other possibilities, but I didn't want to focus on them either. Not now.

I took Biscuit home, fed her, and left her there. Jack picked me up.

Then I had a session of flirtation with Jack and discussion of dog products with all three of the VimPets people, as well as another chance to look around the resort and hope that one of the

269

Ethman relations came up to me and confessed and apologized for allowing me to become a murder suspect.

Neal was out with some friends and not working that night, so he didn't know I was there.

No confessions. Much later, when Jack brought me home, Neal had already gone to bed, so I didn't have a chance to talk with him—which I thought was probably a good thing. I needed to think.

Did I sleep that night? Not a lot. But I did come up with an approach to take with my assistants. Since the next day was Sunday, they would both be around.

But would my sanity?

———

I was resolute the next day as I started baking early in the morning, using some of my proprietary Barkery recipes. I would talk to Dinah immediately upon her arrival, since she was scheduled to come in first. Then, when Judy arrived, I'd take her off by herself somewhere and talk to her too.

Of course my mind had also come up with other possible scenarios. Number one was that Harris had been lying, that no one had offered him my recipes. He had his own agenda, and that included riling me.

But his attitude as he'd told me seemed almost triumphant—hard to disbelieve.

I stepped up the pace of whipping the batter in the deep bowl I was working on, half wishing that it was Harris I was beating so determinedly instead.

Number two alternative scenario was that Brenda had been unhappy enough about the current situation that she'd offered my recipes to Harris. She'd seen me work on them for our opening party and would have had enough proximity to them to copy them. And sell them?

But her leaving town wasn't my doing. In fact, I'd actually helped her by buying her out so she could go take care of her mother without any commitments up here on the mountain. It wouldn't necessarily erase her resentment of my changes, though—even if she'd mostly seemed okay with them.

Then there was number three possibility: Neal. He'd seen me working on a lot of recipes at home so I could bring in nutritious items to the clinic. He'd known where I had them written down. Might he have offered them to Harris—perhaps so an Ethman would owe him and help to preserve his job at the resort?

It seemed a stretch. And I just didn't see my brother doing that. If his job was in jeopardy—and I didn't think it was—he knew his sis would continue to let him live with her while he figured out what was next, like more outdoor expeditions or whatever.

I heard a familiar bark out front. That was unlike my well-behaved Biscuit. Was someone trying to break in?

My imagination was working overtime these days, but that was undoubtedly a result of all that was not imaginary in my beleaguered life. Even so, I put a nice, sharp knife out on the counter at a place where I could grab its hilt if necessary, then went into the Barkery—just in time to see Dinah entering.

"Good morning," I said. "Why are you coming in this way?"

She jumped a little, as though I had startled her instead of the other way around. Maybe I had. "Oh. Sorry. A … friend dropped me off so I didn't park in back. It was easier to come in through the front." She edged forward enough to give Biscuit, who was straining on her leash, a pat on the head—a gesture that earned her back some missing brownie points. Even so ...

The way she'd referred to her friend made me think she had a boyfriend. I'd never really asked either of my assistants about their love lives, but maybe I should have. Was Dinah attempting to hide something ... besides possibly trying to sell my recipes?

She supposedly was a writer. Was she studying people to see how she could use them in her stories? Steal from them? Kill them?

"Coming in this way is fine," I told her, stifling my inner thoughts for now. "Anyway, maybe it's easier to talk out here than in the kitchen."

"Talk?" Her childlike face seemed to grow pale in the still artificial light of the shop. Why?

"Yes," I said firmly. "When was the last time you talked with Harris Ethman?"

She blinked her blue eyes and grasped her large leather purse as if she wanted to use it as a shield. Because she was hiding something, or because my attitude scared her? "At ... at Myra's memorial. I told him I was sorry for his loss."

"And what did you tell him about the Barkery's recipes?" I'd taken a step toward her, still acting aggressive to see her reaction.

"Recipes? I never said anything to him about our recipes. Should I have?"

"No," I said, deflating a bit. "No, that's fine. Go ahead into the kitchen and get ready. We need to do some more baking."

I watched her hurry off, wondering if she'd lied. I didn't think so, but I'd started mistrusting my own abilities to read people and interpret body language around what they were saying.

Well, I still had one more assistant to quiz. Maybe Judy would come right out and admit it.

But she didn't.

By the time she arrived, mid-morning, I hadn't had Biscuit out for a walk for a couple of hours. I used Judy's arrival as an excuse to do so, and insisted that she come along too since Dinah was working in the shops.

We walked slowly along the sidewalk surrounding the grass-covered hills and trees of the parklike town square while Biscuit sniffed and greeted other dogs with nose sniffs and did what she was supposed to.

As we walked I asked Judy the same questions I'd used on Dinah earlier.

Judy also said that she'd last spoken with Harris at the memorial. She acted equally puzzled about my questions regarding the Barkery recipes, and mentioned again that perhaps the shops should have stayed singular—Icing only, since the Barkery seemed to keep gar-nering problems. She didn't go pale in the sunlight, so my suspicions stayed more on Dinah, but I really hadn't gotten enough from either of them to determine which one might have made a sale to Harris.

I needed more.

I needed my sanity, my routine, my normal life—whatever that might turn out to be after all this.

How was I going to fix things?

I wasn't at this moment. Dinah went on break, and I mused about it all as I organized the remaining cookies and cupcakes in Icing's display case.

I still had a few hours of work in my shops before closing time. And today was my last day without a shift at the veterinary clinic.

I wasn't sure how I'd be during my shift there tomorrow. Defensive because of those cookies? I'd definitely not be bringing any dog treats with me for now. When could I again? I needed to somehow redeem myself with my friends at the vet clinic—Arvie in particular.

And Reed? Well, I'd had high hopes not long ago for us forming some kind of relationship. But the kind of relationship we seemed destined for now was solely professional—and I'd still need to redeem myself with him even for that.

A young family came in looking for a special treat. The five-year-old's birthday was tomorrow and he wanted a cake from Icing.

I was delighted to oblige. I took their order for a vanilla cake with chocolate frosting and his name on it. "It'll be ready for you by ten in the morning," I promised.

The child clapped his hands—and I gave him and his older sister each a strawberry cupcake to tide them over. Their parents seemed delighted. So was I. I needed the distraction of something as cute as this.

And I'd make that cake particularly special.

As I walked them to the door, I was surprised, when I looked outside, to see Reed there—not in veterinary apparel but jeans and a Knobcone Heights T-shirt. He held the leash of his dog Hugo. I didn't know his schedule this week, but if he'd worked at the clinic today his shift was apparently over. So what was he doing here?

The only way to find out was to ask him. I followed my customers outside.

"Hi, Reed," I said tentatively. Had he come to chew me out further about my misdeed with the cookies?

"Hi, Carrie." He approached me and I reached out my hand to pat Hugo, looking down at the dog instead of at Reed's face. "Look, I—" He hesitated. "I know what happened was an accident. You wouldn't do anything to hurt a dog, I'm sure of that. And I know you're under a lot of pressure right now. So…" His voice trailed off.

I did look up at his face then. His expression looked pained and maybe wistful, as if he regretted the attitude he'd had. Or was I just hopeful, wishing to see that there?

"So," he continued, "Hugo and I are here to invite Biscuit and you out for dinner, whenever you're free. I'd like to take you to the Arrowhead Diner so we'll be away from here and can talk. They have an outdoor area where dogs are welcome. And—"

His voice had speeded up, as if he was trying to find as many ways as possible to convince me quickly to agree.

I smiled, if only a little, as I raised my hand to interrupt. He stopped talking and waited for my response.

So, for an instant, did I.

But I knew what I had to do—if I wanted to feel comfortable at the clinic again.

And if I hoped to see if there was any possibility of something ever materializing between Reed and me.

"Sure," I said. "Biscuit was just telling me she'd like to try that diner. We'd be delighted to join Hugo and you there tonight."

TWENTY-EIGHT

I LIKED THE ARROWHEAD Diner. It was a family-style restaurant that had apparently, in the past, been built to resemble a train's dining car. At least photos to that effect were hung on the wall inside.

We were outside, thanks to Biscuit and Hugo. The air was brisk and suggested that rain was on the way, but it wasn't predicted to start until late that night.

I'd talked to Jack earlier. He and his trainees had decided to return to L.A. tonight. But he'd be back soon, he promised. I wouldn't have been required to join him that evening anyway, but his absence made my decision to go out with Reed all the easier.

"Arvie recommended this place but I've never been here before," Reed said, looking around. The patio was nearly empty, although the restaurant inside was crowded. His movement was caught by the dogs, who both sat up and regarded him expectantly, as if hoping for treats. But when none were forthcoming they both settled back down.

"I have, although Biscuit hasn't," I said. "It's pretty good."

"Not as good as your cooking, I'm sure." The smile on Reed's face was wide and contagious, so I grinned back. But I still wasn't sure how much to trust him and his now-flirtatious attitude. Not after how he'd acted when he accused me of carelessness about my dog treats.

Justifiably so, but still...

"Thanks," I said, without inviting him back for a home-cooked meal at my place. Not yet, at least. We'd just have to see about whether that ever occurred again.

We both ordered margaritas to start, although my intent was to have a burger for dinner and not any of the Mexican dishes on the menu. When the server brought our drinks, she also took our orders.

After she left, and as I took my first sip, Reed regarded me with what appeared to be concern and asked, "Are you okay, Carrie? I know what happened with the cookies you brought was unintentional and I'm sorry I came down on you so hard. Is that still why you look so sad? Or is it because of the other things you've been going through?"

I knew he was referring to the Myra situation, and I did appreciate his apology. But I found myself needing to vent. "It's everything," I told him. "My being a murder suspect could have led to my carelessness, and I realize that. But now there's something else." I told him about my quandary about who might have offered my recipes to Harris Ethman.

"If Harris wasn't lying about it, could it have been one of your employees?" Reed asked. I related to him that I'd already quizzed both of them and couldn't be sure if it was either.

But as we spoke, something hit me so strongly it felt like a physical blow rather than mental. "One of my employees," I whispered aloud.

Reed seemed to hear what I hadn't said. "One of your employees could have been the one to swap the human cookies for the healthy dog treats at the clinic." His tone was crisp yet full of questions. "I know they sometimes brought your leftover dog treats in the mornings, even when you also brought some in the afternoon."

"But which one would do that? And why? And why offer my recipes to Harris?"

"I haven't a clue—but I think your initial questions to them need to be expanded."

"With something more than just my suspicions," I agreed. "I can't tell you offhand which one brought treats to the clinic that day—assuming it wasn't me. But it was Thursday, right, that Arvie and you discovered the problem with the treats?"

It was. And I believed that Dinah had been working with me at the shops that day, while Judy had had it off. Had Dinah taken the cookies to the veterinary clinic that morning? I would have packed them, but I didn't inspect the package afterward so I wouldn't have known if she'd decided to do something so nasty. I hadn't had a shift at the clinic that day, but Reed had called to ask me to come in, and Arvie and he had scolded me for the mistake... which might not have been a mistake at all.

"I'm not sure if I had a supply of those chocolate chip cookies that day that could have been taken by Dinah," I mused. "But my computer records would give some indication, since all our sales receipts are copied there. We keep chocolate chip cookies around on most days, and I might be able to tell if we had any left over from the day before that Dinah could have brought to the clinic that morning. Or..."

"Or?" Reed was leaning over the table toward me, but he moved back when our food was placed in front of us.

"Or," I said when we were alone again, "there are other possibilities. I usually start that kind of baking early in the morning, depending on whether we have any cookies left from the day before. They're usually fine to keep for a day without worrying about them going bad. I need to review the records for a couple of days. But if we had none left when I came in on Thursday morning, that could be an indication that we'd sold out on Wednesday—or the ones that showed up at the clinic were brought then and stored there."

"Will you be able to tell from that which of your helpers was more likely to have brought them?"

I shrugged. "Not sure, but it may give me more ammunition when I question each of them again, not just about the recipes, but about the cookies … " I looked down at the hamburger on my plate. "Of course, this combining of my two problems could all be in my head, to give me the ability to try to blame Judy or Dinah for my own carelessness. These issues might not be related."

"Then again, they might be." Reed looked excited on my behalf. I supposed he didn't really want me to be guilty of endangering the dogs at the clinic. Well, neither did I.

But I'd reserve judgment on whether I could be exonerated till I at least checked the computer—and spoke with my assistants yet again.

———

I couldn't wait. When we finished eating, Reed returned Biscuit and me to my shops. I'd had to bring a box of hamburger home since my appetite had all but disappeared thanks to the change in my mood. But this was a good change—the anticipation of resolving a couple of problems.

And there was more. It made no sense, but what if all three of my problems were somehow related?

But why on earth would either Judy or Dinah kill Myra, then try to frame me for it?

No, that couldn't be. But my sense of hope had expanded everything.

"Would you like Hugo and me to come in while you check things out?" Reed asked as he pulled up in front of my shops on Summit Avenue.

"No need, but thanks. I don't know how long it'll take." And if I found something that appeared to be an answer, I wasn't sure how I'd sleep that night.

But how could I find an answer just by forming an educated guess about how many chocolate chip cookies I'd had available when?

No, I'd need to talk with Judy and Dinah again, and I planned to figure out the best approach rather than accusing them not only of trying to steal from me but also trying to make me look bad as a vet tech.

"Okay, then." But Reed didn't let me out of the car right away. Instead, he leaned over and gave me one big, sexy kiss.

It felt like whatever our problems had been before, they were now fully resolved. Or was it my own re-stoked optimism making me feel that way?

No matter. I participated in that kiss, and then, picking up the bag containing my hamburger, I got Biscuit out of the back seat, patted Hugo goodbye, and entered the Barkery side of the shops.

Turning on the lights, I waved goodbye to Reed and hooked Biscuit's leash up to her crate. I gave her a hug and then headed through the kitchen, where I deposited my leftovers in the fridge on the Icing side. Then I adjourned into my tiny office.

I turned the computer back on and waited for it to boot up. Was this a fantasy on my part?

Probably. But I had an urge now to fire both my employees and start over. Neither act—endangering dogs with the wrong kinds of treats, or trying to sell a boss's recipes—would wind up in the perpetrator's being thrown in jail. I liked both Judy and Dinah personally—or at least I had. But maybe I needed a completely fresh start here. Maybe who'd done it was irrelevant. Maybe—

There. The computer was finally ready. I got into the pertinent files that contained copies of receipts and started going through them, starting on Monday of this week. And maybe that wasn't even early enough. If one of my assistants had been taking cookies in preparation for leaving them at the vet clinic to make me look bad, she could have been collecting them for a while. They hardly needed to be fresh for something like that.

I heard Biscuit give a woof out front. I'd left the lights on, so maybe someone outside thought we were open. I went back into the Barkery and turned off the lights, giving Biscuit a hug. Then I returned to the computer.

Cookies. We'd baked a lot over the past week—or at least we'd sold a lot. Brenda hadn't kept much of an inventory of her Icing baked goods, so I hadn't started one for either shop. What was important was a tabulation of expenses, including purchases of ingredients, as well as another accounting containing sales and income. But maybe now I'd keep better track of what was baked first, then sold.

I couldn't tell from my records which of my assistants might have been the one to collect potentially dog-harmful cookies. And I realized that this had always been somewhat wishful thinking on my part.

I still could have done it myself, by horrible error.

I nevertheless sat at the computer letting my mind go a bit wild. If I assumed that one of my assistants had done these nasty things, which would it be?

Brenda had warned me that both had had hopes of taking over Icing when she'd left. Could this somehow be an outgrowth of their rivalry?

If so, I could let my imagination move a little further and consider the possibility that whoever had done it might have also wanted to frame me for murder. But that was bizarre. Would either Judy or Dinah really have killed Myra for something as ridiculous as trying to get rid of me?

But as much as I tried, I wasn't able to get my imagination in check. I recalled bits of conversations I'd had with both of them.

And then I realized, if any of this was true, which of them I suspected most.

It was almost as if I'd conjured her up when the back door of the kitchen burst open and one of my assistants came in—holding a gun.

Judy. Of course.

TWENTY-NINE

"WHY A GUN, JUDY?" I felt pleased that my voice sounded relatively normal despite the way my heart was pounding. "You used a leash and rock to kill Myra."

"I caught her unawares with the leash and strangled her till she was unconscious first." Judy no longer looked so pretty and pleasant. Not with her eyes narrowed, her mouth grinning evilly. "But I didn't think that would happen with you, so I came prepared."

"Well, you were right, sort of. I knew it was you who killed Myra." For all of three minutes I'd had some small degree of certainty, at least. "What I don't know is why."

I had stood at her arrival and remained standing at the door to my office. Biscuit had heard us talking and was now barking out in the shop. I had hopes that someone would pass by and call the cops, but why? A dog barking inside a dog bakery didn't mean there was anything wrong.

"Because she deserved it." Judy's nostrils flared as her lips tightened. "You should never have been put in charge of Icing, let alone

283

been allowed to change it this way." She waved her free arm bitterly toward the Barkery part of the kitchen, and I noticed she had some kind of tote bag under that arm. "Brenda told me a long time ago that I was her gem, her perfect helper—but that was before she decided she needed even more help and hired that witch Dinah. But I could live with that—until Brenda said she had to leave town. I begged her to put me in charge, but Dinah wanted it too."

Her gun hand was waving. I had a feeling she was giving me an explanation so I'd somehow understand when she pulled the trigger. The longer I kept her talking, the longer I'd live—and maybe I'd figure out a way to save myself. But I was too far away from any of the drawers to pull out a knife, even if I could get close enough to her to use it before she shot me.

And Biscuit, bless her, kept on barking.

"So you argued about it, I gather," I said. "That's why Brenda decided it was in the best interests of the shop not to choose either of you to run Icing when she left."

I cringed as Judy took a step toward me.

"As if it made any sense for her to sell this place to you and let you ruin it." She was sneering now. "Damn that dog!" Still keeping the gun leveled at me, she backed toward the door to the Barkery. "I'm going to shut her up."

"No. Please." Now I really was pleading. "I'll quiet her down. I promise." I edged past Judy, unable to reach toward the gun, but at least she let me precede her into the Barkery.

It was late enough that the other nearby shops were closed, so the sidewalks and street would be fairly empty. It was unlikely that anyone would see Judy aiming that gun at me. She kept it low enough that it wouldn't be visible around the counter, anyway.

I hurried toward little Biscuit, who, quiet now, wagged her tail.

"See," I said. "She's okay now."

"*Now* being the operative word. Tell you what. Bring her back into the kitchen with us. It'll need to be scrubbed down again before it can be used anyway." Her grin grew even more evil, if that was possible. I knew her intent was to kill me.

What was one more murder to her, even if she got caught?

Besides, if someone else was convicted of my murder, she might find a way to take over the shops after all. Get rid of the Barkery. Turn the premises back into Icing on the Cake.

That gave me yet another reason to want to live—to thwart her in that as well.

I glanced at the front door, wondering if I could run out and survive being shot in the back. It was locked. I'd made sure of it when I'd entered from the street. I might be able to get out, but no one could get in. It was better that way—unless the person trying to get in happened to be a cop. But at least no one else would be in danger.

"Let's go back into the kitchen," Judy demanded.

I obeyed, keeping Biscuit with me. Her being in the kitchen was a minor infraction of the law, especially when compared with what Judy wanted to do.

Once we were all in the kitchen, I said to Judy, "I understand why you were unhappy about the situation here, but why kill Myra?"

"Like I said, she deserved it." My assistant cocked her head slightly. "You asked me before if I was the one to offer your damned recipes to Harris. Well, the answer's yes, but he refused to buy them. When I was leaving his shop I ran into Myra. I was glad at first. She was a much better decision-maker than that wimp of a husband of hers. But you know what she did?"

"No, I don't." But whatever it was, it had led to her death.

"She not only agreed with Harris about not buying those damned recipes, but she was going to tell you that I'd offered them. She—she had the nerve to call me an ineffectual nobody who couldn't have run Icing even if Brenda had offered it to me. And when I said I intended to start my own bakery, she just laughed. Said that the fact that I couldn't even stop Brenda from letting you, an outsider, take over Icing proved my ineptitude." She was nearly crying by then, and her gun hand wavered frighteningly.

"She knew that had to be your hot-button issue, Judy," I said softly. "I had the impression that Myra was a champion of that. It was probably why she picked a fight with me about how my Barkery shouldn't dare to compete with the Knob Hill Pet Emporium."

"Maybe. But I don't care why she did it. I needed to shut her up so she wouldn't tell you. And then I came up with a really ingenious way to get rid of you too—make it look like you were the one to kill her. You made it even easier than I'd imagined by arguing with her. That night was the perfect time to do her in—by going to her place, throttling her first with one of the leashes her dear husband sold at their shop, then bashing her head the way she deserved. Then I left one of your damned dog biscuits beside her so the cops would be sure you were the one who did it. She didn't expect me to jump her, so it was easy."

Now that I knew for sure that Judy had been the one who'd offered to sell my recipes, as well as murdered Myra, the answer to my remaining question no longer really mattered. But I had to ask. "Did you also leave the chocolate chip human cookies at the veterinary clinic so I'd look bad there too?"

Her sudden laugh was like a cackle. "Wasn't that perfect? I followed you there a few times, just like I followed you tonight to your dinner with that vet Dr. Storme so I knew you were here. I saw how you got into the clinic sometimes through the unlocked back door, and then I went in really late one night when hardly anyone was there, only people keeping an eye on the sickest animals. I stuck the box of killer cookies where I knew they kept the treats we brought in. And guess what else I did that night?"

"What's that?" I knew she wanted me to ask but suspected I didn't really want to know.

"I picked this up. Good thing you vet people label things so well." She took a packet out of the tote she carried.

I recognized it immediately, especially when she pulled out a hypodermic needle and small bottle of liquid—all with one hand, since she was still holding the gun.

"No," I said. Once more, the longer she talked, the longer I lived.

But I knew what she intended to do with that.

"This was labeled *Euthanasia, Large Dogs*. You'd know better than me what it is, but I assume it's for putting animals down when they have no chance at recuperation, right?"

"Maybe. But why use that?" My voice was so hoarse not even I could completely understand what I said.

"Because everyone will think it was your veterinarian friend who killed you. Very convenient that you went out to dinner with him tonight."

"But no one there knew us." Would pointing out flaws in her plan help or harm me?

"Some noticed your dogs, I'm sure. And I can get an anonymous tip to the cops. No matter how stupid they are around here, they'll follow up and know that you were with Dr. Storme, and that he'd have unlimited access to this stuff." She waved the hypodermic.

"But he has no reason to kill me."

"Well, neither do I—at least none that anyone would suspect."

She might have been right, although I'd told a few people that I was questioning both Dinah and her. Even so ... well, determining who would be arrested for killing me was a whole lot less important at the moment than making sure I stayed alive.

I wasn't big, but I weighed more than most large dogs. Even so, the pentobarbital that was probably in that vial could do some real damage, even if I survived. Which I might not.

I had to do something—but what?

If I didn't let her inject me, she'd shoot me. Either way, she might also kill Biscuit.

I had come back into the kitchen in front of her and had turned to watch her enter through the door from the Barkery. At the moment, I was closer to the back door than she was. I wasn't facing that direction, but if I turned and I dove for it, could I possibly reach it?

I doubted it, but—

Suddenly I heard a crash behind me. "Attack, Hugo!" shouted Reed's most-welcome voice.

But—"She has a gun!" I screamed, whirling to face them as they came through the back door and trying to protect them with my body.

No need, as it turned out. Yes, Reed was there, but he pulled Hugo back immediately as his place in the door was filled by one of my dear detective friends, Wayne Crunoll. The other, Bridget Morana, was right behind him.

"Drop it," Wayne ordered, aiming a gun at Judy.

When Judy didn't immediately obey, he raised the weapon higher and looked really ready to fire.

Judy must have thought so too. I heard her gun drop. The two cops, followed by some others in uniform, burst into the room and sped behind me.

When I turned, Judy was being taken into custody.

I nearly fell to the floor to hug Biscuit, just as Reed and Hugo ran in too. Reed helped me to my feet and held me tightly.

It was finally over.

THIRTY

It was fairly early on Monday morning. I was in the kitchen, gloves on, electric mixer at the ready while I measured the ingredients for liver biscuits—the ones Reed said were Hugo's favorite. Biscuit loved them too, and they sold well in the Barkery.

Plus, even I liked the meaty aroma.

I tried not to think—much—about yesterday, the last time I'd been in the kitchen, but I had little success with that. I'd already popped into the Barkery shop a couple of times this morning to check on Biscuit, which was unnecessary since all was under control now.

I'd somehow managed to get a little sleep that night and turn up bright and early at the shops. On top of everything else, the rain that had been threatening had finally arrived, but I didn't mind. Getting wet while walking Biscuit was only another sign that we remained alive.

And as exhausted as I was, I intended to keep both Barkery and Biscuits and Icing on the Cake open this entire day, on my own if necessary.

I'd scrubbed all visible surfaces in the kitchen first, including the floor. Not just because Biscuit, now loose in the Barkery, had been there briefly, but because I could—now that my kitchen had been released as a crime scene. I didn't know which might have added more contamination to the room: my dog or the technicians and whatever investigative materials they'd used, plus whatever leaves or mud they'd tracked in.

But though I'd worked intensely, I'd gotten it done fairly quickly so I could get down to the work I really wanted to do.

By myself.

Judy had been the assistant scheduled to come in and help today. And that clearly wasn't going to happen.

I decided to try calling Dinah later, in case she could come in. Or she might wind up calling me first. I'd turned on the TV first thing when I woke up, and the news remained full of the story that had been breaking last night: the arrest of a suspect in the recent murder of Myra Ethman of Knobcone Heights, California. An arrest of a viable suspect in a murder case was apparently big news everywhere.

Especially with the story behind the arrest—an attack in a store in the middle of the night. Lots of angst. Lots of photos from helicopters of the crime scene, which had been under investigation till way into the wee hours. Lots of announcers outside looking serious as they described what they believed had happened there earlier.

And despite my keeping the volume low that morning, Neal had come into the living room and joined me first thing—a rarity for him.

He knew, of course, what had happened.

After my detective buddies arrested Judy and got my initial statement, it had been darned late. I'd needed to go home.

Which I did, more or less. Reed, who'd also hung around and given a statement and received my thanks, insisted on following me to my house. He understood that I needed my car and could drive it just fine. Or so I'd hoped.

But I'd had to go slowly since my whole body was still quivering.

I'd pulled into my driveway and parked there, figuring my shaking could cause me to scrape the sides of my car if I drove into the garage. I grabbed Biscuit's leash and she followed me as I exited.

Reed was right there with Hugo. "You're sure you're okay?" His eyes seemed to scrutinize me for the truth, and his dark, wavy hair was mussed enough that I suspected he'd been running his hands through it.

He'd never looked better to me.

Although...

"I'm fine," I assured him. I'd let him come with me to walk both dogs under the neighborhood's streetlights, and then he and Hugo accompanied Biscuit and me to the door.

I'd no sooner put the key into the lock then the door opened quickly. Neal stood there in sweat pants and a tank top, his usual nighttime wear. "Carrie, are you okay? What happened?"

How did he know that anything had happened? I'd have to ask him that. "Let's go inside," I said.

I didn't kick Reed and Hugo out. I poured us all some water—no caffeine, and no alcohol either at this point. And then our landline rang.

"That's how I know," Neal told me, reading my thoughts. "Some friends and acquaintances called to talk to you and see how you were—probably looking for a blow-by-blow description of what went on tonight, thanks to all those breaking news stories on TV. And there've been a lot of people we don't know, too, from all over the country."

"Media," I surmised, and he nodded.

"I tried calling you, but you must have had your phone turned off," he said. I nodded. "So tell me about it."

I gave a brief narration to my brother about the night's events, with Reed sitting beside me on the couch and adding his two cents' worth now and then.

Both Neal and I asked Reed how he'd happened to be there at the time Judy made it clear she intended to take me out.

"Well, our discussion over dinner did make me wonder which of your assistants was the baddie," he said to me. "And I knew you were going onto your computer to try to figure it out. I wanted to know too. I considered calling you later to ask. I also considered banging on the door and asking you if I could watch over your shoulder. The latter seemed most appealing, especially since I was sitting in my car parked in front of your shops. But when I saw you come into the Barkery the second time, after turning down the lights, and take Biscuit with you into the kitchen—heck, I know you as someone who follows rules, even though you might have lapsed by accident with those cookies."

He raised his hands as if to fend off my objection. "Which we now know wasn't the case," he continued. "But I also saw a movement near the door back to the kitchen and got worried. I figured it would be better to apologize for being over the top if I called the cops when nothing was wrong … so I called them, and they came.

We eavesdropped at the back door. And then I—we—burst in before anything really bad happened."

"Thank you, Reed," I'd said softly, realizing that the look I leveled on him held more than gratitude. He had to really care about me to put himself, and Hugo too, in danger that way—with the cops behind rather than in front of them.

"Wow, sis," Neal had finally said, standing up from the chair facing us and coming over to give me a hug. "I'm so glad you're okay." He'd then put his hand out to Reed for a shake. "And thank you," he concluded, in one of the most earnest tones I've ever heard my brother use.

"You're very welcome," Reed said.

Their interchange had added to my discomfort about … well, almost everything.

What had kept me up for a while despite my exhaustion that night, and kept my mind swirling in the morning as I worked in the kitchen, was that I considered myself an entirely modern woman. I liked to watch adventure movies now and then, sure. But my preference was for those where the superheroes also included superheroines.

I wasn't pleased that I'd been rescued. Not that I had any suicidal notions that I'd have been better off if Judy had succeeded in killing me. Not at all. But I kept wondering what I could have done to fight her off and save Biscuit and me all by myself.

Well, it didn't truly matter. I was okay. Biscuit was okay. I was no longer a murder suspect.

And I was really, really grateful to Reed for all he had done … and I kept wondering what he actually thought of me, to have hung out outside the Barkery like that and then put himself in danger.

Maybe we had a chance at a relationship after all…

I jumped as I heard a noise behind me and whirled, holding the arm of the electric mixer up defensively, its blades whirling. All I accomplished was making a mess of the batter, splattering it around me in the kitchen.

Fortunately, the person who'd come in the back door was Dinah. I didn't have to use the mixer as a weapon.

She laughed, but I also saw tears in her eyes. Her face looked strained, not so youthful. "Oh, Carrie, I'm so glad you're okay," she said. She approached and we engaged in a long hug. "I'm so sorry. I argued with Judy a lot, yes, but I had no idea she would hurt anyone, let alone murder Myra. Or want to murder you." She looked fiercely into my eyes. "Is that true? That's what's on the news."

I moved back a little and turned to reach for some paper towels so I could wipe off the counters and floor where the batter had splashed—yet another bout of cleaning this room today, but easier than the last.

"I can't tell you for sure what's in someone else's mind," I said, trying to act both brave and noncommittal. "But—well, yeah. Judy was definitely threatening me." I paused. "I'm really glad to see you, Dinah. You weren't scheduled to come in today, but—well, can you help out?"

"Absolutely. And any other day you want me, too. Every day, even."

Suspicious person that I was, I wondered if she intended to somehow swipe my shops out from under me. Or maybe it was all good. Now that she'd been shown to be the superior assistant, she intended to live up to that.

We were busy that day, of course. Some people were truly there to buy dog and people treats. Others were there out of curiosity, and Dinah and I nevertheless encouraged them to buy from at least one of the stores. I also got Dinah to prepare the special cake that our customers yesterday had ordered from Icing.

We took our lunches at separate times. Wanting caring company around me, I decided to go to Cuppa-Joe's. Both Joe and Irma gave Biscuit and me big hugs. They had the TV on over the coffee bar area—and guess what was on the news.

I didn't want to get them in trouble for having a non-service dog inside the coffee shop, but I wanted to hear the report—especially since it appeared that Elise Ethman was being interviewed by one of the reporters. I picked Biscuit up.

"Why don't you just come into our office?" Irma asked, sympathy written all over her slightly aging face. "We can watch it there."

"Thanks." I followed her out of the serving area and down a hallway. The office was fairly roomy, and after turning her computer screen around so we could both see it, she sat on one chair while pointing me to another. I put Biscuit on the floor, and all three of us watched the news unfold as one of the servers brought in lunch.

Sure enough, Elise was still being interviewed. She expressed sorrow and disbelief that the person who'd killed her sister-in-law Myra was someone who barely knew her: Judy Zelener. It made no sense to her, and yet she appeared a bit relieved to have learned that the suspect wasn't a relative, either by blood or marriage.

Next, the announcer interviewed Harris Ethman. He, too, expressed sorrow and skepticism. He didn't mention me by name but hinted that the suspect had a connection to another person, her employer, who'd argued with his poor dead wife about their competing businesses. And maybe that person had somehow put the current suspect up to committing the terrible deed. There was some indication, he said, that a leash very similar to the one used to strangle his wife had been bought by that person at his very shop.

Harris's eyes grew even shiftier at that, and my suspicion that he'd forged that receipt he gave the cops grew even stronger. Why? To frame me? To get suspicion off of him? Or had he simply been using the situation to help build his own pet business while trashing mine?

It no longer mattered.

Although at that moment I did have some urge to strangle Harris—not that I'd ever do such a thing.

"You're okay?" Irma asked when I stood to return to my shops. "You're not letting that miserable Harris get to you, are you?"

Even if I was, I didn't need to admit it to her. "I'm fine," I assured her. "Especially now."

But I also realized that I might always have a difficult rivalry with Harris. I'd just have to live with that.

I spent a couple of hours back at the shops, spelling Dinah while she went to lunch. I called the vet clinic and made sure everyone was all right with my limiting my shift that day to one hour. That hour arrived quickly after Dinah's return, and passed quickly at the clinic. I hurried back to my shops with Biscuit and remained there until it was time to close for the day.

Somehow I was surprised when my two detective buddies came in late in the afternoon. They offered no apologies for their earlier harassment, of course, but they did say that things were going well in their current investigation. If I had any further thoughts or comments about what had happened, they would be more than glad to hear them.

I gave them both some free treats to take with them when they finally left—more in relief that they were going than to bribe them to stay away from me. I gave dog treats to Wayne and people-cookies to Bridget.

My cell phone had hardly stopped ringing that day, and I'd put it on mute, just checking it now and then. I'd returned a couple of the calls while sitting in my tiny office during a customer lull. One was to my attorney Ted. "Glad you're not a suspect any longer, Carrie," he'd said. "Maybe you and I can grab dinner one of these nights, just for fun."

Just for flirting, I assumed, now that he apparently didn't need to provide me with legal representation. I liked the guy, so that was a definite maybe.

So was a pending visit from Jack Loroco. He'd heard the news too, in Los Angeles, and had been really glad to hear both that I was all right and that I no longer had cops breathing down my neck.

He told me he'd been informed of his company's decision about buying my recipes—they'd thought the idea was a bit premature, but said they would keep it in mind.

So would I, but at this point I doubted I'd want to sell my recipes. It would be better just to build my own businesses. Maybe some good would even result from my current notoriety. Not that I'd wanted to get publicity this way, but I'd use it if I could.

Jack added, though, that a discussion of the potential future timing for a business arrangement between us would provide a good excuse for him to come for a visit in a few weeks.

That was fine with me.

I pondered, as I hung up, whether I'd still ask Chef Manfred to help create other doggy treats for Barkery and Biscuits—and, if so, how he'd feel about our maybe selling the recipes to VimPets. I would ask him both questions one of these days.

That evening, I allowed Dinah to leave early. Allowed? Heck, I encouraged my very sweet, very dedicated assistant to go home and rest up for the next day, since she insisted she'd be back again then.

"We might need more help soon," I told her. "If you have any ideas for someone else to bring in, let me know."

"I sure will," she said. "Oh, and Carrie?"

"Yes?" There was something in her smile and tone that suggested she was about to say something important. Surely she wasn't going to give notice that she was about to quit—was she?

It turned out to be nearly the opposite. "I'm really sorry about everything that happened—but can we talk about it more sometime? I've already got some ideas, and I might use this whole situation in a book someday—fictionalized, of course."

I laughed. "Of course." But nothing could be stranger than the reality of all that had occurred around here.

When I was finally ready to close up for the night, I walked around all sides of the shop and kitchen. I couldn't help remembering how things had been here last night, and I shuddered yet again.

But I couldn't help feeling a little proud of myself too. I might have needed Reed's help to save my life, but I was actually the one to figure out—with some investigation and discussion and brainstorming—who Myra's killer had been.

In those last minutes before Judy had come in to confront me, I'd recalled her words when we'd talked about my being a suspect in Myra's murder: *I know you didn't kill Myra. Maybe the cops will figure that out too.* I'd assumed at the time that she was just being supportive, but it finally hit me that she'd been telling the truth about what she knew—and that she didn't necessarily want the cops to figure it out. And the partial Barkery biscuit found near Myra's body? Judy certainly would have been able to acquire it easily—and use it to frame me.

I'd also thought of her belligerence in another conversation about Myra, that time with Dinah. Together, these recollections had triggered my last-minute suspicions.

In any event, I was glad I could finally put that murder behind me and go on with my life.

No more detecting for me, and that was a good thing.

But I'd decided to invite Reed and Hugo to my house for another home-cooked meal soon, as an additional thank you for their help.

The End

BARKERY AND BISCUITS DOG TREAT RECIPE

Peanut Butter Dog Cookie Recipe

Into a food processor, place:
1 cup natural peanut butter
1½ cups whole wheat flour
2 eggs
½ cup oatmeal blended to a powder
1 teaspoon cinnamon
½ teaspoon ginger

Blend the ingredients, then add water to bind to a stiff dough.

Roll out the dough between layers of plastic wrap and cut into desired shapes.

Bake at 310°F for around 40 minutes. The cookies will not rise as they have no rising agents.

ICING ON THE CAKE PEOPLE TREAT RECIPE

Rosemary, Lime, and Pignoli Biscotti

2 cups sugar
3 cups pignoli (pine nuts), lightly toasted
2 tablespoons fresh rosemary, minced
1 cup butter, melted
¼ cup limoncello or water
Zest from 2 limes
Juice from 2 limes
2 teaspoons vanilla extract
6 eggs at room temperature
5½ cups all-purpose flour
1 tablespoon baking powder

Mix all but eggs, flour, and baking powder in a large bowl. Beat in the eggs, one at a time. Mix flour and baking powder thoroughly, then stir into mixture. Put mixture into a gallon-sized zip-seal bag, close the zipper, and flatten sideways to fill the bag uniformly. Refrigerate flat at least three hours or overnight. Preheat oven to 375°F, and grease 2 large baking sheets. Slice dough (right through the bag!) into 5 equal pieces. After removing the plastic, dampen your hands and shape each piece into a long loaf ½" high and 2" wide, spacing them 4" apart on prepared baking sheets. Bake until firm to the touch, about 25 to 30 minutes. Let cool 15 minutes, but maintain oven temperature at 375°F. Slice each loaf diagonally into ½" to ¾" slices, and arrange slices cut-side down on the baking sheets. Bake until lightly toasted, about 7 or 8 minutes on each side (this step can be done in batches). Cool on a rack. Makes about 6 dozen.

ACKNOWLEDGMENTS

I'm delighted to be starting a second mystery series with Midnight Ink! Many thanks, as always, to my amazing agent Paige Wheeler, as well as to my fantastic editor Terri Bischoff.

Thanks also to the wonderful people who helped me write and improve *Bite the Biscuit* by reading and commenting on the manuscript. You know who you are!

And I have to admit that, unlike Carrie Kennersly, who stars in the Barkery & Biscuits Mysteries, I'm not much of a cook. I thank some good friends profusely (but without identifying them!) for the recipes at the end of this book.

© Christine Rose Elle

ABOUT THE AUTHOR

Linda O. Johnston (Los Angeles, CA) has published thirty-eight romance and mystery novels, including the Pet Rescue Mystery series and the Pet-Sitter Mystery series for Berkley Prime Crime, and *Lost Under a Ladder* in the Superstition Mystery series with Midnight Ink.